I0564494

JESSICA N. WATKINS

# I LOVE YOU *TOO* MUCH

BLACK
ODYSSEY
MEDIA

WWW.BLACKODYSSEY.NET

Published by
BLACK ODYSSEY MEDIA

www.blackodyssey.net
Email: info@blackodyssey.net

This book is a work of fiction. Any references to events, real people, or real places are used fictitiously. Other names, characters, places, and events are products of the author's imagination, and any resemblance to actual events or places or persons, living or dead, is entirely coincidental.

I LOVE YOU TOO MUCH. Copyright © 2026 by JESSICA N. WATKINS

Library of Congress Control Number: 2025916800

First Trade Paperback Printing: February 2026
ISBN: 978-1-957950-81-5
ISBN: 978-1-957950-82-2 (e-book)

Cover Design by Navi' Robins

To the extent that the image or images on the cover of this book depict a person or persons, such person or persons are merely models and are not intended to portray any character in the book.

All rights reserved. Black Odyssey Media, LLC | Dallas, TX.

This book or parts thereof may not be reproduced in any form, stored in a retrieval system, or transmitted in any form by any means—electronic, mechanical, photocopy, recording, or otherwise—without prior written permission of the publisher, excepting brief quotes or tags used in reviews, interviews, or complimentary promotion, and as permissible by United States of America copyright law.

10 9 8 7 6 5 4 3 2 1

Manufactured in the United States of America

Distributed by Kensington Publishing Corp.

The authorized representative in the EU for product safety and compliance is eucomply OU, Parnu mnt 139b-14, Apt 123
Tallinn, Berline 11317, hello@eucomplianceprtner.com

Dear Reader,

I want to thank you immensely for supporting Black Odyssey Media and our ongoing efforts to spotlight the diverse narratives of blossoming and seasoned storytellers. With every manuscript we acquire, we believe that it took talent, discipline, and remarkable courage to construct that story, flesh out those characters, and prepare it for the world. Debut or seasoned, our authors are the real heroes and heroines in *OUR* story. For them, we are eternally grateful.

Whether you are new to Jessica N. Watkins or Black Odyssey Media, we hope that you are here to stay. Our goal is to make a lasting impact in the publishing landscape, one step at a time and one book at a time. As always, we welcome your feedback and kindly ask that you leave a review. For upcoming releases, announcements, submission guidelines, etc., please be sure to visit our website at www.blackodyssey.net or scan the QR code below. And remember, no matter where you are in your journey, the best of both worlds begins now!

Joyfully,

Shawanda Williams

Shawanda "N'Tyse" Williams
Founder & CEO, Black Odyssey Media

# PROLOGUE

IT WAS THE perfect start to summer, and the yacht party was lit. The sun was shining bright over Lake Michigan as a group of friends partied without a care in the world. Music blasted from the speakers, heavy beats pulsed through the deck, and drinks were flowing nonstop. Everyone was feeling good and tipsy. Some were way past drunk, laughing and dancing.

A few of them had already jumped off the boat. They were splashing in the cool water, relieving themselves from the relentless heat. Others were floating around in the lake on inflatable rafts. It was wild, chaotic fun, just like it was supposed to be for Kayla's birthday party.

"Yo, what's that?" one of the guys shouted from the water. He was pointing to something a few feet away that was bobbing in the lake.

Kayla, who was lounging on a floatie with a drink in hand, glanced over, squinting. "Probably nothin'. People throw all kinds of trash in the lake."

But Marcus was persistent, per usual. "Nah. It looks like a suitcase or somethin'."

Standing on the deck of the yacht, Trey shook his head as he held his beer up to his lips. "This nigga always minding the wrong

1

business." Then he took a swig before shouting to Marcus, "Bro, chill! You better leave that alone. It's probably some drugs in there that fell out of a plane."

Marcus looked back at Trey, grinning. "Then I should definitely go open that bitch up."

"And you goin' straight to jail," muttered Angie who was lounging beside Kayla.

But Marcus being the nosy one, he wouldn't let it go. He swam closer to the suitcase, and as he did, something caught his eye. "Hold up," he muttered to himself as he got a better look. He squinted as he realized what was caught in the zipper of the suitcase.

It was...*hair*.

His heart began to pound against his chest now. "Yo, I think there's hair stuck in the zipper!"

Kayla sat up on her float, frowning. "Hair? Hell nah. You trippin'. You better leave that shit alone, man."

"I'm serious," Marcus said as he continued to swim toward the suitcase. "I'm checkin' this out."

"Marcus, don't! What if it's some weird shit? Just leave it," Angie shouted.

But Marcus was already too close. He grabbed the suitcase, feeling how hard it was to move. Shockingly, it was heavy.

As he tried to pull it open, his hands shook a little. The zipper creaked, and when he finally got it open, he froze.

Inside lay something grotesque. Its eyes were staring blankly at nothing, and its limbs were twisted at unnatural angles. "Oh shit!" Marcus's stomach turned as panic hit him. He couldn't think or breathe.

The body was in a grim state. It had seemingly been in the water for days, and the effects of decay were clear. The skin was pale and bloated. It stretched tightly over the bones in some places, while in others, it had started to peel and loosen. There was a greenish tint to the body, and parts of the skin were dark and discolored from being submerged.

Her face was swollen and unrecognizable to be human. The lips were pulled back slightly, exposing the teeth. The eyes were sunken and clouded over, no longer resembling anything human. Her hair, tangled and matted, stuck out from the zipper of the suitcase and clung to the sides like seaweed.

There was a foul smell, even over the lake water. It was a sickly odor that made it clear the body had been decomposing for some time. The joints were stiff, and her limbs looked awkwardly positioned since they had been forced into the small space of the suitcase.

Marcus's stomach lurched before he screamed, "Oh my God!" He let go of the suitcase and pushed himself away from it as fast as he could, splashing wildly. "What the fuck?"

Kayla saw the look on his face and started freaking out too. "What? What is it?"

Marcus, still swimming away from the suitcase, yelled, "It's a body! There's a body in the suitcase!"

# CHAPTER 1

## AVIANA SCOTT

M IA AND I sat across from each other in a soul food spot in Hyde Park on the South Side of Chicago. Our table was cluttered with mason jar lemonades, half-eaten cornbread, and empty plates. Old school R&B played low through the speakers.

"How was your food today, ladies?" The waitress, Nakia, grinned as her slanted eyes bounced back and forth between Mia and me, waiting for our approval.

"It was delicious," I replied. Then, with a heavy breath, I sat back in the booth and began to rub my belly, which felt like it was being stretched to capacity by all of the food I had just inhaled.

In response, the waitress giggled.

Mia nodded dramatically. "Everything was *really* good."

"I'm glad to hear that," the waitress said and set the black billfold on the table between Mia and me. "Well, here's your check. Take your time, though. No rush."

She walked away with a reassuring, pleasant smile as I glanced at the time on my phone. Seeing that it was half past two o'clock, I groaned. "Well, we do have to rush. We're already thirty minutes late."

Mia waved her hand so nonchalantly that I chuckled. She was unfazed because she and I had laid-back positions at Dream Realty. She was the office manager for the large real estate company based in Hyde Park. With control of the office, she had a lot of flexibility with her hours. As one of the rental agents at the company, she was my boss, as well as my best friend since elementary school, so I'd inherited the same flexibility.

The owners of the company, a pair of Polish twins in their late fifties, usually came into the office in the mornings for briefings with Mia, rental agents, and other staff, so we weren't in a rush, but there were a few Karens in the office that we had to look out for.

Watching Mia glance over the bill, I asked, "How much is it?"

She sucked her teeth and waved me off without taking her eyes off it. "I got it."

"Okay, Big Money," I teased.

"Don't hate," she playfully boasted.

Laughing, I replied, "Nobody is hating."

With her lips pursed, she answered, "It sounds like you are."

"You know I'm not."

She finally let her artificial guard down and admitted with a smile, "I know."

Tilting my head to the side, I leaned forward and lowered my voice. "But how long are you going to keep doing this?"

She cockily shrugged. "As long as it's putting money in my pocket."

Sitting back, I shook my head, not bothering to hide the apprehension in my eyes. "I told you that the more money you make, the greedier you'll get. Don't you think it's time to chill before you get caught?"

Mia's perfectly tinted brow arched dramatically. "You know something about me potentially getting caught?"

Offended, my head reared back. "Don't play with me, Mia. You know I would never say anything—"

"Especially when you're reaping the benefits," she interjected again, raising her brow even higher.

*"Pause,"* I pressed. "Don't try to include me in your scandalous ways, heffa. You've bought me a few lunches and some drinks, but I don't have anything to do with what you're doing."

"Don't forget the bottles we've popped," she quipped.

I sucked my jaws in, running my fingers through my hair. "Touché...Touché, bitch."

*"Mm-humph,"* she snorted as she dug into her purse.

With a playful smirk tugging at the corner of my lips, I lifted my hands in surrender. "You won that. I was just trying to look out for you."

As she placed a few twenties in the billfold, her haughty disposition vanished. She pouted as her eyes found mine again. "I thought you weren't judging me."

"I'm not," I insisted. "I never would. I get it. I just don't want you to get caught. I love you, and I've always got your back, but I can't help you if you're in prison doing five to ten." As I laughed, she did as well.

Yet, as I gathered my purse and phone, worry still lingered in the back of my mind. I had been raised in the Wild Hundreds, a nickname for the Roseland area on the far south side. When I was growing up, the Wild Hundreds had an extraordinary amount of gang activity that caused it to be a high-crime area, so I wasn't unfamiliar with criminal activities. But I was more used to being surrounded by the likes of gangs, drug dealers, addicts, and thieves— crimes more akin to people from impoverished neighborhoods like mine. But Mia was dealing with some white-collar crimes that would likely get her black ass real time if she was ever caught.

Though she and I had full-time jobs, for thirty-year-old women, we weren't gainfully employed. Unfortunately, after high school, we found ourselves in unhealthy relationships rather than in a healthy relationship with college. As a result, we were making seventy-five thousand dollars a year during a time of inflation, scammers, and social media that made money, status, and popularity a priority. So, when Mia revealed to me a year ago that she had figured out how to steal money from Dream Realty, I understood her thirst for more.

Through Dream Realty, she was creating fake invoices for services and supplies. As the office manager, it was her job to approve those invoices for payment. She'd create the invoices and approve them, then when the company paid the invoices, those payments were diverted into a business account that she created using a fake identity she'd purchased from one of her scamming cousins.

At first, she was only doing it here and there to give herself a couple extra thousand dollars when she needed it. However, as time went on, she'd upgraded from an apartment on the south side to one of the more modern and expensive condos owned by Dream Realty in the South Loop. Her clothes became more expensive, and so had her life. I worried that she had fallen so far down the rabbit hole that she would never be able to crawl out unscathed.

But I didn't and would never judge her. Nor would I ever tell a soul. She and I had grown up in the same neighborhood and had gone to the same elementary and high school. Therefore, I knew her struggles and would never forget the obstacles that had been against us from birth. Plus, Mia was single, while I was married to a husband who was paying the bills where I laid my head.

"I won't get caught, I promise." Mia smiled as she threw the strap of her YSL purse over her shoulder. "And I'll stop soon."

I nodded with a half-smile as Mia and I climbed out of the booth at the Soul Food Cafe. Standing at the table, I looked up at Mia since she was quite a few inches taller than me because of the heels she was wearing that day.

I smiled as I softly bumped her with my elbow. "You know I'm never judging you, right?"

The corners of her lips touched her ears. "I know."

"Trust me. I know the feeling of desperately needing and wanting more."

Mia pouted while searching my weary, longing gaze. "Are you worried about getting hired for that new position?"

I'd applied for the property manager position at Dream Realty. I would manage all of their properties across the city. Most importantly, there was a significant salary increase. Though my husband, Damar, took care of our bills, I wanted more for myself. I had always wanted to be a certified registered nurse anesthetist. It had always been a passion of mine to follow in my mother's footsteps. But Damar didn't want me away from him and the home as much as clinicals and studying would take me. And he was now ready for us to have a baby. Earlier in our marriage, Damar's son, Jeremy, was still young, so Damar wasn't ready for a baby. But now that Jeremy was older, Damar had been insisting that we finally grow our family.

"Yeah. But I haven't heard anything yet."

"I heard that the twins will be making a decision soon."

I half-smiled. "Oh, okay. Good."

We traveled through the maze of tables toward the exit. The warm-brown walls were decorated with vintage posters. The aroma of savory spices swallowed us as the chatter of other diners blended with the clinking of silverware and soulful R&B music.

Stepping outside of the restaurant, the May sun bathed us in summer warmth. It felt so good to feel the city finally defrosting.

"You're going to Enchant tonight, right?"

I lightly groaned, rolling my eyes as I walked alongside Mia through the parking lot. "I guess."

She eyed my irritation suspiciously. "What's the problem?"

Frowning, I asked, "Why can't we go somewhere else? We're always there."

"Because our best friend owns it, and we drink and eat for free. Why would we go anywhere else?"

I groaned in response because she knew exactly why.

A taunting grin reached Mia's ears. "Oh, because it's entirely too stressful for you to be in the same space with your husband *and* the love of your life," she mocked me with a laugh as she answered her own question.

I rolled my eyes with exaggeration. "Whatever, Mia."

She giggled while popping the locks of her SUV. "*Mm-humph.* I better see you tonight."

The breeze downtown was so warm. It was the kind of evening that made you forget winter had ever existed. Damar had insisted we take advantage of it being too nice outside to be inside, so after work, he'd met me at home, then I'd jumped in his car, and he'd brought us downtown.

We walked slowly along the Magnificent Mile with our fingers interlocked. Damar pulled me toward a boutique with a glass storefront showcasing designer handbags.

"Let's go in here," he told me, not giving me an option.

I followed him, and the chime of the doorbell welcomed us as we stepped inside.

Damar and I strolled past displays of luxury handbags that cost more than some people's rent. He kept me close with his arm sliding around my waist. He constantly tugged me against him like he wanted everybody in the store to know I was his.

"*Oooh.* Try that one on," he said, pointing to a sleek black tote with gold hardware. "That one look like money."

I slipped it off the display and threw it over my shoulder, then I stepped in front of the mirror. Damar stood behind me, admiring me with a cocky and proud smirk. "Damn. Look at my wife. You look expensive as hell with that bag on your arm, like a basketball wife."

I laughed, blushing.

"Nah, for real. That bag says you're a dope boy's wife. Like you don't check price tags. Like you're used to this life."

I tilted my head, eyeing myself in the mirror. He wasn't wrong. The bag looked good on me. I looked like I belonged in spaces where women sipped champagne while they shopped and didn't flinch when swiping a black card.

He kissed my cheek, pressing his lips close to my jaw. "I work so hard because I want to give you this life all the time. You deserve to have the best every time you even think of it, not just on a special occasion, and I'm going to give you just that. I swear."

I glanced up, startled by the sincerity in his eyes. I hesitated because guilt pinched at my throat, making it hard to swallow. I smiled up into his eyes. "I know, baby."

"You want it?"

"Damar, you don't have to do this," I murmured.

Damar was successful, but he hadn't reached the point in his career that spending this type of money on a handbag wouldn't put stress on his bank account.

"I know," he said quickly, gently tilting my chin so I met his eyes. "I want to, so let me."

The way he looked at me felt earnest. It was desperate almost, like he was doing everything in his power to bridge the emotional gap I'd quietly allowed to form between us, and that made the heaviness in my chest multiply.

I sighed and smiled. "Sure, baby."

His smile stretched wide. "Then it's yours."

As he signaled for the saleswoman, I felt like such a fraud.

I had been complaining about the lack of passion between Damar and me for quite some time. I had been having the same complaint since before we married.

He was a handsome, charismatic man with swag. I could never deny his tall, massive beauty. He was healthy for my broken heart when we met. But I never felt the heart-wrenching longing and need for him that I always felt for my other best friend, Mythic Grey. I hoped that once Damar and I fell in love, once we married, that it would develop. But our chemistry was never a match for the flame that roared in my heart for Mythic.

From the beginning, my marriage with Damar had been mundane. He checked all the right boxes. He was successful, dependable, and a "good man" on paper, but that was it. I thought that the issue was that he wasn't as connected to our marriage because he was so focused on his party promotion business. But a year ago, Damar started to switch things up. Out of nowhere, he started turning up the romance with dinners, flowers, compliments—the things he used to overlook.

I tried to enjoy it. I tried to appreciate the effort he was finally putting in. But the truth was, even with all his changes, my heart kept drifting back to Mythic.

After Damar made the purchase, he kissed my temple, slipped his arm around me, and we stepped back into the evening.

And as I held tightly on to the expensive gift bag, my guilt screamed loudly in my ears, drowning out the carefree laughter and conversations of the people passing by.

As we waited to cross the street, he leaned in and kissed me again.

My eyes fluttered closed, but not for the reasons they should have.

It was Mythic's face that filled the darkness behind my eyelids. I heard his voice and felt his hands. The way he used to look at me like I was both his peace and his undoing. I hated that my body reacted to the thought of him more than to the man actually kissing me.

I pulled back gently and forced a small smile. "You're really making a day of this, huh?"

"Yeah." He nodded, glancing at me like he was searching for something in my eyes. "I just wanna be with you, Avi. No distractions. No bullshit. Just us."

We started walking again. The sidewalks were crowded, but we moved slow, like the city wasn't rushing past us.

Damar's grip on my hand tightened a little. "I know I wasn't always…present. I got caught up with the parties and the scene. The promoting. The attention. I thought providing meant showing up with money and connections. But that's not what you need. And I hate that I had to almost lose you to realize that."

I bit the inside of my cheek, fighting the sting in my chest.

"I've been putting in the work," he said, "trying to prove to you that I'm here—that I'm serious about us. But I can't lie, Vee—" He stopped walking, turning to face me— "it scares the hell out of me that it might be too late. That I waited too long to choose you the right way."

He looked at me like he needed me to save him. But I didn't feel like anyone's savior. I felt like a traitor in heels and lip gloss.

"You didn't lose me." I barely believed my own words.

His thumb brushed against my knuckles. "Then help me feel like I haven't."

I nodded slowly. My lips curled into something that looked like love, but inside me, it was hollow. Damar was a good man. He was willing to fight for what we had.

But my heart was somewhere else—with someone who made me feel like I couldn't breathe without him.

Someone who wasn't my husband.

And no matter how many steps Damar took toward me, I kept drifting farther away.

A few hours later, Damar and I met Mia at Enchant. As soon as we walked through the doors, we went our separate ways so that he could get to work.

Mythic owned the nightclub Enchant while Damar promoted parties there. Damar had been a very successful and popular promoter in Chicago since he'd graduated from college. In the last few years, he'd expanded from promoting small parties to building a full-fledged, lucrative business in the nightlife scene. What started with handing out flyers and hosting club nights had evolved into securing major venues, booking big talent, and locking in sponsorships. His name held weight now in clubs and in other lanes too. He had his hands in event production, brand partnerships, and even upscale private experiences for high-end clients.

When Mythic opened Enchant, Damar was obsessed with getting entertainment control. He had explained that the club was new and hot because of Mythic's street fame, so he had to have a piece.

On the second floor, Mia and I swayed our exaggerated curves along to the beat of the latest rap songs while looking down on the sea of clubbers from our appointed VIP section.

Mia's curves were exaggerated because she had gotten implants and fat transfers applied to a slim, petite frame. Those surgeries had been funded by the money she'd been stealing from Dream Realty. My curves were exaggerated because I was two-hundred and sixty-five pounds on a five-foot-four-inch frame. Though I was a big girl, I wasn't ashamed of my curves. I had never been kicked out of any man's bed because of my weight. Each pound was well proportioned on my short frame, and most of the weight was in my lower body, leaving me with a much smaller upper torso in comparison. However, the new wave of perfect, manufactured bodies with tiny stomachs and invisible waistlines stirred some insecurities every once in a while.

As we danced to the beats and sipped from the bottles of liquor sent over by Mythic, I couldn't shake the knot of nerves in my chest as I spotted him making his way toward us. Suddenly, it felt like the air had been sucked out of the room. His presence was intense, commanding attention without even trying. I found myself holding my breath, and my heart raced the closer he came.

Mia shot me a teasing glance. "Here comes your boo."

I glared at the way she was having so much fun with my misery.

Mythic and I shared a history—one that still haunted me despite the time that had passed. Mia, Mythic, and I had been best friends since high school and were from the same neighborhood. I'd fallen hard and fast for Mythic back then. I'd fantasized about him since meeting him in algebra class freshman year. Junior year, Mythic and I had finally become more than just friends. When he started to flirt with me, I was floored. He had stolen my heart, especially because he was so willing to openly date such a big girl. At seventeen, I didn't even fully understand what love was supposed to feel like, but I knew with him, it was different. Despite his rough exterior, he was attentive, loving, and kind when it came to me. He had this way of making me feel seen, like I was the only person in the room and the only one who mattered. And for the first time, I felt truly safe, like nothing could touch me as long as he was around. When so many immature boys were teasing me about my weight, he adored it and made me feel like the most beautiful, sexy girl in the school.

There was this fire between us that I couldn't put words to at the time. All I knew was he made me feel alive, protected, and wanted in a way I had never felt before. He was always making sure I felt loved, even in the smallest ways.

He reminded me of my father in that way, always doting on me, making me feel cherished. It was like he had this instinct to protect me, and I loved him for it. Back then, I couldn't put a label on it, but now I know that was real love, the kind that wraps around you and doesn't let go. He was the first person to show me what love should feel like, and I'd never forgotten that.

But then he shattered my heart into a million pieces. My parents had always disapproved of our relationship. Mythic's dangerous reputation was well-known in our neighborhood. My parents saw him as an immature troublemaker who would never be right for their daughter. He proved them right when he cheated on me. My young heart was shattered. Despite my obsession with him, my adolescent mind told me that I had to let him go.

I would have never thought that Mythic would still have the ability to take my breath away thirteen years later. He had been the first to penetrate me and the last to ever truly have my heart. Every time I saw him, it was like reopening an old wound, and the yearning and obsession was still raw beneath the surface. Unfortunately, I saw him often. After he and I broke up, he, Mia, and I remained in a tight-knit circle. Being so young, I transformed my heartache into hate for the type of man he was romantically. I swore that he would never be a good man for any woman. I treated him like a playboy, but I continued to long for him. Yet, the fear of being hurt again always held me back and pushed me to pour my attention and love into Damar when I met him three years after breaking up with Mythic.

Luckily, Damar, an older man, who was ready to settle down, had been there to pick up the pieces of my heart. Even while Damar courted me, I secretly pined for Mythic. But Damar countlessly proved to be the more practical choice. He was career-driven and more mature. Meanwhile, Mythic was in the streets, surrounded by women with a focus on his hustle. So, I easily married Damar five years later. But I shamefully never fell out of love with Mythic.

As I watched as Mythic approached, my pulse pounded in my ears. Everything about his six-foot-six towering frame had indecent effects on me. Everything about this man was delicious. My love for him was unreasonable.

As Mythic approached our VIP section, I could feel my heart rate skyrocketing, despite my best efforts to remain composed. His presence always had that effect on me—like a magnet pulling me in, no matter how hard I tried to resist.

"What's good, Mia?" he greeted, giving her a playful side-eye as she poured another drink. "You getting started already, I see."

Mia laughed while playfully rolling her eyes. "You sent them over here for us to drink, right?" she shot back.

They went back and forth for a minute, just clowning like they always did. The whole time, my heart was dancing wildly.

When his attention finally shifted to me, everything else fell away. His eyes locked on mine. It felt like the whole world disappeared and it was just us standing there. All that energy, all that charm focused on me, and I couldn't help but feel his pull on my heart. No matter how hard I tried to play it cool, he always saw right through me.

"Hey, Avi," he greeted me with that signature smirk that sent shivers down my spine. "Found me any condos in the area yet?"

I raised an eyebrow in suspicion as I was forced to tilt my head all the way back in order to look up into his eyes.

He mysteriously chuckled. "What's that look for?"

"You have a beautiful home in the suburbs. What do you need a condo in the city for?"

His smirk widened into a grin as he leaned in closer, his warm breath tickling my ear. "You know me, gotta have a place in every corner of the city."

I chuckled at his cryptic response. "And what's the price point you're looking for?"

When his gaze locked with mine, his eyes twinkled with mischief. "You know my taste, Avi."

I shook my head, unable to suppress a blush. "You're always so damn vague."

He was always discreet and secretive, as most hustlers were. Mia and I never knew in detail what his hustle was, and he preferred it that way, but being from our neighborhood, she and I could guess.

He chuckled softly as his hand lingered on my arm. He leaned against the railing beside me. "And yet you still put up with me."

I glanced at Mia, who was watching our exchange with amusement, before turning back to Mythic. "Every day, I wonder why I do."

He flashed me a playful grin, his touch lingering a moment longer than necessary. "Avi, you know you'll always put up with me."

I despised the way he looked at me. He was, at least, still attracted to me. When it was just him and me, he never hid the adoration in his gaze, which he often locked on me. But it was simply lust because, despite having the body of a Roman god, he had a thing for short, big girls. His current girlfriend, Lelani, and I were neck and neck on the scale.

I rolled my eyes but couldn't suppress the smile tugging at the corners of my lips.

He chuckled as his fingers trailed down my back. "You know you always got my back like a car seat, Avi." Looking up into his eyes, my heart ached with bittersweet longing. Our playful teasing and lingering touches took me back to a time when things between us had been effortless, fiery, and simple. I'd spent so long fighting this and resisting him, but standing here now, every breath and heartbeat screamed the truth that our chemistry wasn't just undeniable; it was inevitable.

# CHAPTER 2

## MYTHIC GREY

**I** **SAT IN VIP** with my eyes locked on Aviana, watching the way she moved on the dance floor, how she smiled, and the way her curvaceous body swayed with the music as she danced with Mia. I was taking in every little detail like I couldn't get enough.

I was infatuated.

My mind was wrapped up in thoughts of her when I saw Damar making his way toward me. For a second, I froze, wondering if he'd noticed the way I was practically devouring his wife with my eyes.

I tensed up, ready for whatever.

"Mythic, what's good, man?" He greeted me like everything was cool.

I relaxed just a little, nodding back. "What's up?"

He hesitated for a second before taking a seat next to me on the back of the couch. "I need a favor. I heard Jeremy's been hanging with the 111 Boyz. You know how wild those dudes are. They ain't nothing but trouble, but I can't get through to him. I was hoping you could talk to him. He looks up to you, respects you, you know? Maybe he'll listen to you."

I nodded slowly, telling him, "I'll handle it." But all I could think about was how much I'd rather take his wife from him than have some heart-to-heart with his kid.

Damar relaxed, nodding with relief. "I appreciate it, man. For real."

We shook up before he walked away. I waited until he entered the stairway before my gaze slid back to Aviana. He had no idea what was really going on in my head. While he worried about his son running with the wrong crowd, I was plotting on what mattered to me most—his wife.

She was my obsession, the one who got away, the most beautiful thing I'd ever laid eyes on. I had broken her heart once, and though she had found refuge in the arms of another, I knew that I could give her a better life than Damar ever could. I had more money, more power, more influence. I could offer her the world on a silver platter, if only she would let me. But Aviana was in love with Damar, and I couldn't bear to take away her happiness, even if that meant longing for her from afar and playing some weak role as her best friend.

I kept staring at Aviana, unable to pull my eyes away. The way she moved, how she lit up the room, was like nobody else even existed. She had that effect on me, and it was hard for me to hide it. As I smiled to myself, I caught movement out of the corner of my eye. My girlfriend, Lelani Dupree, was making her way over. Hopefully, she hadn't caught me stalking Aviana with my eyes, but I wasn't about to explain myself. She'd never had my heart. She was just a satisfactory runner-up.

I glanced up as Lelani walked toward me. After two years together, she still had the power to captivate me with her beauty. She was everything I could ever want—big-boned, curvaceous, with model-like features and skin like rich chocolate.

But as much as I was attracted to Lelani, there was always a part of me that belonged to Aviana.

I tried to make myself content with every woman I'd crossed paths with since losing the love of my life thirteen years ago. Lelani had been the most serious relationship since Aviana. I had finally come to the realization that I would never have Aviana again, that it was time to move on—to find a queen to take the throne of my kingdom. I had been trying to convince myself that Lelani was enough since meeting her. She was loyal, devoted, and beautiful. But deep down, I knew that my heart still belonged to Aviana, and no amount of wealth or power could change that.

I noticed immediately how her steps were slower and cautious, like she was trying to keep her balance. Her usually bright eyes were dull and tired-looking. As she got closer, I caught the strained look on her face and the slight crease between her eyebrows that always showed up when she wasn't feeling right.

I reached for her waist gently, pulling her closer to study her face. "Your head hurtin' again?"

As she nodded slowly, her eyes closed briefly like even the simple movement caused her pain.

These headaches had become constant lately. They were unforgiving and sometimes made her dizzy and nauseous. I had been nervous that she was pregnant, but tests had confirmed that she wasn't.

"Yeah," she said quietly, rubbing her temple. "It's really bad this time. I don't think I can stay. I need to go home."

"Okay, baby. Go ahead," I told her, kissing her forehead softly, careful not to add pressure. "I'll see you at the house later. I have to stay and close up tonight."

A disappointed pout took over her face. "Why do you have to stay late? You got people for that, Mythic. Why can't Tyiesha do it?"

"She can't tonight." I cupped Lelani's face gently, trying to ease her disappointment. "I'm sorry. I know you don't feel good, but I have to stay."

She exhaled slowly, obviously frustrated, but nodded anyway. "Fine. I'll Uber home."

"Call me if you need me," I insisted, gently brushing her hair out of her face. "I'll come straight home the minute I'm done here. Promise."

She nodded again, giving me a weak smile, but before she could say anything else, Mia and Aviana returned from the dance floor.

"Hey, boo," Aviana greeted Lelani.

"Hey, girl!" Mia screeched, causing Lelani to wince in pain.

Lelani forced a smile back. "Hey, y'all. Have a good night," she said a little tightly before she turned and walked away.

As she disappeared into the stairwell, I could feel Mia's and Aviana's eyes on me.

"What's wrong with her?" Mia asked, raising an eyebrow.

"She's not feeling well."

While Mia's head nodded with understanding, Aviana's eyes lingered on me. When my eyes locked with hers, I saw the slightest blush rise on her cheeks, and that did something to me. She was trying to play it cool, but the way she looked at me, the way her face softened just a little, let me know she felt it too.

I held her gaze captive until she quickly glanced away. But not before I caught the subtle curve of her lips, which betrayed a shy grin that told me everything she wasn't ready to say.

As I locked up the nightclub, my homeboy, Taye, was the only other soul there.

"Another successful night?"

I nodded with a proud but tired chuckle as I walked away from the entrance. "Indeed. Everything copacetic with that delivery you made earlier?"

Taye was not only my homie; he was my right hand. He was as skilled in the art of arms dealing as I was. He had also been the most loyal and dependable. He was my second-in-command, overseeing day-to-day operations, and he was a trusted advisor.

"Of course."

"Then why have you had that serious look on your face all night?" I inquired with a raised brow. "You didn't even crack a smile when that thick red bone was trying to give you a lap dance."

Though I chuckled, Taye simply scoffed as he took a sip of his drink while leaning on the bar. I'd known that he had something on his mind all night. Taye wasn't one to hold back when he had concerns, especially when it came to the unpredictable world we operated in.

I joined him at the bar and poured myself a drink. "What's going on?"

Taye sighed, running a hand through his shoulder-length locs. "The King's Men and Viper Crew are at each other's throats, and it's getting uglier by the day."

I nodded, taking a sip of my drink. The turf war between the King's Men and Viper Crew had been escalating for weeks now, and it was starting to spill over into the safer neighborhoods of Chicago. But the issues of the Mexican gangs weren't my concern.

"Yeah, I've been hearing about that," I admitted.

Taye looked at me with a knowing smirk. "You know that both sides are going to be itching to get their hands on more firepower."

I nodded slowly. "And you know I've always stayed neutral. My business is supplying weapons, not picking sides."

Taye's head bobbed up and down, but I could see the worry in his eyes. "I know, but the cartel doesn't play by the same rules we do. They're reckless—impulsive. They don't give a damn about respect or honor. Eventually, they are going to want you to stop providing weaponry to the other. And they are going to pay whatever they have to to get you to comply."

Unlike most of the homies that I grew up with, I did not end up being a drug dealer. I most definitely had a destiny to be a hustler, however. Becoming an illegal arms dealer wasn't something that happened overnight, though. It was a gradual descent into the dark world of illegal deals.

It started innocently; running errands for the local hustlers, including my father, doing odd jobs to make a few bucks here and there when I was twelve and thirteen. But as I got older, I began to see the potential for something more lucrative, something that would elevate me from the streets to the top of the criminal food chain.

When my father was killed, I felt the pressure of figuring out my place in the game on my own. I started small, selling stolen goods and running small-time scams. But it wasn't long before I realized that the real money was in weapons.

I started building connections with others in the underground arms trade. I learned how the business worked and sharpened my skills as a negotiator, smuggler, and strategist.

Before I knew it, I had built a reputation for myself, a name that struck fear into the hearts of my enemies and commanded respect from my allies. I was no longer just a street kid trying to make ends meet, and many people assumed that I was the typical dope boy. I allowed them to make those generalizations. But, I was, in fact, one of the most notorious players in the dangerous game of underground arms dealing.

There were many reasons why my clients chose to purchase weapons from me. Organized crime syndicates sought out my services to acquire weapons quickly and discreetly. I had access to a wider variety of weapons than what was available legally. This included military-grade firearms, explosives, and other specialized equipment that was restricted or prohibited for civilian purchase. Purchasing weapons through legal channels required documentation and background checks, which created a paper trail and revealed the buyer's identity. By buying from an arms dealer, criminals could maintain secrecy and avoid law enforcement. Even for those who purchased weapons for recreational purposes, getting weapons legally was subject to regulations, waiting periods, and other governmental hurdles that delayed the purchase process. I offered a more streamlined and expedited means of obtaining weapons, bypassing the need for paperwork and official approval.

The clients in our world were diverse. Most were the mafia or the cartel. Their greedy appetite for control drove them to seek out the deadliest weapons money could buy.

But it wasn't just the criminals who came knocking on my door. We had clients from all walks of life, from corrupt politicians looking to arm their private security details to wealthy businessmen seeking protection for their illicit dealings.

No matter who they were or what they wanted, they all paid generously for my services.

"For now, we'll just have to tread carefully," I told Taye after a moment of reflection. "My reputation and status in this city are just as lethal as any cartel. They know better than to come at me sideways."

Taye nodded, but I could see doubt lingering in his brow. "Okay. But things are getting tense out there. We might need to start thinking about halting business to both sides."

I clapped him on the shoulder, giving him a reassuring smile. "If it comes to it, we'll handle it, like we always do."

## DAMAR SCOTT

I eased the front door open quietly and slipped into the darkness of the foyer without making a sound. It was nearly four in the morning, and I knew Aviana had been asleep for hours since she and Mia had left Enchant a little after midnight.

My heart was still pumping like I'd had three energy drinks, so I passed our bedroom, walked down the hallway, and slipped into my home office. I shut the door gently behind me. My eyes adjusted quickly to the dimness as I moved toward the rug in the center of the room. Kneeling down, I carefully rolled one corner back and slipped my fingers under a loose floorboard.

It creaked softly as I lifted it up. Reaching inside, I pulled out the phone and pressed the power button, feeling a dark satisfaction as the apple lit up the screen.

This was Aviana's old phone.

Months ago, she'd misplaced it during a small party we'd thrown. We'd both shrugged it off as stolen or accidentally tossed out with the trash. She bought a replacement the very same night, which arrived the next day.

But weeks later, I found it under the couch while looking for the TV remote. Curious, I charged the phone and powered it on. I had been wondering if another man was responsible for the emotional chill she'd been giving me. Aviana had blamed my work schedule on her unhappiness, yet something told me there was another reason for the detachment behind those pretty brown eyes.

That night, I'd scrolled through her messages, searching for proof. At first, I just found boring conversations with friends and family. But then the phone chimed in my hand, lighting up with a new message. And then another. Real-time texts appeared on the screen, and suddenly, I understood. She'd never deleted this phone from her iCloud account. As long as the phone was connected to Wi-Fi, it got every call and text message.

So, I'd hidden the phone, obsessively checking it every chance I got. I even took it on trips with me. It became my compulsive lifeline to further guarantee control over her.

Using the old phone, I'd shared her location with me.

There were tiny, wireless cameras strategically hidden throughout the house where the security cameras weren't. I watched her at my leisure, studying her.

If she was hiding something, I'd know.

I'd even installed a keylogger on her laptop. Every email she typed, every search she made, I monitored from my own devices.

Aviana would always be mine. I'd invested too many years molding her into exactly what I wanted, shaping her decisions, her habits, even her friendships. She thought she'd chosen me freely, but freedom was an illusion I'd carefully crafted.

I leaned back slowly in my leather chair. My eyes were locked on the phone as messages poured in. Aviana was smart, beautiful, and talented. She had qualities I loved when they served me, but ones I had to temper when they didn't. Every time she took a step forward, achieved something, found confidence or strength, I reminded her of her limitations with an indirect comment about her inability to succeed without me, a casual remark of doubt masked as concern, or an unintentional dismissal of her ambitions that she believed to be harmless teasing. Over time, those quiet words sank in, weakening her foundation. I had become the source of her validation and the measuring stick for her worth.

I knew exactly what I was doing.

Because Aviana couldn't leave. She wouldn't. Not when I'd convinced her that no one else would truly understand her or take care of her the way I could. Every carefully timed withdrawal of affection, every cold shoulder I gave her always brought her back to me, needy and desperate for my approval. She thrived on the rare praise I rationed out like expensive gifts and starved with my calculated detachment.

Love was ownership. And Aviana was my most prized possession. I couldn't allow someone else to take her away.

So, I watched. I tracked. I manipulated. It was easy because she never suspected the monster behind my charming smile. And as long as she believed that smile, she would always remain exactly where she belonged, which was under my control, by my side. Forever.

My eyes moved over Aviana's latest batch of text messages. They were mundane conversations about hair appointments, plans with Mia, a new brunch spot her mother wanted to check out.

The phone in my pocket vibrated suddenly. Sliding Aviana's phone onto the desk, I pulled out my own. An unsaved number flashed across the screen.

I grinned cockily as I read the text.

**773-965-9887:** *Did you make it home safely?*

**Damar:** *Yeah. Just walked in.*

I didn't even set the phone down before it buzzed again.

**773-965-9887:** *Thank you for tonight. I really needed that.*

As I typed my response, smugness rolled off me.

**Damar:** *I know you did. Don't worry, you'll get more soon.*

## MYTHIC GREY

A harsh retching sound yanked me out of my sleep. My eyes opened slowly, adjusting to the sunlight. I instinctively reached beside me. My fingers slid over cold sheets where Lelani was supposed to be. I sat up, squinting toward the master bathroom door. It was slightly open, and a sliver of dim yellow light lit the floor.

"Lee?" I called out.

Just as I swung my legs out of bed, I heard the toilet flush, so I decided to just wait. I soon heard the sound of running water, then the vibrations of her electric toothbrush.

A few minutes later, the bathroom door swung open fully. Lelani stepped out slowly, sluggish and exhausted. She padded back to the bed and crawled in beside me, sinking into the mattress.

"You good?" I asked as I shifted onto my side to face her.

"Yeah," she murmured weakly.

I exhaled, frowning. The nausea, headaches, and exhaustion were becoming a nightly thing.

"You sure you're not pregnant?"

"Mythic, I promise I'm not pregnant."

A quiet relief spread through me, and I hated myself for it. Lelani was a good woman. She was the kind of woman who deserved the world. She deserved a man who would celebrate the thought of her carrying his child. But whenever I imagined myself as a father, it was always Aviana I saw holding my child. To picture anyone else in her place felt like betrayal.

"Then you need to see a doctor—soon. Something's not right."

"I know," she admitted quietly. "I'll make an appointment later today."

"Good." I drew her closer, allowing her to curl against my chest. "We gotta get to the bottom of it."

She nodded against me, burrowing deeper into my hold. I stroked her hair gently, feeling guilty for my relief, for my thoughts, for holding Lelani in my arms when my heart wasn't fully here.

# CHAPTER 3

## AVIANA SCOTT

As soon as I stepped out of my car in front of the office building Friday morning, I noticed Mia climbing out of hers down toward the corner. I bit back a laugh, watching her dramatically slip oversized black shades onto her face. She swung her purse over her shoulder with a groan loud enough for me to hear even from a distance.

I shut my car door and locked it with the key fob as I walked up the sidewalk to meet her. "You good, sis?" I teased, nudging her gently with my elbow.

Mia let out another exaggerated groan. "Do I look like I'm good?"

"I mean…" I gave her a playful once-over. "You look like you fought with the liquor *and lost*."

She groaned louder and waved me off. "Don't remind me. Who told me to take that last shot? Oh wait, you did."

"I told you to sip it, not bathe in it."

She rolled her eyes behind those blackout shades. "Whatever. All I know is my soul left my body somewhere around shot number four, and I still haven't found it."

As we walked toward the office doors together, our heels clicked in rhythm on the concrete.

"Pray for me." She winced. "If I make it to lunch without throwing up or cussing somebody out, it'll be a miracle."

I giggled as my phone rang in my purse. When I dug it out, I saw the screen lit up with a video call from Jeremy.

I wiped my hands on a napkin, grabbed the phone, and hit accept. Jeremy's face popped up on the screen with a big, mischievous grin.

"Hey, boo!" I greeted.

"Hey, Avi."

Hearing his voice, Mia quickly snatched the phone from me. She smiled into it. "What up, nephew?"

"Tee Tee Mia, what's good?"

Mia and Jeremy caught up for a minute. "All right. I'll let y'all talk. Love you, J!"

"Love you too, Tee Tee," he said before she handed me back the phone.

Mia hung back, waiting for me to finish my call before she went into the building.

"What's up, Jeremy? What are you doing calling me so early?"

"You think you could spot me twenty dollars?"

I raised my brow, looking at him through the screen. "Twenty dollars for what?"

He leaned back, like he was trying to play it cool. "Me and some of the guys from the basketball team are going to Buffalo Wild Wings get something to eat after school."

I wasn't so sure. "Basketball team, huh?"

"Yeah."

I narrowed my eyes, still skeptical. "You sure about that? I heard you've been hanging with some other folks."

"I promise, Aviana. I'm just going with the guys from the team."

I sighed, shaking my head but smiling. "All right. I'll send it, but don't have me looking crazy if I find out you're with somebody you're not supposed to be around."

Jeremy grinned. "Thanks, Aviana. You the best."

"Yeah, yeah, I know," I said, laughing. "Go have fun, but be smart, okay?"

"I got you. Love you."

"Love you too, J. *Be good*."

Hanging up the phone, I followed Mia through the doors of Dream Realty.

Alfred and Antoni were in the lobby surrounded by the entire office staff, already beginning our morning briefing.

Alfred's welcoming smile beckoned us forward. "*Ah*, Mia, Aviana, right on time. We were waiting on you."

"Oh, really?" Mia asked with a playful smirk as she swayed inside. "What did we do?" she joked.

Antoni laughed along with her. "We were just about to announce the new city-wide property manager position."

I instantly held my breath as I sat in a plush chair meant for waiting clients. Vying for the property management position for months, I had been pouring my heart and soul into every task and project in hopes of proving myself worthy.

As Alfred cleared his throat, my pulse quickened. I glanced at Mia, and she gave me an encouraging nod.

"After much consideration," Alfred began, "we have come to a decision."

My heart skipped a beat as Alfred's gaze swept over the assembled staff, finally coming to rest on Mia. "Mia… congratulations. You've got the job."

Confused, my eyes darted toward Mia, meeting her baffled expression. Her eyes blinked owlishly as the twins inched toward her with proud expressions while the staff began to clap. I swallowed hard, forcing myself to do the same.

"Though we had many qualified candidates, after careful consideration, Antoni and I felt that Mia's exceptional performance as the Hyde Park office manager more than qualified her for the dual role."

As Alfred and Antoni gave Mia congratulatory hugs, I noticed the sympathetic and sorrowful glances she cast my way. Despite my own disappointment, I managed to give her a small smile of encouragement, silently urging her to embrace her victory.

The rest of the staff joined in the celebration, offering their congratulations before the twins finished their morning briefing.

When the briefing was over, Alfred and Antoni bid their farewells and made their exit as everyone else dispersed to their cubicles and offices.

Mia hurried toward me. Her eyes were so apologetic. "Aviana, I didn't apply for the position. I swear. I'm so sorry."

I shook my head, offering her a reassuring smile. "It's okay. You deserve this opportunity, even if you weren't expecting it."

Mia's shoulders sagged with relief as she wrapped me in a tight hug. "Thank you. I'm sorry again."

I continued to reassure her that everything was okay, but happiness for her blended with a bit of envy. I loved my best friend. Yet, while I was genuinely thrilled for her success, I couldn't shake the feeling of being pigeonholed by my own circumstances. Stuck in a marriage where there was no passion and a career where there was obviously no growth, I yearned for the courage to seize control of my own destiny, just as Mia had done.

# DAMAR SCOTT

A few blocks away in Hyde Park, my son, Jeremy, and I were hitting the basketball court, something we'd done since he was little. The sun, finally coming out, beat down on us as we played one-on-one.

*"Ah ight, ah ight, ah ight,"* I chanted as I caught the ball. "I need a break. Let's take five."

"Dang. You can't keep up, old man?" Jeremy taunted with a grin plastered on a face identical to my own when I was sixteen.

"You better pray you make it to my age."

As we took a breather, I wiped the sweat from my face, catching Jeremy's eye. "Listen, I gotta talk to you about something."

Jeremy's smile faded, replaced by a look of curiosity. "What's up?" he asked, leaning against the chain-link fence.

I took a deep breath. "I been hearing about who you've been hanging with. Them streets ain't no joke, and I don't want you gettin' caught up in all that mess."

Though I wasn't a hustler, being a popular promoter, I was tight with many of the dope boys in the city. They knew me well, so they were also familiar with my son. I had heard that he was in the streets, cliquing up with the 111 Boyz, a notoriously well-known street gang with territory in The Hundreds.

Jeremy's expression darkened as his gaze dropped to the ground. "I'm not doing anything wrong, Pops."

I placed a reassuring hand on his shoulder. "I know you're not, son. But I've seen how easy it is to get caught up in that life, even when you're not looking for trouble. But it can seem like you're looking for trouble when you're hanging with the wrong crowd. And I know you've been hanging with the 111 Boyz."

"They're my friends," he protested. "I go to school with them."

This was my reluctance with Jeremy getting older. No matter how much I helped his mother financially, she was insistent on not straying too far away from the neighborhood that she was raised in because she wanted to be close to her mother. Though she and Jeremy lived on a nice block outside of Roseland, I knew that it would be easy for Jeremy to venture into dangerous territories with his friends.

"That doesn't matter. You know how many innocent kids are killed because of their association with the wrong crowd. You've seen it. I love you, and I ain't gonna let you go down that road— not if I can help it."

"So, what you tryin' to say? I'm not supposed to have friends?"

Gritting my teeth, I looked down. I had once been a young boy facing the same fight. For those reasons, I had always wanted my son to grow up differently—in a different neighborhood in private schools. Unfortunately, as two teenage parents, we had been raising Jeremy as we grew up, so Stephanie and I hadn't made the best decisions with the little that we had. And, now that I had the finances to make his life different, Jeremy was nearly old enough to make his own decisions and had already formed bonds with the wrong crowd.

"Find some new friends," I suggested.

As I expected, he immediately sucked his teeth, rolling his eyes up to the sky.

"Why can't you hang out with your cousins?"

"They're lames, Dad."

"They are lames that won't end up in jail or dead."

"Dad," he said, groaning.

No matter how much he grew up, he was still a little boy. I could see the tantrum brewing in his scowl, so I gently squeezed his shoulder. "Okay, okay. We'll spin the block on this later. Let's finish the game."

As I resumed the one-on-one basketball game, I got more worried for him. My bond with my son was incredibly strong; we practically grew up together since I became a father at a young age. Growing up in the tough neighborhood where I saw too many young boys lose their lives to violence, the thought of anything happening to my son was unbearable.

"All right, Pops. See you later." As we stood in the doorway of his mother's home, Jeremy gave me a quick bro hug before attempting to pull away, but I brought him in, holding him a bit longer. I felt defeated, not having gotten through to him earlier.

"I'll talk to you later. Love you."

"Bet. Love you too."

He peeled out of my arms and scurried into the house. A knot formed in my stomach knowing that he was rushing, eager to be around trouble.

Standing in the foyer, Stephanie sighed, looking at my expression. We had already talked about the things I'd heard, so she knew that I was going to try to talk to him that day.

"Well?" she pressed softly.

Frustrated, I leaned against the doorframe and stuffed my hands into the pockets of my basketball shorts. "He wasn't trying to hear anything I said."

She scoffed with a light chuckle. "I'm not surprised. He's a teenager. He doesn't think we know anything."

"Maybe we should consider transferring him to a different school."

Her expression turned into disapproval. "And make him start over in his junior year?"

"Yes. That's an inconvenience worth saving his life."

"I'm assuming you want him to go to a school outside of this area. Who is supposed to take him to school every morning and pick him up? Considering the schedule you have, you won't be able to, which leaves me to do it."

"Or he can live with me and Aviana, as I've been suggesting for the last year."

Immediately, she started to shake her head. "No. Not going to happen. I have nothing against Aviana, but this is my child, and he will be living with me."

Before I could express the protest on the tip of my tongue, my phone started to blare in my pocket. Through my earpiece, my phone announced that Aviana was calling.

Growing frustration made me groan. "I'll talk to you about this later."

I turned my back on Stephanie's defiant smirk and answered Aviana's call while jogging down the porch steps.

"What's up, baby?"

"Hey," she returned with an annoyed sigh.

"What's wrong with you?" I asked as I heard Stephanie's front door close.

She whimpered a bit, which let me know she was pouting. "I didn't get the job."

"I'm sorry, baby."

I wasn't sorry at all. I'd listened to Aviana endlessly talk about that job, pretending to be supportive while quietly hoping she wouldn't get it. The last thing I needed was her gaining too much confidence, feeling powerful, or realizing she could actually succeed without me. Sure, more money from her meant less pressure on me, but it wasn't worth the risk of her outgrowing me—or worse, deciding she deserved better.

I wasn't about to let her outgrow me or us.

"Honestly, I wanted that job, but only because it was my only choice. It wasn't my dream job, though. I want to go back to school," she whined. "I'm thirty. I need a real career. I want to finally apply for nursing school."

My jaw tightened. "That's going to take so much time and energy away from us." I sounded disappointed, just enough to make her second-guess herself. "What about finally having a baby? You're really going to wait four years of school until you're almost thirty-five to have a child?"

She blew an irritated breath, but I cut off any response she was about to have.

"I mean, seriously. By the time you're done, who knows what'll happen? You'll probably be too busy for anything else. Is this really about school, or is it just another excuse to avoid finally having a baby with me?"

"I'm not avoiding anything, Damar," she protested softly.

"Then why do you always need something else? We're good as we are. You know I support you, but nursing school? Sounds like you just want reasons to avoid growing our family."

When she fell silent, I knew I'd planted that tiny seed of doubt. I couldn't let her grow past me. If she did, she might realize she deserved better, and I couldn't risk that.

"I just want you here—with me," I whispered gently, like I was offering comfort instead of control. "Is that so wrong? My business is doing great, baby. I can take care of us. Let's focus on me putting a baby in you sooner than later so that you can go to school in a few years."

"So that I can struggle with studying and taking care of our home with a child, Damar?"

"Baby—"

"I have to go," she quipped with irritation. "I'll see you at home later."

As she abruptly ended the call, I could feel my hold on her slipping. The more independent she became, the less I could control her, and control was the only way I knew how to keep her close. It made me want to tighten my grip and remind her who she belonged to until she never forgot it.

# CHAPTER 4

## MYTHIC GREY

**TWO WEEKS LATER,** I was standing in the mirror, sliding on a tailored designer tee. I was getting ready to check out this condo Aviana swore was perfect for me. But to be real, I wasn't all that eager to see the place. What had me hyped was seeing her. Aviana had been on my mind a lot lately, and today was another excuse to be in her presence.

I reached over to my jewelry display stand, pulled out my gold chain, and slipped it around my neck. It was hot out, so I kept it simple with a white shirt, tailored jeans, and crisp, white sneakers. I grabbed my watch, slid it on my wrist, and gave myself one last look in the mirror.

As I left the bedroom and headed downstairs, I heard her voice before I even got to the steps. Lelani's mother, Rachel, was downstairs, making my mood instantly change.

Rachel despised me. That woman had been a thorn in my side from the day I met her. As soon as Lelani introduced me to her, Rachel saw through the front of me being merely a nightclub owner. She saw me as a gangster and criminal, both of which wasn't good enough for her daughter. But the truth was she was just jealous. She was a bitter, older single woman who never had a man take care of her the way I took care of Lelani.

I made my way downstairs, hearing their voices get louder as I approached the living room.

Lelani was ruffling through her purse. Rachel was perched on the edge of the couch as if she were waiting on Lelani.

Rachel barely looked at me when I walked in. She gave me a quick, dismissive hello that dripped with her usual coldness.

I scoffed, shaking my head as I looked at her, then turned to Lelani. "I'm heading out. I'll be back later." I leaned down, pulling Lelani close and kissing her slowly.

Lelani smiled up at me, but Rachel shifted in her seat, clearly annoyed. That was the reaction I was looking for. I gave Lelani one more kiss, then straightened up and shot Rachel a quick glance before heading out the door.

## AVIANA SCOTT

As I led Mythic through the lavish penthouse on 21st and Indiana, my heart raced with longing and anxiety. Being in this intimate space with him ignited a familiar ache in my core. But I pushed the thoughts aside, focusing instead on the tour.

"Check out this view, Mythic," I said, eagerly gesturing toward the floor-to-ceiling windows that framed the sprawling cityscape below. "It's one of the best views in the city."

I was proud to show him this place. It was just like him—stylish, sleek, and dripping with swag.

Mythic stepped closer, his gaze lingering on me for a moment. He murmured, "Impressive," before turning to take in the view.

I swallowed hard and cleared my throat, trying to speak around the lump of seduction Mythic had made form. "And the kitchen," I continued, leading him toward the sleek, modern appliances. "It's equipped with top-of-the-line stainless steel appliances and granite countertops."

As I spoke, I could feel Mythic's eyes on me. "I can think of a few ways to put this kitchen to good use."

His teasing tone caused a flush to creep up my cheeks. I busied myself with pointing out the other features of the penthouse, desperate to keep my composure. But with each playful remark from Mythic, the tension between us exploded.

As we strolled through the penthouse, Mythic's admiring gaze lingered on each impressive feature of both the condo and myself.

"This place is something else," he remarked, looking around with genuine awe.

"Are you looking to move back to the city?"

He chuckled at my nosiness. "Nah. I just need a secure spot for when I don't have the energy or time to drive to the burbs."

I smiled, trying to ignore the fluttering in my chest at the sound of his voice. "So, this place would be perfect. It's definitely one of the nicest in the area."

But it was when we reached the master bedroom that Mythic's eyes widened as he took in the expansive space. "Wow," he breathed. "This bedroom is insane."

I chuckled at his reaction, pleased at the sight of his genuine enthusiasm. "Yeah. It's definitely a standout feature."

As Mythic continued to explore the details of the penthouse, watching him sent a thrill flowing through me.

I turned to face him, my pulse pounding in my ears. "So, what do you think?" I asked, forcing myself to meet his gaze.

"I love it. Send me the paperwork as soon as you get back to the office."

Grinning, I squealed. I was going to get a nice commission check from this lease. "I knew you would like this place."

He studied me for a moment. His eyes lingered on me for longer than I could take. I swallowed hard as I felt myself blush.

"It's perfect, Avi," he said softly with his eyes still locked on me. "Just like you."

My face flushed, and I defiantly smiled from ear to ear against my will. I couldn't take his eyes on me, and I couldn't breathe, so I spun on the heels of my gold sandals and led the way out of the bedroom.

"Avi." His deep rumble caused my caramel skin to litter with goosebumps. Entering the kitchen, I felt his soft yet firm grip on my elbow. Swallowing hard, I reluctantly turned around. Still holding my elbow, he sat on a stool at the island. He then brought me between his large, long legs.

*I can't breathe.*

"What's wrong with you?" his deep roar asked sweetly.

I gulped, swallowing the lust bubbling over. "What makes you think that something is wrong?"

"You're trying to smile, but it's a sadness behind it."

Sighing, my eyes drifted away. "I didn't get the job I applied for."

He finally let me go, and my skin cried out for his touch. "Sorry to hear that."

"They gave it to Mia."

His face covered with sympathy for me. "Wow."

"Most likely to cut costs. I'm happy for her, but it still stings. I really wanted it."

He let go of my elbow. His hand softly slid down my arm and then held my hand tenderly. Giving it a slight squeeze, he said, "I know."

I leaned into his comfort. "I feel so behind. I see everyone flourishing in their careers or entrepreneurship, and I want that for myself."

"What's stopping you?"

"Damar doesn't want me to go back to school."

"Why not?"

"Because he's ready for us to have a baby." I blurted it out, hoping that it would stop him from looking at me with those eyes.

He swallowed hard but managed a loving smile. "But what do *you* want?"

"I want to go back to school."

"Then do it. Damar will just have to fall in line."

His authority made my brown skin tingle. I yearned for his embrace but knew that it was a place I would never return from, so I fought the urge.

Pulling into the parking lot of Dream Realty, my eyes narrowed. As they focused on the figures standing in front of the office, my heart started to pound violently. My breath caught in my throat at the sight of federal agents surrounding the building.

"Let me call you back, Jeremy," I rushed.

"Okay," he said before I hung up.

Without a second thought, I hurried out of my car and rushed inside.

But before I could step through the doors, my eyes widened in shock at the sight of more FBI agents escorting Mia out of the building with her hands cuffed behind her back.

I looked behind her through the glass walls. Other staff members and agents watched from the other side—appalled—from their desks and peering out of their office doorways.

"Mia!" I blurted as I rushed toward her. "What's going on?"

An officer stuck out his arm, keeping distance between us. Her eyes met mine. Anger and accusation burned in her glare.

"Really, Aviana?" she spat. "Are you that upset that I got the job instead of you?"

Shock rooted me to the spot that I was standing in. "What are you talking about? No!"

Mia's expression was so hardened with conviction as she shook her head. "You lying ass bitch," she seethed, her voice laced with betrayal as the cops led her away. "I trusted you!"

I blinked slowly, staring at her anger-fueled accusations with shock and disbelief.

As Mia was being led to a car, I walked inside the building in a daze of confusion and worry. The entire office was eerily quiet, like everyone was holding their breath. I stood there, frozen, watching through the window. Her head was low, but there was no real shame on her face.

Then I heard my name. "Aviana."

I jumped a little, and my heart hammered wildly. Antonio was standing in the doorway of his office. I hadn't even noticed him there. He had this serious look on his face, the kind that made my stomach drop.

"Come into the office," he sternly told me.

My legs felt like lead as I walked past him into the office. I couldn't lose this job. Though Damar had been splurging lately, we weren't comfortable enough with his finances to trust that he could carry us. He still spent money frivolously, and the promotion business was too unpredictable.

Alfred was already sitting at the desk with an expression just as serious as Antonio's.

"Sit down," Antonio said, gesturing to the chair in front of the desk.

I sat, feeling a knot tighten in my stomach. My palms were sweaty, and I didn't know where to look. Antonio stayed standing, arms crossed over his chest, while Alfred leaned back in the chair watching me carefully.

"Did you know anything about what Mia was doing?" Antonio asked as his eyes narrowed.

I acted obliviously the best I could. "What was she doing?"

"Stealing money from the company," Alfred answered.

"Really? How do you know this? You just promoted her."

"We received an anonymous tip right after her promotion. We had our head of finance do some digging. He found many questionable transactions, so we contacted the authorities who quickly linked the stolen funds to Mia."

I swallowed hard, feeling the heat rise in my chest. "I didn't know. I swear, I had no idea."

Alfred leaned forward slightly. "Are you sure about that, Aviana? Because you were pretty close to her."

I tried to force down the lump in my throat, which was suddenly so dry. "Yes, she's my best friend, but I didn't know she was stealing anything. I don't have anything to do with what Mia did. I've worked hard here. I love this job. I enjoy working with my clients. I can't lose this."

Alfred's eyes softened a bit, but he still didn't break his gaze. "You understand how serious this is, right? We need to be able to trust the people who work here."

I nodded quickly. "I understand. I swear I had no idea what Mia was doing. This job has been a blessing to me, and I'd never do anything to risk that."

Antonio and Alfred exchanged an unreadable look that made my heart race even more. They both stared at me for what felt like an eternity, like they were waiting for me to crack.

Finally, Antonio nodded toward the door. "Get back to work."

His voice was still so tense that it sent chills down my spine. However, I was so relieved.

Yet, it was short-lived.

"But understand this," Alfred added with his eyes locked on mine: "Mia is still under investigation. If anything comes up that connects you to what she was doing, you'll be facing charges too. Do you understand?"

I nodded swiftly. "Yes. I understand."

"Good," Antonio clipped. "Now get back to work."

I stood up with legs that were still shaky. I quickly made my way out of the office, hoping that Mia's bullshit hadn't rubbed off on me.

# CHAPTER 5

## AVIANA SCOTT

**AFTER BEING CHARGED,** Mia was released on bond until her court date. Since, she had been accusing me of telling either the twins or the authorities about her embezzling money from the company.

"I'm fighting federal charges because of you! I'm going to prison!"

As I paced the carpet in my bedroom, my stomach began to turn. "Why do you keep saying that it's because of me?"

"I know you told on me, Aviana," Mia spewed through the phone.

"Why are you so insistent that it was me? Maybe they just figured it out."

This was beyond bizarre. Mia had been my best friend for fifteen years. We had never had as much of a disagreement. Now, suddenly, she was so sure that I was deceiving her in such a heinous way.

"There was no way that they could have figured it out," she growled. "I've been meticulous for a year. You snitched because you were jealous that I got that promotion instead of you."

"Mia, I promise—"

"I swear to God," she gritted threateningly, "you're going to feel this, Aviana. I just lost everything, and I'm going to make sure that you do too."

"Mia…" I paused when I heard the end of her line go completely dead. "Mia?"

I pulled the phone away from my ear, staring at it. Blinking slowly, I felt tears coming to my eyes. As I began to sniffle, Damar left his spot at the foot of our bed.

"It's okay, baby," he tried to assure me as he slipped his arms around my waist.

"No, it's not." My voice cracked. A rush of overwhelming confusion and grief caused me to rest my head on his chest. "We've been best friends for nearly twenty years. Why would she assume that I would do something so devious to her over a job? She won't even give me the benefit of the doubt."

"She's reaching, baby. She has to blame somebody. She shouldn't have been doing that dumb shit anyway."

"I would never do something like this over a job," I insisted. "I wanted the raise, but it wasn't going to change my life. The money wasn't worth sending her to jail over."

"I can't believe you've been keeping what she's been doing from me," Damar softly fussed as he rubbed my back.

I looked up at him with watery eyes. "She's my best friend. She asked me not to tell anyone."

"Well, you see where that got you."

Sucking my teeth, I softly called his name in warning, "Damar…"

"Okay. I'm sorry. This night is supposed to be about us anyway, so let's stop thinking about Mia and her drama."

"That's going to be hard since she thinks I'm the cause of it."

"Can you at least try? You wanted me to give us some dedicated time, and I'm trying to do that."

"You're right." Taking a deep, soothing breath, I forced a smile. "I'm sorry, baby."

He smiled into my sorrowful pout, causing his bedroom eyes to twinkle. That convincing, charismatic expression reminded me of why I had fallen for him ten years ago.

He took my hand, leading me out of the bedroom.

In his quest to create a perfect evening, Damar went all out and arranged for a personal chef to whip up a dreamy candlelit dinner just for us. As we stepped into the dining room, I was spellbound by the transformation. It felt like we'd stepped into our own cozy, intimate restaurant. The table was a vision of romance, decorated with fragrant flowers that danced in the soft candlelight.

"It's beautiful in here," I swooned.

Damar's proud, cocky smirk made my center thump.

As we sat down at the beautifully set table, the warm glow of candlelight casting a soft ambiance over the room, I felt much-needed comfort. The aroma of the chef's cooking filled the air, tantalizing my senses with the rich scent of lobster bisque. The dining room had been transformed into a romantic, private restaurant, complete with elegant table settings and delicate floral arrangements.

"Aviana," he said softly, his eyes filled with tenderness as he reached for my hand across the table, "I know how much you wanted that job, but please don't forget that you are capable of achieving anything you set your mind to. You're talented, resilient, and deserving of anything you want in life, and I'm here to help you achieve it."

I felt a lump form in my throat as his words soothed the ache of disappointment that had been gnawing at my heart. "Thank you, Damar. I needed to hear that."

"I want you to have everything you've ever dreamed of. We're going to make it happen. I'm going to hurry up and put this baby in you so that you can go back to school, and I'm going to hustle so that you can have all the help you need so that school and raising our child won't be such a chore."

"Thank you, baby."

He smiled with an unwavering gaze as he continued to speak. "And as for Mia… She's just hurt and lashing out right now. You've always been there for her. It's not even in your character to do what she's accusing you of. She'll realize that soon."

As I nodded, I finally felt reassurance settle over me. "I hope you're right."

Damar squeezed my hand gently. "I know I am."

The soulful melody filled the air. Damar's eyes lit up as he recognized one of his recent favorite songs. A playful smile danced across his lips.

Unable to resist the infectious rhythm, Damar started to bob his head to the beat. His fingers tapped lightly on the table. He glanced over at me, his gaze sparkling with mischief, and extended his hand toward me with a charming grin. "Come dance with me, baby."

"Of course," I replied with a smile, taking his hand as he pulled me up from my seat.

As we moved together to the rhythm of the music, Damar led with effortless grace, his movements smooth and confident. With each step, he exuded a magnetic charm that drew me closer to him, melting away any lingering worries or doubts. Our bodies moved as one, swaying to the intoxicating melody with a sense of unity and connection.

As the song reached its crescendo, Damar spun me around gracefully before pulling me close once more, his gaze locked with mine.

Looking into my eyes, he softly chewed on his bottom lip. His large hands then cuffed my ample butt cheeks. Staring deep into my orbs, he acted as if he was going to pick me up.

"You better stop," I warned.

"Girl, this is light work."

I smirked cockily. "Just because I carry it well doesn't mean it's not heavy."

Damar seductively raised a brow. "Doesn't matter how heavy it is, I handle it well."

## MYTHIC GREY

Looking up at the warehouse, Taye blew out a long breath. Then he slowly turned toward me as I sat in the driver's seat of my G-Wagon.

"You sure about this?"

Chuckling, I shook my head. "You're thinking too deep about this."

"You're not thinking deep enough."

One corner of my lips rose into a taunting smirk. "You never have these reservations when we're working with other clients."

"Because these clients are different. The Mexican cartel is notoriously ruthless. They live by a different code. They kill for minuscule reasons. If they think you crossed them, they will want your head...*literally*, your head."

My head tilted back as I let out another deep chuckle. "I got this."

Nodding slowly, Taye put his hand on the handle of the passenger door. "Okay. Let's roll."

As Taye and I emerged from the sleek black SUV, I appreciated his caution. His apprehension was realistic. The Mexican cartel operated with brutality and unforgiving principles. In their world, loyalty was bought with blood, and betrayal was met with swift, unhinged, brutal vengeance. But I had always operated in principle. And I feared no one.

The gravel beneath our feet crunched with each step, stirring up a cloud of dust that danced in the air like ghosts. As we approached the imposing, weather-beaten metal door, it groaned open with a mechanical creak. My gaze swept up, noticing the surveillance cameras perched overhead.

A hulking figure emerged from the shadows of the doorway. His massive frame was meant to be imposing, but we were similar in size. Sweat glistened on his brow, mingling with the grime that coated his skin. His long, unkempt hair hung in greasy strands, concealing his menacing features beneath an oily veil. But his eyes bore into mine with an intensity that was meant to intimidate me.

With a curt nod, he stepped aside, wordlessly granting us entry.

As Taye and I stepped into the dimly lit warehouse, the overwhelming scent of motor oil and gunpowder hung in the air.

Pablo and Felipe emerged from the shadows. Their faces were masked with unreadable expressions. They were the lieutenants of the Kingsmen.

"Mythic," Pablo greeted with a low, gravelly voice. "Taye."

Taye answered with a quick, sharp nod.

"Felipe," I acknowledged with the same brisk nod.

Felipe waved a hand toward two metal chairs parked at a wooden table, gesturing for us to have a seat.

As we all sat, I got straight to business. "What can I help you gentlemen with?"

Pablo's lips curled into a faint smirk. "Getting straight to business. I like that." A smile spread to his ears, revealing a chaotic scatter of teeth. "Let's talk numbers."

"We offer quality," I stated firmly, "and quality comes at a price."

Felipe's eyes narrowed, but I could see a glint of respect buried beneath the hostility.

"Here's what I can offer you," I began, "AK-47 assault rifles, five hundred dollars each. Glock handguns, three hundred dollars each. RPG-7 rocket launchers, two thousand dollars each."

His interest now piqued, Felipe raised a brow. "And what about ammunition?"

I leaned so far back in the chair that its front legs rose in the air. "Ammunition prices vary depending on quantity," I explained. "But for bulk orders, I can offer you a discount. One thousand rounds of 7.62 millimeter ammunition for the AK-47s three hundred dollars. Five hundred rounds of nine millimeter ammunition for the Glocks, $150."

Felipe sat up, placing his intertwined hands on the table. "And explosives?"

"For your standard C4, I can offer you a rate of five hundred dollars per kilogram," I stated matter-of-factly. "But if you're looking for something with a little more kick—say, RDX or TNT, you're looking at a higher price point. RDX will run you about eight hundred dollars per kilogram, while TNT is a bit pricier at one thousand dollars per kilogram." I paused, letting the numbers sink in before continuing. "Again, if you're interested in bulk orders, we can negotiate a discount. And if you have any special requests or specific preferences, we can accommodate those too— for the right price, of course."

Felipe and Pablo exchanged a glance, silently conferring before turning back to me with a nod of approval. "Those prices sound reasonable," Pablo conceded.

"Excellent," I replied. "I'll need half upfront, with the remaining balance due upon delivery. Cash only, no exceptions."

"Deal." Pablo grunted, extending his hand across the table.

I clasped it firmly, sealing our agreement with a handshake.

After quickly hammering out the details of the delivery, Taye and I stood to make our exit.

Before leaving, I fixed a firm glare on both men. "Gentlemen, let's get one thing straight: I'm in the business of arms dealing, not gangs. I don't pick sides, and I won't be swayed by loyalty or allegiance." Their eyes narrowed slightly, but they remained silent, waiting for me to continue. "If you want to do business with me, understand that I do business with whoever *I* see fit. The only color that I see is green."

There was a moment of tense silence as they processed my words. I could see the defiance flicker in their eyes, but ultimately, they nodded in reluctant agreement.

"No innocent bystanders," I told them. "I don't deal in weapons for the slaughter of innocents or children. I refuse to have my name stained with their blood."

Many arms dealers didn't have the moral convictions that I did. But having grown up in the hood, I had seen far too many innocent people, especially children, die by the hands of careless criminals. This was the specific reason why I never sold weapons to the young gangs in my old hood that had no rules or morals. I couldn't control how the weapons that I sold were used, but my clients knew that if they were tied to any murders of the innocent or youth, they would no longer have my services and would pay hefty consequences.

"Understood," Pablo forced through tight lips.

I locked a steely glare on them. "I'll be in touch when the delivery is locked in. Good day, gentlemen."

Taye's and my heavy footsteps echoed through the warehouse as we neared the imposing metal door. The hulking figure, drenched in sweat, who had granted us entry swung the door open, releasing us back into the warm night.

As we approached my truck, Taye waited until we heard the metal close behind us before asking, "You think they'll play by the rules?"

"I am the only respected and reliable arms dealer on this side of the country. To get my quality and my prices, they will have to travel west or even out of the country, so they have no choice but to play by my rules. They don't have a choice if they want to be able to fight their war."

Hour later, I sat at the bar at Enchant, scrolling through Aviana's Instagram like some kind of stalker, as if I hadn't seen these same pictures countless times already.

Every time I tried to pull my eyes away, my thumb just kept swiping, moving to the next picture. I relished in the way her eyes shined in that way that always got to me. Then there was a shot of her in that red lace dress, looking innocent, as if she had no clue how fine she was. The more I stared, the more I felt like I was losing it.

I knew I had to get it together. Aviana was married. She wasn't mine anymore, but I couldn't stop thinking about the way her touch lingered when she showed me that condo the other day. But she had her life, her husband, and I had whatever I had with Lelani.

I was deep in my thoughts when I heard someone call my name. Before I could even react, I saw Lelani standing over me, and I hurriedly closed the app.

"What you doin' here?" I asked, trying to play it cool as she walked up.

Lelani slid onto the barstool next to me with an unreadable expression. "Dinner ended early. I wasn't ready to go home yet, so I had my mom drop me off."

I leaned in and kissed her quickly. As she sat, I was already putting my phone back in my pocket, pushing the thoughts of Aviana out of my mind. I tried to focus on Lelani—on being here in the moment with her. But that lingering feeling of Aviana's touch, the way she looked at me the day before, stayed with me, no matter how much I tried to shake it.

As the clock crept past midnight, I perched on the second-floor balcony of Enchant.

Enchant had become more than just a nightclub; it was a sanctuary for those seeking refuge from the mundane and the ordinary. My reputation allowed everyone to party peacefully in this domain. At Enchant, rivals partied alongside one another without fear of violence.

At thirty years old, it was starting to feel like I was living on borrowed time in the criminal world. It had started to feel as if it was time to put my intelligence into a new hustle that would be as lucrative but less dangerous, so I had invested in Enchant. Its success was birthing a new venture for me. I was hoping that soon, I could transition from a notorious arms dealer to a successful club/restaurant owner with nightlife locations all over the city.

I stood above it all, watching the scene below with that same satisfaction I always got when I looked out over Enchant. This place had become the spot, a real force in the nightlife game. The bass pounded through the floors, shaking the walls like the whole building was alive. The deejay had the crowd in a zone, locked into the beats, swaying and grinding.

The dance floor was packed. Bodies were moving in sync. Laughter, whispers, and the music blended into one. Some people were straight wildin', standing on couches with their hands in the air like they were trying to touch the ceiling.

Lelani was still at the bar, hanging out with the bartenders she'd gotten tight with since we got together. Bottle girls were zigzagging through the crowd, holding trays full of bottles, heading to VIP.

The whole place was flowing like a well-oiled machine, and as I watched over my kingdom from above, I felt a swell of pride at what I had built.

My attention was soon drawn to a figure moving with purpose through the tight crowd. Mia's determined stride set her apart from the sea of partygoers. Her attire made her even more noticeable. Unlike the other women who flaunted their beauty and body in revealing outfits, Mia was in leggings, a baggy t-shirt, and gym shoes. Her unkempt hair added to her distinctive appearance.

I leaned over the banister as I watched her engage in a brief exchange with Butch, one of the bouncers stationed near the flight of stairs that led to the second floor. Their conversation seemed tense, punctuated by animated gestures and furrowed brows. And then, Butch pointed in my direction, directing Mia's gaze toward the second floor where I stood.

My curious eyes locked on Mia as she ascended the stairs with angry strides.

"What's going on?" I asked with brows knitted together as she marched toward me.

"Your snitch-ass friend!"

Her abrupt anger caused me to take a small step back as she closed the space between us. "What are you talking about?"

"You mean you haven't talked to her?" she quipped angrily.

Still confused, I inquired, "Aviana? No. Not since she showed me the condo yesterday." Eyeing her frazzled disposition oddly, I asked, "What happened?"

Her chest dramatically rose up and down as she paced in the small space between where we stood between the railing and a VIP table. "I was arrested at work yesterday. It was the Feds!"

My eyes bucked as my jaw dropped.

"Exactly!" she snapped, arms flailing in the air.

"What were you charged with?"

Thinking of the answer made her cringe. "Wire and bank fraud, money laundering, identity theft—"

"Shit." I exhaled loudly.

She winced. "My lawyer told me that I'm facing ten years."

My eyes ballooned wider. "Gawd damn. How much money did you take?"

She peered at me reluctantly. "Almost a hundred thousand."

"Gawd damn, Mia!" I barked.

"I know," she whined.

"I told you to stop doing that shit."

"I would have never gotten caught had your friend not told on me!"

"Why do you think she said anything? She hasn't even mentioned it to me because you have her thinking that no one else knows."

Her pursed lips pressed to the side as her hands went to her hips. "Well, I know you would never tell, so it had to be her."

"Or you just got caught slipping," I suggested.

"I didn't slip. The bank accounts aren't in my name. My paperwork was immaculate. I was careful. It had to be her. She's been wanting more for herself. She's so unhappy. She was judging me for what I was doing. I think that me getting that promotion over her just sent her over the edge."

I shook my head, refusing to agree. "It's not in Avi's character to do something like this. She loves you to death."

Mia scoffed. "Well, she obviously loves me to fucking prison too."

"You're trippin'. You need to calm down."

"I can't," she snapped, still pacing with chaotic breaths.

I leaned against the railing, asking her, "What are you going to do?"

"I don't know," she whined as she ran her fingers through her frazzled, unkempt mane. "I was able to get a good lawyer, but then they froze my accounts today, so I won't be able to make the next payment to her. But she's convinced that the Feds are going to make an example of my black ass and give the maximum time. This is a federal case, Mythic. They aren't going to let me off easy. And I can't even negotiate a deal because there are no other or bigger players in this. It was all me."

"You know I'll help you pay for the lawyer."

I would have gladly helped her with anything, but her stubbornness prevented me from lending a hand. Just like the prideful demeanor of many women we had known since childhood, she insisted on handling things independently, without my assistance. While she didn't mind accepting small gifts or complimentary bottles from me, her ego prevented her from allowing her best friend to support her entire lifestyle.

She pouted with a sigh. As she gazed up at me, I saw the fear in her cat-like orbs. "Thank you, My—" Her phone started to ring in her hand, taking her attention. Seeing the number, her eyes widened. "Th–Thank you, Mythic," she stuttered as she looked at the phone.

"Everything okay?"

"Y–Yeah," she said, prying her eyes off her phone. "I just…I have to go. I have to go take care of something," she rushed.

Furrowing my brows tightly, I nodded. I watched her now hurried demeanor as she shoved her phone into her pocket and started to back away. "I'll call you later."

I nodded as she rushed away. "Yeah. Do that."

# MIA GREEN

My phone was ringing again as I entered the stairwell of Enchant. Finally out of Mythic's sight, I took it out of my pocket and answered Damar's call. "Where the hell have you been? I've been calling you all day!"

"You expect me to answer while I'm with Avi? She's a wreck! Why would you accuse her of snitching on you?"

"Who else did? That jealous bitch told on me."

"Calm down," he gritted. "Meet me at the spot."

"I'm on my way."

As I paced the living room of the condo, my mind raced with fury and frustration. I was filled with rage and felt so betrayed. And every second that Damar sat on the couch appearing unmoved and unfazed made my frustration grow wildly.

I had done all of this for him, but now he had nothing to say. Watching him casually scroll through his phone was offensive. Walking up to him, I snatched it out of his hand and threw it on the couch. "Damar, do you even hear me? I know Aviana snitched to the twins." Fuming, I started pacing again. "There's no other explanation. She's the one who blew my cover. I should have known she was a hating ass bitch. She didn't get that position, so she got me fired."

I stopped pacing and spun to face him. My eyes blazed when I realized that he had retrieved his phone and was sitting there casually responding to a text message. "I'm facing federal charges, and you're just sitting there like you don't give a damn? I had everything lined up for us, and now it's all falling apart because of *her*. I'm done playing nice. I'm going to make sure she pays for this. I'll make her life a living fucking hell."

Damar remained silent with his expression indifferent. His continued lack of response only fueled my anger. I threw my hands up in exasperation. "Do you even care? I was the one who followed your damn advice, who risked everything based on what you said. You taught me how to steal that money. You helped me spend this fucking money, and now you act like it's nothing?"

Damar shook his head slowly with raised brows. "I told you *how* to do it. That's all I did."

My shoulders slumped seeing his own fear of possibly being wrapped up in this.

"Baby, we can run away," I offered desperately. "You have some of the money. We can run away together—me, you, and the baby."

His cold eyes watched me as if I were being ridiculous. "Mia, we can't be on the run like we're drug lords. It's the Feds. We'd have to run to Africa to keep them from finding us. You knew the risks when you started doing this shit. I only told you what to do, but I'm not involved in this shit anymore."

"You think you can just act like you had nothing to do with any of this?" I spat, feeling his betrayal make me physically sick. "I'm the one left facing the charges while you get to sit back and enjoy your life? What about everything we have? You want nothing to do with this now, but you were right there with me when it all started." My hands started to shake as I nervously ran my fingers through my hair.

Watching Damar's uncaring attitude was like a dagger to my heart. I thought we were in this together, that we shared something real. We were supposed to save the money, start fresh, and build a life far away from all the lies and deceit. But now that the shit was hitting the fan on oscillate, he was being dismissive and cold, as if I was just a small inconvenience to him.

His lack of concern was intolerable. It felt like every dream I'd ever had with him was shattered in that instant. I had given him everything—my loyalty, my trust, and my love. And now, as I stood there, it hit me with brutal clarity: It had all been a lie. He never cared about me the way I had cared about him. All those whispered promises—the stolen moments of passion— meant nothing to him.

The realization ignited a rage so fierce it felt like a beast clawing its way out from within. I felt tricked. I could feel it swelling in me, making my hands tremble and my heart race. I wanted both of them to pay for this betrayal—Damar *and* Aviana. This wasn't just about revenge anymore; it was about unleashing the fury that was currently swallowing me whole.

The thought of Damar's dismissive attitude and the way he had turned his back on me made my blood boil. He would not get away with this. I would make sure that every last person who had contributed to my downfall would face consequences. My rage had become uncontrollable, and it wasn't going to stop until I had taken everything from everyone who had ever wronged me.

"You didn't have anything to do with this?" I taunted him with narrowed eyes as I slowly licked my lips, tasting the rage coating them. "You don't want to leave with me? *Cool.* I'm telling Aviana everything—how we've been sleeping together for the past year, how you're the one that talked me into embezzling, how you've been spending the money with me and fucking me in this condo every chance you get. I'll make sure she knows exactly who you are and everything you've done."

Damar's face darkened with a flash of anger. "I wish the fuck you would. You're not going to say shit."

I glared at him, my heart pounding with fury and hurt. "What's wrong with me telling her? I thought you were leaving her. I thought you loved me. I thought she was a fat bitch who couldn't make your dick hard."

Damar slowly stood. I should have been scared of the rage that I saw in his eyes, but I was too filled with my own fury to pay it any attention.

"You think I'm going to just rot in prison while everyone else lives their lives freely? Fuck that!" I went on, "Don't think for a fucking second that I won't do whatever it takes to get back at Aviana and make you pay for how you're playing me."

"You're not going to tell Aviana shit." His voice dripped with a cold, unfeeling certainty.

Damar's harsh words sliced through my rage, cutting deeper than I ever expected. Something snapped inside me. I was no longer the woman who had once dreamed of being his partner in crime, the one who had envisioned a future together. All I wanted now was for the pain to end. The betrayal, the heartbreak—it was all too much. I wanted everyone involved to suffer like I was suffering.

I lunged for my phone on the coffee table. I needed to call Aviana, to expose Damar and everything he had done. But Damar was right behind me, his desperation clear as he tried to twist the phone from my grasp. His eyes, usually so confident and commanding, were now filled with a frantic fear that only fueled my determination.

As we wrestled, my fingers gripped the phone tightly. "You really love her, don't you?" I spat, my voice shaking with anger and betrayal. "I told you about her feelings for Mythic, and you still want to love and protect this fat bitch. It's so obvious now that you were just using me. All those promises, all that love—you were just playing me."

His face contoured with growing fury. "No shit. I just wanted the money, and your stupid ass fell for it," he roared as his hands forcefully yanked at the phone. "You're not telling her anything."

The intensity of his rage made me even more stubborn. There was no way that I was going to let him get away with this. I fought back with everything I had, struggling to keep hold of the phone.

My emotions were a raging storm, and my movements became frantic as I tried to break free.

"Nigga, I'm telling her everything." I brought my face so close to his that we were nose to nose. I could feel the hot rage and tension exploding between us. "I'm showing her our text messages, and I'm *especially* showing her every video of you eating my pussy from the back. I'm going to ruin your life the way you ruined mine. You were supposed to love me…" Against my stubbornness, I choked up as I thought of the life growing in my belly. "It was supposed to be me, you, and our baby. Avi deserves to know. You can't keep hiding me and my baby."

## AVIANA SCOTT

The next morning, I woke up to so many threatening text messages from Mia that I couldn't read them all.

**Mia:** *You were my friend. I trusted you.*

**Mia:** *I can't believe you did this to me.*

**Mia:** *I lost everything, so you have to lose everything too.*

**Mia:** *You ruined my life, so I'm going to ruin yours.*

**Mia:** *Watch your back, fat bitch.*

"This is insane." I sighed with tears in my eyes. I gripped the steering wheel, staring blankly out of the windshield of my parked Jeep.

I had been trying to get in touch with Mia since receiving the messages that morning. No matter how vile she was toward me, I willed myself to believe that this was only her anger talking. I felt as if I could get through to her, she would calm down and realize that she was being ridiculous. But she wouldn't answer any of my calls.

Still, I kept trying. Before getting out of my car, I tried to call her again. I bit my bottom lip nervously, reluctantly waiting for her rage to answer, but still hoping that she did.

But, again, I got her voicemail.

"You've reached Mia…"

Blowing another frustrated breath, I hung up and tossed my phone into my purse. I had read the first barrage of messages over and over all morning in pure disbelief. Mia's unwillingness to give me the benefit of the doubt was heartbreaking and baffling. I couldn't understand where this sudden rage toward me and distrust in my loyalty to her had come from.

I sat in the car for a minute, just staring at the steering wheel. I was so frustrated and confused. I didn't understand how Mia could believe that I would do something like this to her.

I sighed, picking up my phone and dialing Damar.

He answered on the second ring. "Hey. What's up, baby?"

"Damar," I whined.

"What's wrong?"

"Mia has been texting me all morning. She really thinks I snitched. She's accusing me of setting her up, talking about how I betrayed her. I'm lost, Damar. I really don't get it. I would never do anything like that to her. She's acting like I'm the enemy. After everything we've been through, why does she think I'd stab her in the back?"

"Bae, you know how people are when they feel like their back is against the wall. She's just grasping at straws, trying to blame somebody. It ain't about you."

Feeling the frustration growing, I rubbed my temple. "But why me? She knows I'd never come for her like that. I don't know what to do. She keeps texting me, but she won't answer the phone."

"Just ignore her. She'll get over it eventually. And if not, fuck her. You've been a great friend to her. If she'd turn on you like this, you don't need her."

I let out a long breath. "Yeah…you're right." Then I asked, "Where have you been all day? You were gone when I woke up."

"I went to the gym. Had to get it out the way early 'cause I got a lot to handle today."

"You could've at least let me know you were leaving."

He chuckled softly. "You were drooling, baby. I didn't want to wake you up for nothing. You already had a long night."

*"Mmmph,"* I mumbled, still feeling frustrated.

"Look," he said gently. "Don't let Mia's mess get to you. She'll figure it out, and everything will calm down."

"All right," I said reluctantly as a I blew a heavy breath. "I'll try."

"Good girl. I'll catch up with you later, okay?"

"Yeah." I hung up and sat there for another moment because my frustrations were still simmering.

Broken, I climbed out of my Jeep and made my way toward my parents' house on 109th and Vernon. Despite the familiar sights and sounds that surrounded me, there was an eerie stillness that hung in the air. It was a temporary calm. The block was resting after a Friday night, but soon the storm of activity would inevitably descend upon the neighborhood again.

But for now, on this quiet Saturday morning before noon, the neighborhood was sleeping, as if holding its breath in anticipation of what the day would bring. I paused for a moment, taking in the sight of the familiar houses and streets bathed in the soft glow of morning light. Despite the changes that had swept through Roseland over the years, there was still a sense of home here, a feeling of belonging that anchored me to this place and its people.

I used my set of keys to let myself into the house. As I stepped inside, the savory scent of sausage greeted me. My mother sat on the couch nearby in the living room.  Her warm smile lit up her face. "Hey, baby."

"Hey, Mama." Entering the living room, I bent down and kissed my mother on the cheek. She lifted her hand, holding my cheek as she pressed hers into the kiss.

"C'mon. Let's eat. We were waiting for you."

Nearing her late sixties, my mother's body was starting to show its age. She wasn't able to stand as quickly. Seeing her body's resistance, I looped my arm with hers and helped her stand, then we made our way through the small living and dining area toward the kitchen.

The house was unchanged, frozen in time since the day I'd left at nineteen. Every piece of furniture, every picture on the walls, remained exactly as I remembered it. It was as if time stood still within these walls, preserving the memories of years gone by.

In the kitchen, my father rushed about, which was a familiar sight. Cooking had always been a ritual he took pride in. The clatter of pots and pans, the sizzle of food on the stove filled the air.

Standing at the stove, he looked over his shoulder with a smile. "Hey, baby."

I smiled as I unhooked my arm from my mother's and approached him. I hugged him from behind and kissed his cheek. "Hey, Daddy."

I closed my eyes for a millisecond, appreciating the nostalgia of being home. I needed the embrace of my parents and the familiarity of this place. I needed the reminder of who I was, my morals, and the flash of reality because Mia's fury had caused me to forget.

"I'll make your plate, baby," my mother told me. "Have a seat."

Sitting down at the table, I felt the relief of the homey, familiar surroundings.

"Aviana, did I tell you that Reverend Johnson's daughter is having another baby?" my mother asked.

I chuckled, shaking my head, as my mother went on. "She insists on embarrassing her father."

"That's what PKs do." My father laughed heartedly as he sat down across from me.

As I listened to my parents gossip about Reverend Johnson's daughter, Sheila, I couldn't help but feel a pang of sympathy for her. I too had been a preacher's kid, so I understood the urge to act out.

"Can you believe it?" my mother exclaimed as she set a plate with an omelet with a side of sausage and grits in front of my father. "This is Sheila's fourth child with her fourth baby's father. She's making a mockery of her father's position in the church."

My father nodded solemnly with his brow curled in dismay. "It's a shame, really. Reverend Johnson has always been so strict with Sheila, but it seems like she's determined to defy him at every turn."

"I can't help but feel sorry for her," I interjected quietly as my mother set breakfast in front of me. "She's only twenty-one. I'm sure there is a lot of pressure on her from her parents and the church."

My mother sighed. "I know, Aviana, but Sheila has always been fast and defiant since she was a little girl. She doesn't realize that trying to go against her father is only making things harder for herself."

As my parents continued to discuss Sheila's situation, I fell silent. They would never understand the suffocation of growing up under the pressure of trying to meet their expectations, especially given that they themselves had married at the tender age of sixteen.

I couldn't shake the feeling that I had ended up in my mundane marriage partly because I was trying to fulfill the expectations ingrained in me since childhood. The desire to please my parents, especially in matters of love and marriage, had always affected every decision I made.

Thoughts of Mythic lingered like a bittersweet ache. I was still drawn to him, as I had been back then. But the disapproval I imagined from my parents had always kept me from fully embracing the passion and excitement Mythic offered.

I always wondered if I had made the right choice. I often wondered if I had followed my heart instead of bowing to the pressure of my parents' expectations, would my life have turned out differently. Regret, as it always did, gnawed at me. But dwelling on what-ifs only caused me more suffering. All I could do was accept the path I had chosen and find peace in the small moments of happiness my marriage had, even if they fell so short of the passion and excitement I'd had with Mythic.

Stepping out of my parents' house, every nerve in my body came to life as soon as I spotted Mythic walking up the block. It wasn't surprising to see him in the neighborhood. He still had ties there. But his presence never failed to send my nerves into a frenzy.

As our eyes met, a jolt of electricity shot through me. My heart pounded unsteadily in my chest.

With shaky hands, I approached him. Mythic stood tall and imposing. His presence cast a shadow over me as I stopped in front of him while standing on the sidewalk in front of my parents' home.

My breath hitched. His appearance kidnapped my attention, demanding it. It dared me to find the ability to look away. Despite his bad-boy swag, he was still angelic in a fitted white tee. Diamonds glistened in his ears and on his neck, competing with the sun.

"Avi." His voice was so smooth and deep, sending shivers down my spine.

"Hi, Mythic." My voice was weak as my heart raced with excitement.

My stomach lurched with regret knowing that Damar never made me feel this way.

He took me into his large embrace, smothering me with his woody scent. The familiar pull of obsession tugged at me. He was so intoxicating that it swallowed me. His irresistible grip on my heart tightened around it.

"Why haven't you called me?"

Pushing back against his chest, I looked up at him with a wrinkled brow.

He answered my silent inquiry. "Mia came to the club last night."

I pried myself from his embrace. Frustrated, I began to charge toward my car. "She told you? So, she seriously thinks that I did this?"

Mythic followed close behind me. "Of course she told me. We're tight. *You* should have told me."

"I was going to. But it's not something that I felt I should talk about over the phone, especially since she's being investigated."

Looking back at him, I saw Mythic nod. "That's smart."

"You don't think I really told on her, do you?"

His steps halted. His head tilted dramatically as his striking glare anchored on me. "Hell no, Avi. I know better."

I swallowed hard, forcing myself to focus on reality. "Then why doesn't *she* know better?"

Mythic shrugged. "I think she's just lashing out. She's frustrated and has to let it out on someone."

"But on me?"

"When people are going through something, they often lash out on the person closest to them."

Sucking my teeth, I pouted. "That's fucked up."

"Don't worry about it. She'll figure out that she's tripping soon enough. Her lawyer will figure out the evidence against her, and she will realize how she got caught up. I've been trying to call her to talk some sense into her, but she hasn't been answering all day."

"It shouldn't take all of that for her to realize that I would never do something like this."

"I know." He slightly poked out his hefty bottom lip, mocking my own expression. Then he softly grabbed my chin, causing my body to quake. "It's going to be okay."

I craned my neck to meet his towering height. I had to squint up at him as the sun's rays blinded me.

"You okay?"

Looking up at him, a current of emotions rushed through me. His mere presence stirred up a longing that I had tried to suppress for years. The yearning I felt for Mythic was unlike anything I had ever experienced, and it was a force that I could no longer deny.

But I had to.

Standing there, I felt like my parents' and God's eyes were on me, ridiculing me.

"I'll be okay." I forced my eyes off him and unlocked my Jeep with my key fob.

"I know you will." I could hear his sexy, deep rumble as he followed me.

As we reached the curb, I paused when I noticed a car speeding down the block. I was instantly relieved as I realized that it was Mia's Audi. I looked back at Mythic, who gave me a reassuring, supportive smirk.

As the car slowed to a stop in front of me, I discreetly smiled, grateful that Mia was at least willing to talk.

As her tinted window began to roll down, I stepped forward, saying, "Hi, M—"

But Mia's arm shot out of the window, clutching a glass bottle with a flaming cloth rag, which made my whole body freeze. She hurled the bottle through my driver's side window. The window and bottle shattered on impact, engulfing the Jeep in flames.

"Oh my God!" I shrieked, just as Mythic's large arm snatched me back. We stumbled over the curb, tumbling into my parents' yard.

Panicking, I scrambled to escape the inferno. The heat and smoke choked me as I crawled away from the wreckage. Gasping for air, I felt Mythic's presence shielding me from the chaos.

As the adrenaline began to subside, he gently lifted me to my feet. His concerned voice cut through the confusion. "Are you okay?" he asked as he scanned my face and body for any injuries.

Gasping for a steady breath, I couldn't find words as I stared at the flames engulfing my Jeep.

All hope of reconciliation with Mia vanished in that moment, replaced by a blinding reality of her unhinged wrath.

# CHAPTER 6

## MYTHIC GREY

Finally, Aviana was able to find words "Y–Yeah." She nodded slowly, blinking owlishly at the flames. "I–I'm okay."

But I wasn't. As I watched the flames swallow up Aviana's car, a fear hit me so deep I could barely breathe. My heart was pounding like I had never felt before. In that split second, knowing her life was in danger, it was like my whole world flipped upside down. The idea of losing her shook me to my core. I couldn't even wrap my mind around living in a world without her. Just the thought alone had me spiraling, damn near panicking.

Suddenly, she erupted into horrific coughs as she stared at the flames with a bewildered expression.

Taking her hand, I led her several feet away from the flames.

"Oh my God!" Her mother's shrieks tore our awed gawks away from the flames toward Avi's parents' home. Her parents were storming down the porch. Their terrified stares darted between Avi and what was transforming into the corpse of her Jeep.

The fire on the Jeep raged. Flames shot up, licking at the sky like they were trying to swallow it. Thick and dark smoke was everywhere.

"Avi!" her father called out as he approached her with open arms. "Jesus! Are you okay?"

Even her father taking her into his arms caused jealousy to erupt in my gut. I wanted to be the one to protect her.

"I'm okay, Daddy," she breathed into his chest, as her mother wrapped her arms around her as well.

"This is ridiculous! Who did this?" her mother shrieked.

Still in her father's arms, Avi looked over her shoulder at me with conflict in her eyes.

"Some neighborhood kids playing around too much. I'll take care of it," I told them.

I knew that Aviana's hesitation was in putting Mia in more trouble than she was already in. That's how loving and humble Avi was.

Her parents watched me silently. There was some appreciation in their eyes, but behind it was the same judgment they'd had toward me as Avi and I were growing up. They knew that I was the same type of gangster that they despised.

Her father gave me a sharp nod and then continued to embrace his daughter. Her mother replied with a short, "Thank you," before giving Avi back her attention.

"I called the fire department," I heard from a window nearby. Looking around, I saw Miss Bernadine, the neighbor to the left, with her head sticking out the window.

"Thank you," I told her with a nod.

As her parents continued to comfort Aviana, I watched her with more intensity than I ever had.

Physically, I could see that she was unharmed, but I was still in shambles. Aviana wasn't just a part of my life; she was my entire world. She was my everything, the very essence of my existence, and the idea of anyone or anything harming her shook me. That realization hit me hard—like a freight train slamming into my chest—knocking the wind right out of me. From the moment we were children, she had been a constant presence that I had taken for granted. But now, having faced the possibility of losing her, I couldn't imagine a future without her in it. I knew in that moment that I would do anything to protect her, to keep her safe.

But as Damar's Bronco sped chaotically toward the scene, I was reminded that that wasn't my job. She didn't want me to be her protector; she hadn't since I'd broken her heart.

As she watched him park with curiosity, her mother answered her questioning stare. "I called him as soon as it happened."

Aviana only nodded as she peeled herself out of her father's embrace. Damar jumped out of his SUV. The smoke made his broad, towering frame a shadowy approach. He stared at the fire in disbelief as he hurried toward Avi.

Watching him throw his arms around her lit a jealous rage in me that consumed me with a fire so intense, it felt like it was roasting me from the inside out. I despised the way the sight made me feel like I was being torn apart. I felt out of control, which was a feeling I rarely experienced and one that I was determined to quash before it consumed me entirely.

I hated leaving Avi at her parents' house, but I couldn't take watching Damar fail at protecting her anymore. The fire department had arrived to put out the blaze a few minutes later. Watching them douse the flames, I knew I had to let Damar handle Avi now. As much as I wanted to be there for her, he was her husband. It was his job to take care of her, not mine.

As I drove through the neighborhood toward the expressway, I noticed Jeremy standing on a street corner with a group of 111 Boyz. They were huddled together, their faces hidden by masks and hoodies, looking ridiculous in the summer heat. I pulled over, the engine rumbling to a stop as I parked by the curb.

I got out of the car and walked up to them. My presence instantly commanded respect. My reputation in this part of town preceded me, and these kids knew better than to fuck with me.

I grabbed Jeremy by the arm and pulled him a few paces away from the group. The others fell silent. Their eyes shifted nervously as they watched us.

"What's up, Mythic? I do something?" Jeremy asked, acting shifty.

"Did you?" I urged, raising a brow.

"N–Nah."

"Then why you hanging with niggas that be on bullshit?"

"I…*uh*…I—"

"Shut the fuck up and listen to me: You gotta make better decisions. Hanging out with these young niggas and running the streets is not gonna get you anywhere good."

He glanced at me, shifting his weight from one foot to the other, his hoodie pulled low over his face. "Yeah, Mythic, I hear you," he muttered, but his gaze kept darting away, not really meeting mine.

"You think this is a game, man?" I continued. "Being in the wrong crowd, doing the wrong shit—it's not just about you. It's about everyone around you. You think you're invincible, but being in the wrong place at the wrong time can get you locked up or worse. Innocent people get hurt or killed every day because they're caught up in stuff they had no business being a part of."

Jeremy shuffled his feet, his attention clearly wandering. "Yeah, I know. That's why I don't be on shit. I just be hanging out."

I scoffed, stepping closer to him, making sure he felt every word I said. "You just be hanging out, huh? You're young, and you're still figuring things out, but listen to me: You can't afford to mess around with the wrong people. It's not just about street cred or whatever. It's about your future, your life. You need to make smarter choices and hang with the right crowd."

He nodded slowly, but his expression was distant. "I get it, Mythic."

Yet, I continued to scowl at him.

He chuckled nervously. "I do."

I could see he was hardly taking it in, probably too wrapped up in his own world to fully grasp what I was saying. But I had to try, for Avi's sake if nothing else. "Just think about what I'm telling you," I said, giving his shoulder a final, firm squeeze. "This isn't just about you now. It's about how you want your life to turn out. Don't end up being another young nigga dead or in jail because you was hanging with the wrong people."

With that, I turned and walked back to my car. I had only done that for Avi. She loved Jeremy like he was her own son. If it had been up to me, I would have let Damar check his own fucking kid.

I'd been on the second floor of Enchant for a few hours, nursing my drink and staring down at the first floor. It was early, and there was just a few people scattered across the bar. I knew it wouldn't stay this way for long. Tonight was one of Damar's nights, so the crowd would be packed soon.

As I watched the scene below, my mind was a million miles away, stuck on thoughts of Avi. The image of her being held by Damar kept replaying in my head over and over. It was like a damn loop that I couldn't escape. Almost losing her had done more than shake me up; it had doused the fire I felt for her with gasoline.

I was obsessed, and I *hated* it.

Everything in my life was under my control—my business, my empire, my reputation. I dictated the pace, set the rules, and made the calls. But when it came to Avi, I was powerless. I hated how vulnerable she made me. The thought of her, especially in Damar's arms, was constant torment.

I tried to push it aside and focus on the club. But no matter how hard I tried, my mind kept drifting back to her, to the way she looked at me, to the way I felt whenever I was near her. I was a man used to control, and yet, here I was, completely at the mercy of my own feelings for her.

*"Fuuuuck."* A low, regretful growl escaped my throat as I eyed Aviana following Damar into the spot.

I stiffened. It was like my muscles had a mind of their own, reacting to her presence in a way I couldn't control. I hated how my whole being unraveled at the sight of her. The way she could unsettle me so effortlessly was unnerving.

When she spotted me and flashed that smile, it infuriated me how oblivious she was to the intensity of my feelings for her.

I watched her approach the VIP section. She had changed out of the casual leggings, t-shirt, and gym shoes she'd worn earlier that day. Now, she wore what was supposed to be a basic t-shirt dress, but on her, it was anything but ordinary. The fabric clung to her curves in a way that left little to the imagination, accentuating her voluptuous figure with every move she made. The way the dress hugged her curves, the generous swell of her hips, the gentle roundness of her stomach, and the confident way she carried herself made it look like a high-fashion piece from a runway show in New York. My dick rocked up as hard as the steel of the railing that I was leaning against.

"What are you doing here?" I asked, trying not to let my irritation show. At that moment, it was a blessing and a curse to see her. "You should be resting after the day you had."

She glanced up at me, and I could see that her eyes were soft but tired. "Damar didn't want to leave me alone, so he made me come with him."

She stood close enough that I could smell her sweet fragrance. It made it even harder to focus. Her presence was so close, it was almost unbearable. I found myself staring at her, my gaze fixed on her face, drinking in every detail.

Avi shifted slightly, as if sensing my intense scrutiny. Her voice broke the silence with a nervous edge to it. "Why are you looking at me like that?"

Her question cut through my haze.

I couldn't take it anymore. I had to put an end to this. "Avi, you can't come to the club anymore."

Her eyes widened in shock. "What? Why not?"

I took her hand and pulled her into the stairwell. I paced a few steps before turning to face her. "Because of how I feel about you." Her eyes ballooned more, and I saw her breath hitch as I went on. "I can't think straight when you're around. You drive me insane, and I need space. I need you to stay away because nothing can happen between us. You're happily married, and I have to respect that."

Her face was a picture of disbelief. Her mouth was slightly open as she processed what I'd just said.

I was naively waiting for her to deny her marriage and tell me that she felt the same, but she didn't. Instead, she looked at me with sadness. "Please don't push me away." Her voice trembled slightly. "I've already lost my friendship with Mia. I don't want to lose you too."

I could feel the pull between us. The tension in the air grew thicker. I wanted to argue more, to convince her to leave, but something else was happening. Our eyes locked, and I could see the same desire reflected in her gaze that I felt in mine.

I towered over her. "You don't want me to push you away?"

She blinked up at me. "Please don't."

"Then tell me that you feel the same about me," I said, making her breath hitch.

Before I knew it, we were inches apart, our breaths mingling. I could feel the heat from her body. I leaned in, desperate to close the gap between us, to finally taste those lips I had been craving. But just as our lips were about to touch, she pulled back, her eyes wide and filled with nervous uncertainty.

"I–I have to go," she stammered.

She turned and hurried away. As I watched Avi scramble down the stairs, I was about to call after her—to try to make her stay, to complete that kiss—when I saw Lelani standing at the bottom of the stairwell. I had no idea how long she'd been there. Lelani was always popping up at the club whenever she wanted to.

Avi was so engrossed in her quick exit that she nearly crashed into Lelani. As soon as she recognized Lelani, her eyes grew wide with shock. "Oh my God, I'm so sorry!" She fumbled with her words, trying to regain her composure, but Lelani's expression remained unreadable. "Hi–Hi, Lelani."

Lelani's lips were pressed tightly together as she nodded a curt greeting.

I could see the way Lelani's gaze followed Avi. Once Avi was out of sight, I moved down the stairs. Lelani climbed the stairs and met me in the middle.

"What was that about, Mythic? What's going on with you and Avi?"

I tried to play it cool. "Nothing. I was asking her what she was doing here after everything that happened earlier. She needs to be at home. I was just looking out for her."

Lelani didn't look convinced. "*Mm-humph.* It didn't look like you were just looking out."

I met her gaze and forced a shrug, trying to deflect. "You're being silly. Stop trippin'. Anyway, what are you doing here? How was your doctor's appointment?"

"He ordered an MRI and blood tests since there was no obvious cause for the persistent headaches. He told me he'd review the results and contact me within a few days.

I was driving past the club and just wanted to pop in and say hi. I'm not staying. I'm not feeling well."

"Another headache?"

"Yeah."

I grabbed the back of her head and kissed her forehead. "Go home and get some rest. I've got to holler at Tyiesha about something. Let me walk you to the door."

She nodded and took my hand. As we walked down the steps, I discreetly took a deep breath, relieved of that close call. I wasn't in love with Lelani, but I was a gentleman. I didn't want to purposely hurt her, especially over a woman who belonged to someone else.

I needed to get my head right and put some distance between me and Aviana.

# CHAPTER 7

## AVIANA SCOTT

**T**HE NEXT MORNING, I woke up to the familiar touch of Damar needing his morning release.

I moaned, stirring in my sleep, as his fingers softly played with my essence.

Finally, my eyes fluttered open. My sleepy gaze fell on his devilish one.

"Good morning," he smoothly told me before kissing me.

"Good morning," I spoke into our kiss.

I wanted to feel the passion radiating from him. I wanted to want this, but my mind was everywhere. As he lay kisses down my neck and began to play with my breasts, I wasn't aroused. Frustrations over Mia and Mythic were way louder than any desire I should have felt at that moment.

"Baby..."

He knew the reluctance in my tone, so instead of answering me, he continued to kiss down my body. He French-kissed my stomach and started to lay soft pecks over my navel to my center.

His tongue gently parted my lower lips. He took his time savoring my juices before gliding up to my clit. My back arched, and I hissed as his lips met my love button.

He moaned as he sucked.

He started giving my clit slow, open-mouth sloppy kisses. He teased the pearl with his tongue. He sucked and drooled over it, only to lick up the drool and go back, kissing and sucking the pink bud. His tongue gently speared into my pussy as he sucked my clit, rubbing my inner walls, thrusting inside of me.

Slowly, my frustrations faded away. I started to writhe and moan, thrusting my hips to meet his demanding mouth.

His tongue was plunging in and out of me as he slurped up the wetness. I moaned at his filthiness as he moved back to my clit, sucking hard at the tight bud.

I came apart, screaming in ecstasy, hips thrashing, juices pouring from my pussy as he continued to gently suck and slurp at my clit, helping me through the orgasm and tonguing me through the aftershocks.

"Oh my God," I breathed as the orgasm faded.

As I attempted to catch my breath, Damar's naked body climbed over mine. He hovered over me, watching me with adoring, lust-filled eyes.

"Are you ovulating?"

I blinked at the random question. "H–Huh?"

"Are you ovulating?" he repeated as he rubbed his length along my lips, lubricating it with me.

"No. Not yet." Then I giggled. "You are so insistent about getting me pregnant all of a sudden."

"It's time, baby. I told you, I'm ready."

His expression was loving as he brought his head to my center. He penetrated me slowly, keeping his eyes on me as he started to ride me.

A few hours later, I was driving through the city in Damar's Bronco. Damar usually slept in on Sundays after a long night at the club, so I was able to use his truck to go to church. Having grown up with religious parents, I never missed a Sunday when I was young. Even as an adult, I tried not to miss a Sunday, especially if I didn't want to hear my parents' mouths.

This Sunday, more than ever, I needed to be there, though. The events of the past few days had left me feeling unsettled, and the stress was unbearable. I had always known that Mythic was attracted to me, but I never imagined that he harbored deeper feelings. His confession last night took me completely by surprise. It was a revelation that both thrilled and terrified me. The kiss we almost shared had ignited a fire inside me, but my morals had pulled me away. I couldn't let myself be swept up in that moment, no matter how much I ached for it.

Despite the passion I felt for Mythic, I was still committed to Damar who might not set my heart on fire like Mythic did, but he had been loyal and loving. Our marriage wasn't perfect; we had our problems, but they didn't justify betraying him or disgracing myself by pursuing something with Mythic. I respected Damar too much to throw it all away for a man who was still living the playboy lifestyle, professing feelings for me while in a relationship.

I thought about how leaving Damar would not only hurt him but also disappoint my parents. They had always been proud of my stable life and the good man I had chosen. I couldn't face them if I left all that behind for someone like Mythic. The stability and respectability that Damar represented were important to me, and I couldn't just toss them aside. I felt obligation to my husband, to my family, and to myself.

The phone rang, jolting me out of my thoughts. I glanced at the screen and saw it was Carol, Mia's mother.

"Hi, Carol," I said, steering with one hand and holding the phone with the other.

"Aviana, hi."

My brows curled as I noticed that Carol's voice was filled with worry.

"I was wondering if you've seen or heard from Mia. I haven't been able to reach her since Friday."

"The last time I saw or talked to Mia was Saturday."

Carol's sigh was filled with concern. "Well, she hasn't been home since Friday, and she stopped sharing her location with me. I'm really starting to get worried."

I swallowed hard, fighting the urge to spill the details about what Mia did to my car Saturday. "I'm sorry, Carol. I haven't heard from her either."

"She told me about the charges. I'm worried she might be on the run." Carol blew a worried breath. "I just don't know where she could be."

I felt a pang of guilt, knowing that Mia had blown up my Jeep. It was hard to believe she would be in such a state of desperation, but it was clear she had been hiding. "I can't say for sure, but if she's avoiding everyone and not answering her phone, she might be laying low somewhere in the city."

Carol sounded more distressed now. "I just wish I knew where she was. It's not like Mia to disappear like this. I hope she's safe."

"Me too," I said, trying to offer some comfort. "If you hear anything or if there's anything I can do, please let me know."

"Of course," Carol replied. "You do the same, please."

# MYTHIC GREY

That afternoon, when I walked into the house, the first thing I noticed was the sound of soft, muffled sobs coming from the living room. When I saw Lelani on the couch, her shoulders shaking with each sob, I instantly cringed.

Since the incident in the stairwell the night before, she had been distant and short with me. It was becoming clear that she had more than likely seen me and Avi in a compromising position. Guilt gnawed at me. I was so lost in my obsession with Aviana that it was breaking Lelani.

I knew I couldn't keep dragging such a good girl through this. She deserved better. I was never the type of man who wasted a woman's time or purposely ruined her, so I made the decision right then to end it right then and there. I walked over to the couch and sat down beside her, taking a deep breath as I prepared to break her heart.

But before I could say a word, her trembling voice cut through the air.

"There's something I need to tell you," she murmured.

I froze.

"I just got off the phone with my doctor." Her voice was trembling as I sat beside her on the couch.

I placed a soothing hand on her thigh to help settle her. "What did he say?"

She swallowed hard, finally lifting her tearful eyes to meet mine. "My MRI results came back. They found a tumor in my brain."

"A tumor?" My voice barely came out. "Are they sure?"

She nodded slowly. Her tears now slid freely down her cheeks. "He said based on how it looks on the MRI, it strongly suggests cancer. My blood tests show signs too. He said it all points to cancer."

As she broke down, I could feel her fear. It was so evident that I could almost touch it. I knew that she was already envisioning a painful death because her aunt and grandmother had lost their fights with breast cancer years ago.

I tried to stay cool for her. I put my arm around her and brought her into my arms. "What are the next steps?"

Lelani took a deep, shaky breath against my chest before answering. "He said I have to meet with a neurosurgeon next. They'll probably need to do a biopsy, which is surgery, to confirm it officially. Then most likely another surgery to remove or reduce it. Then after that, most likely chemo or radiation…or both." She paused, trembling slightly.

I held her tighter. "You'll get through this. I promise. You're going to beat this shit."

She sobbed quietly against me, clutching at my shirt. "I'm so scared. I don't want to die."

The pain in her eyes tore at my heart. My feelings now seemed insignificant in the face of what she was going through. Despite my feelings for her, she had always been loyal to me, so she deserved my support. I owed her to be her rock, the person she could lean on, and suddenly, my own needs felt so small compared to the battle she was about to face.

## AVIANA SCOTT

Monday morning, I was leading an Asian couple, Jin and Mira, through yet another condo in Bronzeville. My patience was stretching thin as we made our way through the third unit of the day. While women were usually the picky ones, Jin was actually the nitpicker. His eyes darted around the place critically, picking apart every little detail. Mira, on the other hand, looked on with a resigned, irritated sigh. Her excitement from the earlier showings was long gone.

"This room seems a bit small, don't you think?" Jin asked, wrinkling his nose as he inspected the master bedroom.

I forced a smile, trying to keep my frustration at bay. "Well, it's actually a pretty standard size for this type of unit. You get more space in the common areas here, which is great for entertaining."

Jin nodded but didn't look convinced. I could feel my irritation. Every time I showed him a place, it was like nothing was ever good enough. I was trying hard to remember that I was in this line of work because of the big commission checks.

Mira's eyes met mine in a silent apology as we followed Jin out of the bedroom. I could see she knew Jin was being difficult, and she seemed to genuinely appreciate the effort I was putting in. I wanted to give her a nod of encouragement, but Jin's next comment cut through my thoughts.

Arriving at the kitchen, Jin asked, "Does the kitchen have any more counter space? We like to cook a lot."

I forced myself to take a deep breath, running my fingers through my hair to calm the growing frustration. "The kitchen's got a good amount of counter space for the size of the condo. It's all about how you organize it. You could always add an island or a cart for extra prep space."

Jin's face remained impassive as he continued to scrutinize the details. I watched him, wondering if he'd ever be satisfied.

As Jin and Mira disappeared into the walk-in pantry, I heard yet another notification on my phone in my purse. The notifications had been relentless since I'd entered the condo. Since I was finally alone, I pulled my phone from my purse and unlocked it, only to see a flood of fire alarm alerts from my Ring camera. My pulse quickened as I swiped to view the live feed.

Smoke was billowing from my bedroom, but I couldn't see anyone inside. Panic took over, and I started to hyperventilate.

Suddenly, Jin's voice broke through my haze. "Did you hear me?"

I blinked, realizing with a jolt that Jin and Mira had emerged from the pantry. "I'm—I'm sorry, I didn't. But I have to go." Jin looked slightly annoyed, but I was too frantic to care. "I'm so sorry, but I have an emergency at my house. I need to leave right now."

Without waiting for a response, I turned and hurried out of the condo.

Standing outside my home, surrounded by the wail of sirens and the crackle of flames being doused, I felt like I was trapped in some surreal episode of *The Twilight Zone*. The firefighters worked urgently to tame the blaze that had erupted in my bedroom, but the scene seemed to move in slow motion, like I was watching it through a foggy lens.

I hugged myself tightly. My mind was numb.

I had looked at the footage from our indoor cameras over and over.

There hadn't been a break-in. Being my best friend, Mia had the code to get into the keyless entry at the front door, but it triggered the alarm since it was set. The cameras had captured only a hooded figure slipping inside. The footage showed the figure heading straight for the bedroom, where the smoke soon began to billow after the figure left.

Damar stood beside me, reeling from the sight of the smoke and damage. His face was a mask of anger and frustration. "This bitch is crazy!" he barked. "Mia's lost her fucking mind!" He turned toward the police officers who had just taken our statement. "Y'all need to do your fucking jobs and find that bitch before I do."

I had assumed that Mia was just letting off steam when she bombed my car, so I didn't give the police her name. But after this, I told them everything.

I placed a hand on his arm, trying to steady him. "Damar, calm down. I know you're upset, but yelling at the police won't help."

He turned to me, his eyes blazing with anger. "How can I stay calm when she's doing this? This is some crazy shit."

I took a deep breath, trying to keep my own anger in check. "I get it, I really do, but it won't solve anything."

He took a long, deep breath. Though his nostrils still flared, I could see the anger slowly dimming in his eyes. He pulled me into a gentle embrace, and his strong, big arms wrapped around me.

"I'm sorry, Avi. I can't believe Mia is doing all of this just because she got caught up."

I held him tightly, my own heart pounding as I gently rubbed his back, trying to soothe both of us. "It's okay. Obviously, she doesn't want me to tell the Feds what I know. She's just trying to scare me."

We stayed like that for a while, wrapped in each other's arms, the noise of the sirens and the sight of the fire fading into the background as we focused on finding peace in each other. Though Mia was unraveling dangerously, at least, it seemed, she was pushing me and Damar more passionately together.

After the fire was finally under control and the police had finished their initial investigation, a fireman led us inside, past the charred remains of our bedroom, which now looked like a disaster zone. I could see the damage was contained to the bedroom, but there was a lot of it.

As I surveyed the room, my heart sank at the sight of our summer clothes completely ruined. The contents of the walk-in closet were now a heap of ashes and drenched fabric. I was relieved, though, that our winter clothes had been safely stored in one of the guest bedroom closets.

The fireman noted the burn patterns on the floor and walls, which showed signs of where the fire had been purposely started. He explained that the way the fire had spread rapidly from a specific point and the evidence of accelerants pointed strongly toward arson. He mentioned the lack of natural spread, the way the flames had been concentrated, and the presence of unusual burn marks. All of these factors led him to conclude that someone had intentionally set the fire.

As I stood in the middle of the smoke-stained devastation, my heart ached knowing that Mia could do such a thing.

As we finished gathering what we could from the house, Damar and I headed to a hotel. The fire had shaken me up, and though we'd managed to salvage a few important items, the damage was extensive enough that we agreed staying in a hotel was the best move until we confirmed that there was no structural damage and that the air quality was safe.

After we checked into the Sophy Hotel in Hyde Park and settled into our room, I was looking forward to unwinding and relaxing with Damar. After everything we had been through, I wanted nothing more than to rest in the comfort of this nice hotel and spend some quality time with my man. But as he moved to grab his keys, I felt a sinking disappointment.

"Where are you going?"

Damar paused, looking apologetic. "I have to support another promoter tonight. It's important for business. It's a good opportunity, and I can't pass it up."

I frowned in shock and disappointment. "You're leaving me alone after everything that's happened?"

"I'm sorry, Avi. I know it's been a rough weekend, but this is crucial for the business, and it's really important now that I have to remodel our bedroom." He chuckled in an effort to lessen the blow, but that shit didn't work, so he sighed, saying, "I'll be back as soon as I can. Promise."

I let out a frustrated sigh. I rolled my eyes, clearly annoyed, and turned my back to him as I pulled the covers up over me. I got comfortable, hoping just maybe I'd find some comfort and peace in the softness of the hotel linens.

I heard him approach, but I kept my gaze fixed on the TV remote, stubbornly flipping through channels in an attempt to distract myself. He leaned in, pressing a soft kiss to my cheek.

"I'm sorry, baby," he spoke against it so close that I felt the brief warmth of his lips, but it did little to ease the frustration gnawing at me.

I responded, the sound more of a dismissive scoff than a real reply. *"Mm-humph."*

# CHAPTER 8

## MYTHIC GREY

STEPPING OUT OF my Aston Martin, I headed toward the back door of Enchant. My mind was still stuck on Lelani's diagnosis. Lelani never hid how much her aunt and grandma had suffered with this same disease. I had met her not long after her aunt passed away from breast cancer. Soon after, her grandmother got her diagnosis. So, I saw firsthand how that anxiety was eating at Lelani. It was always in the back of her mind. She'd talk about it like it was inevitable, and now, it was coming to fruition. That fear she had been running from was right in front of her now, and, suddenly, it was hanging over everything.

Even though our relationship was far from perfect, and my feelings weren't as deep as I'd like them to be, I was ready to be there for her. Despite knowing that Lelani might not be the love of my life, my loyalty compelled me to offer whatever support she needed.

Though I was lost in my thoughts, years in the game had taught me to always keep my head on a swivel. Because of that, I saw the figures approaching in the darkness. The lieutenant of the Viper Crew, a notorious Mexican cartel, stepped forward from the shadows, flanked by his henchmen. His name was Diego Moreno, a man known for his ruthlessness.

Diego's presence was menacing enough to put fear in any man's heart, but I wasn't one to flinch. I was just as ruthless, and fear had never been a part of my game. His dark suit stood out in the dim, neon-lit parking lot, and the bright club lights reflected in his shiny shoes.

His henchmen, armed and ready, stood like silent, menacing statues just waiting for a signal.

As soon as Diego and his crew emerged, my security team sprang into action. They materialized from the shadows like ghosts with their weapons drawn and ready. The tension in the air was suffocating with unspoken threats and potential deaths. I could hear the clicks of my team's safety switches being flipped off.

Diego's gaze locked onto mine. I met his stare with equal intensity. The dim light from the streetlamps shined on the grim expressions on both our faces.

The silence was deafening, broken only by the distant noises of the city and the occasional shuffle of feet. My mind raced, trying to piece together the purpose of this confrontation while keeping it cool. Diego's eyes never wavered, and neither did mine. We stood there, locked in a menacing stare, each of us measuring the other's gangsta.

Finally, Diego cracked a slow, menacing grin. "I come in peace. Just want to talk, Mythic. Your men can put their guns down."

I glanced at my security detail with their weapons still trained on Diego and his crew. With an icy and unyielding bark, I told him, "My security never lowers their weapons when there's a threat."

Diego's eyes narrowed. "I'm here to discuss the explosives you sold to the Kingsmen."

I arched a brow high. "Since you're not a Kingsmen, that's not your business. Does your boss know that you're stepping to his distributor like this?"

"Manuel doesn't micromanage his most trusted lieutenant. Now…those explosives you offered the Kingsmen were used to wipe out a lot of our crew and our people."

I smirked. "I didn't *offer* such powerful weaponry to the Kingsmen. If they were smart enough to ask for what they needed, that's their business. Business is business, Diego. I provide whatever my clients ask for. I told you before, you don't tell me how to run my fucking business. I don't have shit to do with cartel business. You don't run shit; I do. You're *my* client."

Diego's grin faltered as his eyes flashed with anger. His voice dropped to a dangerous growl. "Watch your mouth, Mythic. You're treading on thin ice."

"Treading on thin ice?" I chuckled cynically. "If you keep pushing me, I'll just break that shit. I don't deal in half-measures. You got an issue, step your game up and take out them motherfuckas that's wiping out your people." My laughter that followed made Diego's fury ignite.

He yanked his gun from its holster. His fingers tightened around the grip as he aimed the barrel at my head. The muzzle pressed dangerously close as I let out a dark, defiant laugh that seemed to fuel Diego's rage.

In one swift motion, I disarmed Diego, knocking the gun from his grip. The weapon clattered to the ground. Without a second thought, I gripped Diego by the collar, and in a single fluid motion, I drew my blade from my waistband and slashed his throat. The blade cut through flesh and muscle, and crimson blood poured from the gaping wound like a fountain. It sprayed across the pavement, pooling around Diego's feet as he fell.

His eyes widened in shock and pain, but the life drained from them quickly. He gurgled, struggling to breathe, but the blood flowed too freely, choking him as he collapsed to the ground. His crew, caught off guard by the sudden violence, scrambled in panic. Before they could fully react, my security opened fire. Their shots were muffled by the silencers on their guns. The bullets cut through the air with deadly accuracy, and the henchmen's bodies slumped to the ground in lifeless heaps.

As Draven stepped over the fallen bodies, his expression was rigid with concern.

"Boss, you sure this was the right move?" he asked. "We just took out a member of the fucking Mexican cartel. We're about to be at war with these motherfuckers."

I barely spared him a glance. "I'll handle the cartel. They're not a problem."

Draven's eyes widened slightly, but he nodded, accepting my assurance despite his obvious apprehension. "What do you need us to do?"

"Get these bodies out of here. Clean this mess up before the club opens. And make sure that all the cameras in the area are wiped clean."

Draven and his team moved swiftly as they began to drag the bodies.

As Draven's team worked, I approached the locked doors of the club. I unlocked them and pushed them open, stepping inside. I walked through the entrance, my mind already shifting back to the night's plans. The blood on my hand glistened in the darkness of the club. The casual swipe of my hand against my black tee to remove the blood from Diego's throat felt almost routine.

As I sat in my office at Enchant, the bass from the club below was muffled but still throbbed through the floor. I barely registered it as I held the phone to my ear, listening to Aviana rant fearfully on the other end.

"The fire started in the bedroom. All of our summer clothes are ruined. The firemen said it looks like arson. We saw a hooded figure on the cameras, but it was obviously a woman, and Mia has the code to get inside. I know it was her. I can't believe this is happening. Mia is going too far. She set the fire, Mythic. She's trying to ruin me."

My hands clenched into fists on my desk. "Avi, try to calm down."

She took a deep breath, though it did little to steady her voice.

"Fuck," I growled. "It's not unusual for people to go to extreme lengths when they feel betrayed or threatened, especially if they're facing federal charges. Mia really thinks you're the reason she's in this mess. She's out for revenge."

"I just don't understand why she's doing this. She was my best friend, and now she's acting like a madwoman. What the fuck is she going to do next? I can't believe this shit."

"I'll make it my priority to find her. You're right, she's going too fucking far. She knew what she was doing could get her locked up. She was being greedy. And she gotta be a stupid motherfucka to think you would snitch. I'm going to find her and knock some sense into her ass."

"Please do." Aviana's voice was flooded with fear. "I'm scared, Mythic. I don't want to keep looking over my shoulder."

"I got this," I reassured her, though my blood was boiling. "I'll track her down and deal with this. You know I always got you, Avi."

I heard her take another shaky breath.

"Just stay safe," I said, trying to keep my tone calm but failing. "I'll call you back once I've got something. Just keep your head on a swivel and stay indoors."

"Okay," she mumbled.

My rage was simmering as I ended the call. I couldn't believe Mia had the audacity to do this.

I dialed Timmy's number, and he answered on the first ring. "What's up, boss?"

"Timmy, get to my office ASAP," I said, hanging up before he had a chance to respond. I turned my attention to the monitors displaying various angles of the club. My security team had everything locked down, but I had a habit of keeping a close eye.

Timmy, my intelligence analyst, burst into my office almost immediately. The door swung open, and the thundering bass of the club briefly flooded the room before Timmy shut it out with a firm hand. He looked at me with a mix of curiosity and urgency.

"What's up?" Timmy asked.

"I need an update on Mia. What you got for me?"

I had asked Timmy a few days ago to get me a location on Mia since she had gone into hiding.

He settled into the chair across from me, pulling out his tablet. "It's like she vanished off the grid. We've checked everything we could. She hasn't used any credit cards or made any transactions since she disappeared. I've combed through her financial records. Nothing there. No sign of cash withdrawals, no suspicious activity."

Frustrated, I leaned forward. "What about her phone?"

Timmy shook his head, tapping on his tablet. "Her phone hasn't pinged anywhere since Saturday. We've traced its last location, but she must have either shut it off or thrown it away. There are no records of her at any airports or transportation hubs. It's like she just disappeared."

I combed my forehead as my patience began to wear thin. "Have you checked with other local sources?"

"Yeah. I cross-referenced with surveillance footage from her usual spots around the city. Nothing. It's like she's gone underground..." As Timmy continued, I barely heard him. My focus suddenly shifted to the camera on the entrance of the club. My eyes locked onto a familiar figure slipping through the crowd.

It was Damar.

I couldn't believe Damar was at the club while Aviana was a wreck alone in a hotel room. The anger I felt was immediate and consuming. My protective instincts flared up, overriding everything else.

"Timmy," I interrupted sharply, cutting him off mid-sentence. I stood abruptly, causing the chair to scrape against the floor. "I need to make a run. I'll catch up with you later."

Timmy looked up, concerned. "Everything okay?"

"Yeah," I assured him, already heading toward the door. "Just keep digging. We need to find her ASAP, and let me know the second you get any lead."

Without waiting for a response, I stormed out of the office.

# AVIANA SCOTT

The knock on the hotel room door sent anxious nerves through me. My breath hitched with anticipation, and my nerves were all over the place. I glanced at my reflection in the mirror in the plush surroundings of the luxurious hotel room. I was dressed in a cozy pajama short set, comfortable yet far from the glamorous outfits I usually wore. My hair was pulled up into a messy high bun, and I could only hope it didn't look as disheveled as I felt.

I took a deep breath, trying to steady the uproar of emotions erupting inside me. The fire had been overwhelming, and Damar leaving me alone had made it worse. And now, with Mythic on the other side of the door, I felt like my nerves were strung tight.

I walked over to the door, each step feeling heavier than the last. My fingers hovered over the handle, and I hesitated for a moment before twisting it open. The anticipation of being alone in this beautiful hotel room with the man who had a hold on my heart was too much in addition to all the other shit that was happening.

As I opened the door, I was instantly encased in Mythic's musky, masculine scent. I closed my eyes for a moment, letting the aroma sweep over me. His tall, commanding frame glided past me and into the room. My eyes lingered on his powerful legs as he settled on the couch in the living room of the suite. Suddenly, I had a wild yearning to straddle him.

I sat beside him, noting the furrow in his brow and the tension in his shoulders. "What's wrong?" I asked gently.

"I'm worried about you."

I shook my head. "No. Something else is wrong."

He hesitated for a moment. His eyes shifted, as if he were deciding whether to answer or not.

Finally, he spoke, "Lelani... Her doctor told her today that she has a tumor in her brain. It's most likely cancerous."

I gasped. "Oh my goodness. That's the reason for all the headaches she's been having?"

He nodded sadly, and my heart ached for him.

I reached out, placing a comforting hand on his arm. "Oh my God. Mythic, I'm so sorry. She's young and strong, though. She'll be able to fight this."

He shook his head with a frustrated glare. "I don't know how to handle this. I don't know how to support her. It's just...it's overwhelming. I feel so helpless because this is something I can't control. But I feel so fucking selfish for feeling that way. If I'm overwhelmed, I know damn well she is."

Feeling a rush of sympathy, I drew him into my arms. He accepted the embrace, pressing his face against my chest as I leaned back against the large arm of the couch. His massive arms encircled my waist, pulling my soft body flush against his hard frame. I began to rub his back soothingly, trying to offer some comfort.

We held each other in silence for what felt like a couple of forevers.

"I feel so guilty." His words came out muffled as he spoke into my chest. "Because I really can't focus on her."

"Why?"

"You know why, Avi."

Mythic looked up into my eyes, and my breath hitched. Mythic was a man who always got what he wanted—who never lost. I had stopped our kiss before, but the look in his eyes now told me he was intent on finishing what we had started.

Tonight, however, I didn't feel the same reluctance. Instead, I felt so vulnerable and scared, and his presence had managed to soothe any of it. So, when he leaned in and took my lips with his, I didn't resist.

He groaned into my mouth, and immediately, the reluctance between us vanished, and so did the stress and worry that we were just grappling with. Tasting him made everything feel so much better that it no longer existed, and he kissed me as if it were the same for him. He thrust his tongue down my throat and explored my mouth and lips with his own. Passionately, we moaned and moved our bodies against each other's.

His firm grip sat me up. With ease, he lifted the pajama shirt over my head. I was weary, and guilt started to creep in, but he began to kiss it away, placing those soft lips all over my breasts. He took each nipple into his lips. The moisture of his mouth soothed the aggression of each suck. Then he placed soft pecks down my body, making a trail from between my breasts and over the imperfections of my belly.

My back arched under the vibrations that each kiss sent through my body. My head fell back, and my eyes stared at the ceiling. I wrestled with the many emotions rolling through me. Fear, guilt, shame, and need took over me. But I soon felt his mouth on my clit. His lips sucked it in to meet his tongue, which played with it slowly and carefully.

All resolve left my body. I gasped and melted into his oral fucking. He had pushed my small shorts aside to get access to his feast. My heart thumped harder and harder as I let out a faint whimper. With every pass that his tongue made over my clit, I leaked.

My nipples hardened watching the man of my dreams, the man who defined longing, the man who portrayed what passion was, drink me with eagerness. He was feasting on me as if I were heavenly.

My body rippled with pleasure. My legs shook, and my back arched.

When he removed his face from between my thick thighs, it and his beard glistened with my cum. He then licked his lips, savoring my taste.

"Oh God, Mythic," escaped me in a moan of need and disbelief.

"You taste so good, baby," he spoke into my juices. "Please don't make me stop."

I cringed. "But Damar might come back."

With his eyes fixated on mine, he licked my clit slowly, sucking my pearl. I shivered, feeling my center leaking down to the crack of my ass.

"I got eyes on him at the club. When he makes a move, I'll get a call. Now, relax and let me eat."

His yearning was humbling. Such a man of his stature needing to taste me was unfathomable. But in that moment, he wasn't the gangster, and I wasn't the married woman. We were Avi and Mythic, the two teenagers who fell in love and never truly fell out, who were just pushed apart by juvenile mistakes and decisions. So, I allowed him to pull my shorts down. He then stood up and dropped his joggers. His smooth, brown length was so hard that the veins in it looked 3D.

As if not to give me time to change my mind, he hurriedly dropped to his knees. He took his left hand and scooped some of my juices on it, then he slid that hand over his length, lubricating it. He took my thighs in his grip by his elbows and positioned my dripping center in front of him. Using his hips, he brought his dick to my center and forced me down on it.

He groaned in response to my tightness on his shaft. He started thrusting slowly. I grabbed his back and dug my fingers into his skin, trying to take all of him. He quickened his pace, and my pants matched his rhythm. As he thrust his dick into me, his body pushed against my clit, causing me to quiver with pleasure. My moans grew louder, and he quickened his pace more until we could barely breathe.

I could feel every inch of him filling me. My back arched, my legs shook, and I screamed with pleasure. At the sound of my oncoming climax, he thrust his dick as far into me as he could.

I inhaled so loudly that the sound of my breath bounced off the windows, which reflected Chicago's skyline. I didn't know what I should have expected from Mythic, but I felt foolish that I was shocked that he started to drill me. He drove every inch so far into me that the tip of his head kissed my cervix. I took the beating eagerly. My center spilled sweet juices in appreciation of finally feeling the passion that it had been missing since before I had gotten married.

His penetration felt so good that I loudly sang his praises, making sure that every inch of the suite heard how good his dick was. It was too big to handle and a chore to take, but I forced myself to take every intense stroke because the good came with the bad. He made me orgasm more than my husband could even research how to.

## DAMAR SCOTT

I'd been at Enchant for hours, showing support for Richie. He promoted parties here on the nights I didn't, so I had to come through. In this business, promoters had to support one another. It was all about networking, building connections, and making sure the money kept flowing between us. That's how we stayed on top.

But it was late now, and my mind was back on Aviana. I knew she was mad as hell at me for leaving her at the hotel, and I had to smooth that over.

I made my way over to Richie, dapped him up, and told him, "I'm out. Gotta get back to the wife."

He nodded. "For sure."

I headed toward the exit, ready to get outta there and fix whatever was waiting for me back at the hotel.

But just as I got to the door, JD, one of the bouncers, stepped in front of me.

"Yo. You can't leave right now," he told me.

I frowned, looking at him sideways. "What you mean I can't leave?"

He didn't flinch, didn't even blink. "All the exits are sealed. We got a situation outside."

Now, I was curious and annoyed. "What kind of situation?"

JD leaned in slightly, keeping his voice low. "A fight broke out outside. One of the dudes said he's goin' to his car to grab a gun. We ain't letting nobody out 'til it's handled."

"C'mon, man. Just let me dip out real quick. I gotta go."

JD crossed his arms. "Nah. Can't do that, Damar. Ain't nobody leavin' 'til it's safe."

I looked over at Tyrell, another bouncer standing nearby. I hoped he might back me up, but all he did was shrug like his hands were tied.

I let out a frustrated breath, feeling trapped. "Are y'all serious? I got somewhere I need to be, man."

JD didn't budge. "I'm not playing, bro. Stay inside."

Shaking my head, I turned back toward the club.

## AVIANA SCOTT

"Are you okay?"

My heavy eyes darted toward him as he cleaned his seed from my stomach with a soapy towel. They were weighed down with exhaustion. Mythic and I had fucked for two hours, taking our frustrations out on each other sweetly and making up for lost time. But now I had cum a countless number of times, and he had finally given me mercy by cumming.

I couldn't look at him. I gnawed on my bottom lip as I stared up at the ceiling. "Of course not." Watching him wash his cum away from my stretch marks made me cringe. "You need to leave."

The passion was gone. The aura of lovemaking had subsided, and reality had set in.

"Why? Talk to me. What's wrong?"

I groaned, sitting up. "What do you mean what's wrong? *This*. This was wrong!"

"Did it feel wrong?"

I winced. "No." Then I swallowed hard, fighting to allow my morals to win the battle against my yearning for him. "But I'm married, and you have a girlfriend who is sick."

Mythic looked at me with eyes filled with a blend of pain and yearning. "And despite all of that, I love you."

His words dripped with affection. I winced, feeling a pang in my chest at the sight of such raw need and want in his eyes. It was too much to witness. "Mythic, please..." My voice trembled as I tried to find the right words.

"No. Fuck that," he interrupted, shaking his head with determination and desperation. "I love you, Avi—"

"Mythic, I am married."

His face fell, a flicker of hurt crossing his features. But he stubbornly pressed, "Do you love me?"

The question struck me like a physical blow. I could feel my heart pounding as I tried to maintain my composure. "I am married," I could only insist.

He didn't relent, his eyes locking on to mine. "Answer the question."

I swallowed hard, feeling tears prick at the corners of my eyes. "I'm married, Mythic. Please."

He seemed to deflate slightly, his shoulders slumping as he took a step back. "That's your answer?"

"Yes," I whispered.

He opened his mouth to argue, but thankfully his phone chimed with a notification. After unlocking it, his gaze focused on it as if he were reading something. Then his face painted with frustration. "Damar left the club. They couldn't hold the doors any longer."

"Shit," I breathed.

"So, that's it?" he pressed.

His need made me wince. "Mythic, *please*."

"Ah ight. Bet. I'll let it go. Only because I love you."

The finality in his tone cut through me as he turned away, making my eyes water.

As Mythic dressed quietly in the dim light, I lay there, unable to bring myself to look at him. The sound of his movements, the rustle of fabric, and the occasional clink of his belt buckle were the only indications of his presence. I had waited for this moment for years, and now that it had finally happened, I felt a deep, gnawing sense of guilt.

The pleasure I had just experienced was unlike anything I had known, but it left me feeling even more conflicted. I hated that Mythic made me question everything about my marriage.

When I heard the jingle of keys, my breath caught in my throat. I looked at Mythic regretfully. The sight of him took my breath away. He was a vision of raw, unrestrained beauty, and the tears began to flow at the sight of him. His gaze was filled with comfort and concern, but it only made me feel worse.

I turned away from him, my tears flowing freely as I began to weep. Through my sobs, I begged him, "Just go…please…just go."

My voice was broken, and I felt like a fraud for the pleasure I had felt and the heartache I now faced. I just wanted to be alone with my turmoil, to figure out how I had let myself get here.

With my back turned to him, I heard Mythic's heavy footsteps as he left the bedroom. I held my breath, my entire body tense with anticipation and dread. Each step seemed to echo the finality of our moment together, and I was overwhelmed by a deep sense of loss and regret.

The sound of the suite door opening and closing was both a relief and a fresh wound. As the door clicked shut behind him, I let out a ragged sob. My heart broke with the yearning for the man I truly loved. I clung to the bedding as my sobs grew louder.

## DAMAR SCOTT

I pressed my foot harder on the accelerator, cutting through traffic like a madman. My grip on the steering wheel was so tight my knuckles ached. Streetlights blurred into streaks of color as I shot down city streets.

I'd gotten sloppy tonight. I had been so busy drinking with Richie that I hadn't checked Avi's old phone in hours. When I finally remembered to pull it out, standing by the door waiting for security to let me out of the club, my heart stopped.

Mythic had asked for our hotel room number, and she had given it to him.

I squeezed the wheel harder with my teeth clenched so tight it hurt. At first, I'd brushed off Mia's slick comments about Aviana having feelings for Mythic. I figured she was just playing games, trying to get under my skin and into my bed. But then Mia had played those damn recordings between her and Aviana that shattered my ego. Hearing Aviana's own voice confess her feelings for another man stung so badly that I slept with Mia, taking revenge in the pettiest way possible.

But no matter how badly Aviana hurt me, I wasn't letting Mythic have her...ever.

That's why I'd been pushing so hard to get her pregnant. Avi had the kind of values that made it almost impossible for her to leave her marriage. So, if we had kids, she'd definitely be trapped forever, no matter how badly her heart longed for someone else.

I knew they hadn't crossed that line yet. I'd pored through every message on that old phone obsessively. They never mentioned anything beyond friendship. Her feelings for him were obviously something she just told Mia about, but that almost made it worse.

Mythic had real money and power. He could buy Aviana the life she dreamed of and deserved—a life better than the one I could give her. That was something I couldn't stomach.

The thought of Aviana moving on and having a better life made me physically sick. I'd built my entire sense of worth on possessing her. She wasn't just my wife; she was my trophy and my greatest achievement. Losing her wasn't about love anymore, it was about pride and control.

No matter what it took, no matter who had to get hurt, Aviana was mine. She belonged to me. I knew it was sick, but Aviana wasn't something I could just let go of. Losing her to Mythic wasn't even an option. I'd rather burn the whole world down first. I'd killed to keep her, and if necessary, I'd do it again without hesitation.

# THREE DAYS AGO

# CHAPTER 9

## DAMAR SCOTT

As MIA AND I struggled violently over her phone, her voice rose to an ear-splitting level as she yelled accusations and threats at me. My patience was gone and had been replaced by a fury that pushed me toward the edge. Listening to her threaten to shatter the careful world I'd built made me see red.

She was serious this time. I could see the reckless fire in her eyes that told me if I didn't do something immediately, she'd ruin everything. I wasn't about to let Mia tear my world apart, not when I'd sacrificed so much to keep Aviana exactly where she belonged.

"Nigga, I'm telling her everything. It was supposed to be me, you, and our baby. Avi deserves to know. You can't keep hiding me and my baby."

I knew that Mia hoped that the reminder that she was carrying my child would soften me, but it had done the opposite. Suddenly, my anger turned violent. My fist collided with her temple, and pain exploded behind her eyes. She looked as if the world had spun around her. Her grip on the phone loosened, and she blinked as if her vision was blurred. She fought to stay conscious, but I watched as the darkness closed in on her.

She slumped to the floor as she passed out from the knockout.

Panic consumed me, pushing me into a rage that was manic. More than my fear of her telling my wife everything, I knew that Mia was so pissed that she would tell the Feds of my involvement with the embezzlement. I couldn't afford to let her reveal everything to Aviana or the Feds. I was desperate and thinking irrationally. I needed to silence her and to keep my secrets buried.

My initial efforts to try to silence her had failed. Two weeks ago, I had come up with the plan to make an anonymous tip to the twins at Dream Realty. Considering how much money she'd stolen, there was no way that she would avoid prison time. I hoped that once Mia was arrested, she would be so in love with me that she would never turn me in. But then we found out that she was pregnant. She was even more determined for us to be together then. She thought we were Bonnie and Clyde, but I didn't want to lose Aviana, so I made the anonymous tip. I hoped that once Mia was arrested, she would want to terminate the pregnancy, but she only became more determined than ever.

I dropped to my knees beside her. Her body was limp and unconscious. Desperate, I gripped her neck with my hands. My fingers tightened around her throat. Her skin was warm, but I could already sense her life slipping away. The choking sounds that escaped her lips were the only indication that she was still alive. I squeezed harder with desperation driving me.

Her breathing grew more ragged.

Then it stopped altogether.

My heart drummed in my chest as I realized I had actually done it. But I couldn't deny the relief I felt. Still, I was shook that I had actually taken a life.

I was still shaking as I stood up. Panicked, I rushed into the bedroom nearby. The only sound in the condo was my unnerved breathing and rushed footsteps. I dragged the large suitcase from the corner of the room and into the living room.

As I stood over her body, I crouched down to ensure that she was in fact dead. Checking her pulse, I confirmed that she was no longer alive. With trembling hands, I lifted her into the suitcase. The sound of her bones cracking as I contorted her body to fit inside was sickening. I gagged, fighting to keep the contents of my stomach inside. The suitcase seemed too small, but I forced her in.

I struggled with the zipper. I had to sit on it to get it closed.

When I finally did, I stood there, breathless and horrified at what I had just done. I started to question my own sanity. Staring at the suitcase, I knew I had to get rid of it and make sure that no one ever found out what had happened here. My hands were slick with sweat. My mind raced as I tried to figure out my next move.

I wrestled with the suitcase as I drug it out of the condo. Every creak of the suitcase sounded so loud in the silent hallway.

When I reached the elevator, I was already sweating. The metal doors slid open. I was so lost in my own head that I didn't realize I wasn't alone until I saw Paul step in behind me. He was an older black guy who lived down the hall. We'd exchanged a few words before, but never anything more.

I tensed up as the elevator door closed behind us. I tried to maintain a casual demeanor, nodding my head in greeting. "What up, Paul?"

"How you doin', Damar?" He looked at me with kind, but curious eyes. "How's everything going?"

My throat was dry, and I struggled to keep my voice steady. "Good as they can be."

Paul's gaze lingered a moment too long, and he frowned slightly. "You sure you're okay? You look a bit off."

I forced a tight-lipped smile. "I'm fine. It's just been a long-ass day."

He chuckled sarcastically. "I've had plenty of those, and you'll have plenty more."

I scoffed at the irony.

The elevator descended slowly, each floor feeling like an eternity. I could feel Paul's concerned eyes on me. I shifted from foot to foot, trying to distract myself, but the feeling of the suitcase handle in my hand felt like a lead anchor around my legs.

Finally, the elevator came to a stop at the lobby. "Well, this is my stop." I tried to sound casual as I drug the suitcase toward the opening doors. "Have a good night."

Paul nodded, but his concerned eyes remained fixed on me. "You sure you're all right?"

"Yeah, yeah, I'm fine," I insisted.

I rushed out of the elevator and headed toward the parking garage.

I didn't look back as I hustled toward my car.

An hour later, I was quietly slipping into bed with Avi.

She was sound asleep. Her gentle snores interrupted the quiet of the room. Her peaceful face was framed by a loose strand of hair that fell over her cheek.

I was jealous of how content she looked. There was no way that I could get any sleep. My thoughts were all over the place.

I was confident that no cameras had caught a glimpse of Mia coming or me leaving. The condo Mia had gotten for us was an older building on the east side near the lake. It was a place that was perfect for our little secret because it had no cameras in the lobby and the neighbor across the hall didn't have a Ring camera, nor did we.

I pulled the sheets back gently, not wanting to disturb Aviana, and slid in beside her. She stirred slightly but settled back into a deeper sleep.

As I lay there, my mind was anything but at ease. My thoughts drifted to Mia's lifeless body, now hidden in the trunk of my car, still in the suitcase. The image of her stiffening form filled me with a cold dread. I needed to figure out how to get rid of her for good without leaving any trace.

I tried to sleep, but that was impossible, so I just lay there for hours, figuring out the perfect way to make all of this go away. When I finally did, I slipped out of bed before the first light of dawn.

The drive to the lake was a blur. The city was still, and early morning fog made it look ghostly.

When I reached the pier, I parked.

Taking the suitcase out of the car was just as hard as it had been putting it in. The dead weight was heavier than I ever could have imagined.

The silhouette of my boat was dark against the pale morning sky.

I loaded the suitcase onboard and drove out onto the lake. Once I found a spot far out, I secured an anchor to the suitcase. With a quick glance around to ensure no one was watching, I heaved the suitcase overboard. I watched as it sank, feeling my stomach churn as I realized I could never go back from here.

Returning to shore, I pulled Mia's phone from my pocket. I began typing threatening messages to Aviana, pretending to be Mia. I figured this was an additional way to cover my bullshit so that none of this ever came back to me.

Days passed in a haze of deceit. I made Aviana's life hell, all while pretending to be Mia. I thought that as long as everyone thought that Mia was still alive, it would be harder to prove that I had killed her if her body was ever found.

The threating text messages were just the beginning. I had convinced one of my other side pieces, Marlene, to go by Avi's parents' house in Mia's car and blow up Avi's car, then I had convinced her to go into my and Aviana's home and set it on fire. She was built a lot like Mia, so I knew that Aviana would automatically assume it was her when she saw her on camera.

I was surprised at how far I was willing to go, but I couldn't stop. I was driven by this warped need to stay in control and to keep my secrets buried so that I never lost Aviana.

I had one more loose end to tie up. The sun was starting to come up as I parked a block away from Marlene's crib. She danced late at a strip club, so I knew she'd just gotten home a few hours ago. By now, she'd be passed out.

Marlene was always about her bread. That's all she cared about. So, when I offered her some money to torch Avi's whip and burn down our house, she was game. But, in case she ever grew a conscious or if Mia's body was ever found, I didn't trust her to remain loyal to a nigga who would only have sex with her after the club and wouldn't even take her on a real date.

I pulled my hoodie low over my head and slipped around the back of her place. The back window was always cracked open because the latch was broken. She had fussed a few times about her landlord not getting it fixed. I eased it up slow and climbed in carefully.

I crept down the hallway with my gun gripped tight in my hand. I stepped carefully past piles of laundry and heels tossed around the floor. Her bedroom door was open just enough for me to slip inside without touching it. She was sprawled out, face-down, barely covered by her sheets. I raised the gun, aimed, and squeezed the trigger. The blast was louder than I expected, but she didn't even have a chance to flinch.

I stepped toward Marlene's body. Standing over her, I leaned closer to make sure she wasn't breathing. Blood seeped steadily from the hole in her head. Bits of brain matter were splattered across the pillow. Her chest shuddered a few more times, but each breath was weaker than the last, until she finally went still. I watched closely, making sure she was gone before I stepped back, satisfied.

Being a stripper, she had plenty of thirsty dudes running in and out of her place all the time. I knew once the cops found her body, the suspect list would be endless. She would be just another dancer caught up in some bullshit. The police would brush off her murder and soon forget about her case.

Before I dipped out, I went straight to the spot I knew she stashed her cash. I opened her top drawer and grabbed the thick stack of bills inside to make it look like some desperate dude from the club came through, shot her, and robbed her.

I slipped out of her place just as quietly as I'd come in. Pulling my hoodie lower, I walked quickly toward my car.

# PRESENT DAY

# CHAPTER 10

## AVIANA SCOTT

**A**FTER **MYTHIC LEFT** the suite, I lay in bed sobbing until I realized that I had to pull myself from the bed and shower before Damar got back.

I hoped the hot water would wash away more than just Mythic's scent and sweat. As the steam encircled me, I tried to cry out my guilt and the desperate need for him. My fingers scrunched into fists, clutching the shower tiles, but the tears wouldn't stop.

Mythic had exceeded every fantasy I'd ever imagined. Having him inside me again was more than I could have ever dreamed of. Years of maturity had only refined his touch. Each stroke was more precise and electrifying. He explored parts of me that Damar had never even come close to understanding. I had always known that passion was missing between me and Damar, but last night had confirmed it. Damar paled in comparison; he couldn't hold a candle to the intensity and depth of what Mythic offered.

No matter how much I scrubbed, I couldn't cleanse away the yearning that his presence left behind. The way he made me feel protected and wanted was like a flame that smoldered even when he was gone. It burned a hole in my conscience, reminding me constantly that I'd betrayed not just Damar, but myself.

When I heard Damar come into the suite, I prayed he wouldn't notice that I was still awake. I hoped to God he wouldn't try anything sexual. I turned my back to the bedroom door and wrapped myself tightly in the covers like a cocoon, hoping the darkness would shield me from what I'd done.

As he stumbled in, I held my breath. When he climbed into bed, I could smell the tequila seeping from his pores. Soon, he was snoring softly beside me. I quietly let out a long sigh of relief. I lay there with my back to him, staring out at the busy street below. The lights of 53rd Street twinkled like distant stars. Cars honked now and the occasional late-night pedestrian moved like shadows against the streetlights. The distant noise of sirens pierced the stillness of the night.

Tears continued to stream down my face, saturating the pillow. As the night wore on, my eyes never closed. My heart ached with every beat, and sleep refused to come. Though my husband slept next to me, I felt alone in the bed. My thoughts were a jumbled mess of what-ifs and should-have-beens, and I was haunted by the memory of Mythic's touch.

A few hours later, the sunlight filtered through the hotel room's curtains. As I stirred awake, I realized that I had managed to get a few hours after the sun had risen. The last time that I had looked at the clock before closing my eyes, it was almost six in the morning.

There was a brief moment where everything felt right. It felt like I was a devoted wife about to start my day, heading to work, and that Mia would be there asking me where I wanted to go for lunch.

But as I slowly opened my eyes, the illusion shattered. I wasn't in my cozy bedroom at home; I was in this foreign hotel room, surrounded by the unfamiliar. The memories rushed back—the fire, the chaos of Mia's arrest, and Mythic's epic penetration.

His presence lingered all over me. I could still feel him inside of me.

I turned my head to the side, hoping to see Mythic, but instead, I was met with the sight of Damar lying beside me. He stared up at the ceiling. His face was a mural of weariness and frustration, catching me off guard. I was convinced that he somehow knew about my betrayal.

My pulse quickened, but I forced those anxiety-filled thoughts away as I rolled over to face him. "Are you okay?"

He glanced at me with a weary look and sighed. "Yeah. I've just got a lot on my mind."

I discreetly swallowed hard. "Like what?"

"It's nothing you need to worry about." He brushed it off with a shrug of his shoulder. "It's business stuff. But there's something I've been meaning to tell you."

I leaned in, raising a brow.

When he placed a hand softly on my waist, I relaxed, but only for a second before I felt like I didn't deserve his tenderness.

"I want you to finally fulfill your dreams and go to nursing school."

I was taken aback. I sat up a bit, raising a brow so high that it felt like it touched my hairline. "Really?"

He softly chuckled at my animated shock. "Yes, love."

"What changed your mind all of a sudden?"

He looked at me with a sincerity I hadn't seen in a while. "I want you to be happy, Avi. I feel like I'm holding you back. Go to school. I'll pay for everything."

My head dramatically reared back. *"Whaaat?"*

He grinned. "Yes. I got you, baby."

I was still reeling from the shock. "But what about the baby? I thought you were ready for me to get pregnant."

He shifted a bit. "I am. But we can do both. I'll work hard so that when you get pregnant, you can quit working if you want to. I'll make sure that you have enough help with the baby so that you can focus on school. I'll even get a bigger team so that they can take up the slack and I can spend more time at home."

I stared at him, trying to process the sudden shift in his attitude. "Are you sure about this, Damar?"

He nodded confidently. "Yeah. I just want you to be happy. That's what matters most to me."

I cuddled close to Damar, feeling the warmth of his body against mine and major guilt. "Thank you, baby."

"You don't have to thank me," he said as his fingers began to softly caress my scalp. "I'm your husband. It's my job to make you happy, and I'm going to get much better at doing that."

I sighed as shame and guilt swallowed me. I snuggled so much closer to him that I could smell the remnants of cologne and alcohol from last night.

"What do you want to do about getting another car?" he asked. "Do you want another Jeep?"

I frowned as I thought about it. "I want something else. I love it, but the ride is so bumpy."

He chuckled. "Because it's meant for the terrain, not the city."

"True. I'm ready for a smoother ride."

"Like what?"

I shrugged. "I don't know.'

"I'll help you look."

Guilt made my stomach turn, but I forced a smile, looking up into his sexy, dark eyes. The thought of Mythic loitered my mind, but Damar's love for me was so apparent, and he was committed to our life together. His touch might not have the same fire as Mythic's, but his steady, unwavering affection was real.

I told myself it was foolish to risk everything for a what-if with Mythic, but deep down, I knew the truth. The longing for Mythic—the way he made me feel—was such a big difference to the routine comfort I was settling for with Damar. It was clear that my heart was torn.

As I held Damar close, I tried to find contentment in the life we had built together. His steady presence, his promises, and his love were real and solid. But as I nestled against him, I couldn't shake the feeling that I was merely fooling myself. The truth was, my heart was still consumed by Mythic, and spending last night with him had only given him the gas to truly set my heart on fire.

## MYTHIC GREY

I stared at the Instagram blog post on TheRealChicagoMedia with an amused smirk. The post was a list of missing men, all of Mexican descent. I recognized them as the Viper Crew members we'd taken out Monday night. The guys on my security detail were pros at what they did. They'd made sure those bodies were never coming back to haunt us. My team had covered every angle and detail. We were experts at making bodies disappear without a trace.

I scrolled through the comments, scanning the wild theories. One commenter was convinced that the Venezuelans who'd recently migrated to Chicago were behind it all. Another claimed it was a turf war between rival gangs.

I kept scrolling with a smirk at the corner of my mouth, envisioning each of their bodies falling one by one like dominoes.

Lelani walked into the living room and somberly headed for the door. She was hesitant and nervous with fear painting her face. It hit me hard seeing her like this, knowing I couldn't be there for her.

She watched me reluctantly, sighing deeply. "My mom is outside."

I scoffed, shaking my head. "I can't believe I can't come to this appointment with you."

She bit her bottom lip reluctantly. Her eyes and body looked tired because of the battle she was fighting. "You and my mother fight like cats and dogs—you know this. I need to focus on the treatment, not you and her bickering and talking shit to each other."

She had a consultation appointment with her neurosurgeon this morning to prepare for her biopsy. When I started to get dressed for her appointment as well, she had the audacity to tell me that I couldn't come because her mother was.

I threw my phone on the couch, giving her my undivided attention. "You know I want to be there for you. I hate sitting here while you're dealing with this. This shit's not cool."

Lelani pouted, appearing helpless. "Please, Mythic. I need this day to go as easily as possible. My mom already refuses to miss an appointment."

"I know how to ignore her."

"That's the problem. I don't want to feel that tension. This isn't about you or her. It's about me trying to make it through this."

I clenched my fists, fighting to keep my anger in check because I knew it was selfish to add to the stress she already had. "Fine. I'll chill. But I'm not okay with this shit. I want to be there for you. Ain't no way you should be going without me."

Lelani's expression softened a little. She walked over and laid her soft lips on top of mine for longer than a peck. "I know you want to help," she said with our foreheads touching. "I appreciate it. Just let me handle today in my own way, okay? I'll call you as soon as it's over."

I nodded, though I was still frustrated. "Ah ight. Call me if you need anything."

She gave me a small, reassuring smile. "I will. I promise."

I watched as Lelani walked out the door, fighting the urge to disregard her needs. Each step she took stomped on my pride. I was a man who prided himself on being a protector, yet I was sitting here letting her go through this without me.

I felt like a hypocrite, though. I wanted to be there for her, but deep down, I knew it was more out of obligation than genuine desire. A real man wouldn't let someone he cared about get this type of treatment without him. But as much as I tried to focus on that, my mind kept drifting back to Aviana.

Ever since I walked out of her suite on Monday, her memory was haunting me, sitting right there in the back of my mind. Being with her—finally getting that close—only made things worse. My obsession ran deeper now. It dug into me like a hook I couldn't get free of.

But she was loyal to her husband. We hadn't talked since she told me to leave, and the space between us made me want her more. I kept replaying the feeling of her against me, her smile, everything about her. It was on loop, and no matter how much I tried to shove those thoughts aside, it wasn't happening. It was like trying to put out a wildfire with a cup of water.

I spent the morning lounging around the house, taking it easy. Most of my mornings and afternoons were chill and relaxed since the real action always kicked off when the streets came alive at night. The quiet was a welcome change from the chaos that came with my line of work.

As I was sinking into the comfort of my couch, my phone rang with a call from Timmy.

I hurriedly picked up. "Tell me you got something for me, Timmy."

"I do, but it's not what you want to hear. I got an update on Mia. She's gone completely off the grid. It's like she vanished without a trace."

"What do you mean vanished?"

"Her phone hasn't pinged anywhere since Saturday. There hasn't been any sign of her at any airports, no activity in her bank accounts. It's like she just disappeared."

I frowned, leaning forward. "No money withdrawals? Nothing?"

"*Nothing,*" Timmy confirmed. "It's as if she dropped off the face of the earth. Her accounts are untouched."

Mia disappearing like this seemed dramatic, but she was facing time that most couldn't handle. If she had a large amount of cash stashed somewhere, she could have run to avoid the charges. She had no ties to Chicago. No kids. No husband. So, considering the heat she was under, it made sense.

I understood. Hustlas and murderers did it all the time, and Mia was on the verge of being both. But because of her obsession with Avi, I didn't trust that she was done trying to get revenge, so it was a must that I find her.

"Keep digging, Timmy. I want to know if there's any sign of where she might be."

"Got it. I'll keep you posted."

As I ended the call with Timmy, I heard the front door open and looked up to see Lelani walking in. The sight of her was a punch to the gut. She looked even more pale and distraught than usual. I stood from the couch, quickly ending the call, and moved toward her.

"You good?" My voice was filled with concern as I followed her closely. She didn't say a word. Her face was distorted with discomfort as she rushed into the master bedroom, then straight into the master bathroom.

"Lelani?" I called out as I trailed behind her.

As I pushed open the bathroom door, she didn't answer. Instead, she collapsed to her knees in front of the toilet. I watched helplessly as she leaned over and began to vomit violently into the bowl. Her body shook with the force of it, and I could see the strain and pain etched on her face.

As she continued to heave, I sat next to her on the edge of the tub and gently placed a hand on her back, trying to offer some comfort.

The sound was painful, like she was trying to expel more than just the contents of her stomach. Each heave seemed to come with a new wave of discomfort. I could feel her body trembling under my hand, each lurch making me cringe with helplessness.

Her gagging grew more violent. Her body continued to convulse, but nothing else seemed to come up. The bathroom was filled with the sound of her struggle, and I could see how much it was taking out of her.

Finally, her body stilled, and she collapsed against the toilet with tears streaming down her face. "I can't do this."

# CHAPTER 11

## AVIANA SCOTT

THE RICH, FRUITY scent of mango filled the bathroom as I scooped a generous amount of body butter into my hands with my phone cradled between my shoulder and ear. I had just gotten out of the shower, so steam still swirled around me.

"Have you heard anything from Mia?"

Mia's mother, Carol, sighed heavily. "No. I haven't heard a thing. It's so unlike her to just drop off the radar. I don't understand why she wouldn't at least reach out."

"I know. It doesn't make sense," I replied, smoothing the butter over my legs. "I just hope she's okay."

It wasn't hard for me to be genuinely concerned. Mia and I had been besties for years, so I was close to her mom. Despite Mia's attempts to ruin my life, I was truly worried for her mother.

"It's like she's vanished." Carol's voice trembled slightly. "I know she's scared. She has to be running from the Feds."

"Yeah. I really think that's what's happening, that she's running scared."

"I can't think of any other reason," Carol replied as frustration seeped into her words. "She knows prison is on the line. She's probably panicking and going off the grid."

"I agree, but I wish she'd reach out so you know that she's okay. She could at least let you know that she's safe."

"Exactly. No matter what she's done, she knows that I will be here for her. I just don't get why she wouldn't at least try to contact me."

"Me either," I admitted. "I just hope she comes to her senses soon so you can stop worrying."

"You're so sweet for being concerned about me and Mia, especially after everything she's done to you," Carol said with a hint of disbelief in her voice. "I couldn't believe it when the police questioned me about Mia after your house fire. You're so kind to still check on me."

"Despite what she's done to me, I'm still worried about you. I don't have children, but I can only imagine how hard it is to have no idea where your child is. I just wish she'd reach out. It's hard to believe she would go this far."

"I know." Carol's sigh was filled with regret. "I'm really sorry for how things have turned out. Mia has always been impulsive, but *this*...this is something else."

As I smoothed the body butter over my skin, I noticed my stomach felt less bloated, and I could tell it had gotten smaller. I was losing weight, likely due to all the stress I'd been under since Mia's arrest.

"I'm just so worried about you, Aviana," Carol said, pulling me back to the conversation. "You need to take care of yourself, especially with everything happening."

"I'm trying," I assured her. "But honestly, I think the stress is helping me shed some pounds." I giggled slightly.

"Stress isn't a good weight-loss method. You need to take care of yourself first."

I smiled weakly. "I know, Carol."

As I glanced at the time on my phone, I realized it was almost time for me to leave for work. I reluctantly wrapped up the call with Carol. Just as I hung up, the bathroom door creaked open, and a groggy, naked Damar strolled in, clearly not yet fully awake.

He walked behind me, lifting the toilet seat and started to relieve himself.

"You and Carol need to stop looking for Mia," his sleepy voice croaked. "It's obvious she's run and doesn't want to be found."

"But she should at least find a way to get in touch with her mom. It's not right to leave her mom hanging."

"That's not how hiding works, Aviana," he replied, flushing the toilet.

He washed his hands before leaning over to plant a quick kiss on my cheek.

"I just think she needs to reach out. It's hard to believe she'd leave without a word."

His eyes were filled with sympathy for my naïveté. "Sometimes people do stupid, unrealistic things when they're scared."

I let out a slow breath. "I just hope she's okay."

Damar shrugged. "You're worried about somebody who didn't give a fuck about killing you." I winced at that realization. Seeing my discomfort, his tone softened. "I'm sorry, baby. It's the truth. She's been trying to ruin your life over an assumption. She's obviously not thinking clearly, so just let it go, and focus on you." Then he slowly smiled, creeping up behind me. He slipped his arms around my waist. Our eyes locked through the mirror. "Focus on us." His deep rumble-spoke against the sensitive skin on my neck. "Focus on applying for nursing school and having our baby." Then he began to place sweet, wet kisses on my neck.

Guilt made my stomach turn. I could still feel Mythic all over me.

I giggled nervously. "Stop, bae. I have to get ready for work."

He growled lowly as he stepped back with eyes focused on my hips. Holding his bottom lip tight between his teeth, he softly smacked my butt cheek. "Well, you better hurry up and cover up before I have you face down, ass up."

I managed to blush as he finally tore his eyes away from mine and left the bathroom. As soon as he disappeared, I let out a breath that I didn't even realize I was holding.

## DAMAR SCOTT

My mind was all over the place as I headed south toward the city. Stress was riding with me. Trying to cover up Mia's murder while keeping up this front as the innocent husband was wearing me down. It felt like I was carrying around the weight of a mountain. Every single day felt like I was walking a tightrope, trying to balance everything just to keep my lies together, keep Aviana by my side, *and* stay free.

From Damar and Aviana's lack of messages since he'd been at the hotel, it didn't seem like the visit was anything more than friendly. But I knew that he was everything I wasn't. I had to pull her back to me, give her what she wanted to keep her focused on us. I was determined to get her pregnant, though I was dreading it. I had no plans of taking care of another crying ass baby. My plan was to trap her with the baby. I wouldn't be there for her like I'd promised or provide her with any of the help that I said I would. Then she'd have no choice but to drop out of nursing school and stay home with the baby. I could control her that way, keep her close, and ensure she wouldn't have the freedom to consider Mythic or anyone else.

My plan seemed to be working. She was still with me, still loved me. But the lies I was weaving were growing thicker, and the more I thought about it, the more suffocating it became.

As I drove through the streets, my eyes narrowed at a familiar sight.

"What the fuck?" I muttered to myself as I stared closer, trying to make sure that my eyes weren't playing tricks on me.

Unfortunately, they weren't. Jeremy was walking with a group of the 111 Boyz.

Without thinking, I slammed on the brakes and pulled my car over to the curb.

I jumped out and stormed toward him. "Jeremy! Get in the car," I barked.

He turned to me and was shocked at first, then his expression turned defiant, as if not being embarrassed in front of his guys was more important than obeying me.

I stepped closer as my anger rose. "I told you to stop hanging with these niggas. Get your dumbass in the car." I grabbed him by the shoulder and pushed him toward my ride.

The force of it surprised him, making his eyes bulge. "Dad, chill," Jeremy yelled, pulling away from my grip.

I could see the fire in his eyes. He was itching to push back, and it made my blood boil.

"You wanna hit me, nigga?" I dared him, stepping closer.

He had the nerve to stand his ground. For a minute, I thought he might actually throw a punch.

His friends watched with wide eyes, some snickering.

Jeremy squared his shoulders defiantly. "You can't just tell me what to do."

"Watch me. Get in the car, Jeremy. *Now*. Don't make me embarrass you further in front of your homies."

Though these 111 Boyz were shooters and thoughtless criminals, they stood back, not interrupting.

Sucking his teeth, Jeremy stormed toward my car. His tantrum further proved that he wasn't mentally ready to hang with real killers.

Once Jeremy begrudgingly climbed into the car, I hopped in the driver's seat and sped off.

"The fuck is wrong with you, boy? I told you to stop hanging with them niggas."

Jeremy sat in the passenger seat, arms crossed and pouting, refusing to say a word.

"It's time for you to live with me," I decided. "Clearly, you're not listening to your mother or me, so maybe a change of scenery will help you get your head on straight."

That was when Jeremy finally found his voice. "I don't want to live with you."

I scoffed as I pulled into a gas station. "You don't have a fucking choice. That's what you've misunderstood. You don't make decisions for yourself because you're a fucking kid. You're just pretending to be grown. You don't know shit."

Before he could reply, I got out of the car and slammed the door. As I paid for the gas, I ran a frustrated hand over my face. Everyone around me was slipping through my fingers. First, Aviana was defying me; now, my own son was out here disrespecting me, acting like my word meant nothing. I was losing control, and that shit was unacceptable. I'd built my whole life around authority and respect, around people knowing not to test me. Now, it seemed like nobody respected my gangsta anymore.

As I finished pumping the gas, I tried to clear my mind of the tension so that I could talk to Jeremy calmly when I got back in the car. I knew that I would have to get him under control the same way I had gotten Aviana—through manipulation.

As I slid into the driver's seat, I noticed Jeremy bent over, searching for something under the seat.

"What are you looking for?"

"I dropped my phone," he muttered defiantly as he rummaged around.

Suddenly, he sat up, looking completely confused and taken aback. "What are you doing with Tee Tee Mia's phone?"

Confused, I glanced over to see him holding Mia's phone, the unmistakable purple wallet case catching my eye. My blood ran cold, but I forced myself to keep my composure. "That's not Mia's phone," I said nonchalantly.

I tried to grab it, but he snatched it back as he shook his head. "I know it is. It has the purple case she always had on her phone." He opened the wallet and pulled out her ID, then he held it up for me to see. "See? This is Tee Tee Mia's ID."

I started to panic as I stared at the ID. I had securely taped the phone under the seat, but it had obviously fallen at some point. My chest rose and fell rapidly as I scrambled to think of a way to deflect this. "Jeremy, just give me the phone."

His brows knitted together as he studied me. "Why do you have her phone, Dad? What's going on?"

I took a deep breath, trying to figure out how to handle this while driving toward Stephanie's house. "Listen, it's complicated. Just…let's talk about it when we get to your house. Right now, I need you to trust me."

But suspicion was growing wildly in his eyes. "She's missing," he said as if he were putting the pieces together. "I heard you saying that Mia has been doing all of this crazy stuff to Avi. We need to get this phone to the—"

His words lodged in his throat when I reached over and snatched the phone from his grip. As I sped through the city, I could feel Jeremy looking at me curiously, watching me unravel.

Jeremy picked up his phone from his lap, and I felt a sinking sensation in my stomach.

I tried to hide my panic as I asked him, "What are you doing?"

"Checking my text messages," he replied defiantly. "Why do you have Mia's phone, Dad? I don't understand why you won't answer the question."

Frustration was building up inside me, ready to explode. He was so fucking disobedient and hardheaded. He had no idea of the severity of the situation or the lengths I would go to to hide the truth.

"Jeremy, put your phone down," I gritted.

"Why?"

"Put your fucking phone down, Jeremy!"

He backed away, looking confused as my anger erupted like a storm.

I pulled into an alley as I tried to figure out my next move. Overwhelmed, I snatched Jeremy's phone from his hands. He looked at me with confusion clouding his eyes.

He was so green, so confused. He had the audacity to try to take the phone back. I pushed him into his seat, holding him by the collar of his shirt.

"Stop, Dad. Let me go. What's your problem?" he shot back, pushing against me.

We began to tussle. The struggle escalated as I fought to keep control. I was so desperate. This wasn't just about the phone anymore; it was about protecting my freedom, my life. I couldn't let him expose me. I had to end this before it spiraled further out of control. If anyone found out that I had this phone, it would connect me to Mia.

Suddenly, it felt as if my soul had detached from my body, hovering somewhere above while I was lost in desperation and rage. My hands found Jeremy's throat, and I squeezed, my fingers curling around his flesh like a vice.

Tears pooled in my eyes, blurring my vision, but I couldn't look away. I felt the frantic thump of his pulse against my grip, the hysterical struggle for air as I tightened my hold. I could feel his esophagus beneath my fingers, the soft flesh giving way to the pressure.

Even as I choked the breath from him, Jeremy's eyes remained locked on mine, filled with confusion and trust, as if he believed I would come to my senses, that I would stop before it was too late. But the panic in me drowned out that glimmer of hope. Each desperate gasp he took only fueled my rage, and I squeezed tighter, feeling his body begin to go slack.

I could taste my tears as they slid out of my eyes, down my cheeks, and between my lips. I didn't want to kill my own son, but he'd made me do it. Still, I wanted to stop myself, but the fear of being caught for Mia's murder was stronger. Jeremy now knew too much. If he told anyone about this phone, he would open up a can of worms that would never close.

Finally, Jeremy's body went limp.

Suddenly, my adrenaline skyrocketed. I jumped out of the car and rounded the trunk. I flung open the passenger door. Jeremy's unconscious body tumbled out. It hit the dirty gravel with a sickening thud.

My breath quickened as I scanned the alley. Luckily, it was empty and quiet.

I lurched toward the glove compartment, yanked it open, and took out my gun.

I began to pace. I groaned in frustration as I struggled to come to terms with what I felt I had to do. But I couldn't turn back now. I had to do what I had to do.

I banged my fists against the sides of my head. Tears streamed down my face, mixing with sweat. I wasn't crying because I had killed my son. These were tears of anger because he had forced my hand.

Finally, I paused, taking a deep breath to get my shit together. With tears still streaming down my face, I turned toward my son. I gnawed on my bottle lip as I aimed the gun at him.

To make it look like the usual violence of the inner city had taken his life, I put two bullets in his head.

I let out a guttural groan as his blood started to spill on the gravel surrounding him. I bent down, resting my hands on my knees. But I couldn't get caught for this either, so I sprinted back to the open driver's side door. I quickly slid inside, unable to catch my breath. My leg was shaking uncontrollably as I floored the gas pedal and tore out of the alley and into the street.

# CHAPTER 12

## MYTHIC GREY

TAYE AND I were rolling through the burbs on our way to a cigar bar to have a meeting with Manuel, the boss of the Viper Crew.

Taye leaned back in the passenger seat, glancing over at me. "This shit between the Urban Enforcers and the Crimson Order is getting outta hand. Fury made a dumb move starting that war."

I chuckled as I nodded in agreement.

Fury, the boss of the Urban Enforcers, had kicked off a war with the Crimson Order two weeks ago. He had murdered top lieutenants of the Crimson Order in order to gain drug territory. Since, he had been losing many of his crew in the war that he had initiated and was now losing.

"That whole move was dumb from the jump. The Enforcers ain't got no claim to that turf, but Fury wants to run everything."

Taye chuckled, but it wasn't out of amusement. "You know what's coming next, right?"

I glanced at him with a curious raise of my brow.

"You know he's gonna try to come to you asking to buy weapons. He needs the firepower if he's gonna hold on to any of that territory. And you're the man with the connects."

I let out a low laugh, shaking my head. "I ain't doing business with that nigga. He's reckless as hell. He ain't got no control over his crew, and that's why they've been out here wildin' out, killing innocent people. I don't do business with bosses who can't keep their soldiers in check."

Taye nodded, leaning forward a little. "That's real. His crew's full of these young trigger-happy dudes that don't know how to move smart. They just wanna shoot anything that moves."

"Exactly. Fury's an immature leader. He's not thinking long-term, not thinking about how to build and protect what he's got. All he cares about is making noise, and that's why he's losing control. If I give him weapons, he's gonna tear the whole city apart, and I'm not putting my name on that."

Taye smirked, glancing out the window. "I figured as much. But you know he's gonna try, though."

I shook my head again. "Ain't enough money in the world to make me deal with Fury."

"Facts." He grunted. Then as we approached the parking lot, he asked me, "You really think this meeting is a good idea? After everything that went down with Diego and his crew, I'm not sure we should be doing this."

"Manuel isn't stupid enough to pull a hit here, not in a snooty suburb like this in broad daylight. It would be too messy. He knows better than that."

Taye shot me a skeptical look. "You really think he'll just sit down and have a conversation like nothing happened?"

"Absolutely," I replied confidently as I parked. "Besides, Draven and the rest of the security team are tailing us. We're not walking into this blind. Most of our team are already positioned inside, ready for anything."

As I turned off the ignition, I surveyed the parking lot. I spotted the vehicles of my security team discreetly parked in various spots.

Taye still wore that worried expression. "I just don't like the idea of walking into the lion's den after what happened at the club. You slit one of his lieutenant's throats."

My brow arched cockily. "He doesn't specifically know what I did since we killed everybody."

Taye's eyes narrowed, scolding my smug smirk.

"We control the situation, not Manuel," I told him, seriously. "Just keep your head on straight and follow my lead."

As I climbed out, I cleared my mind. Although my team had gotten rid of the bodies, I was sure that someone in the Viper Crew knew that Diego was coming to Enchant to meet with me that night. My team and I figured that this request to meet with the boss of the Viper Crew had something to do with his missing men.

As Taye and I stepped into the cigar bar, the thick, pungent stench of smoke soaked into the fabric of our clothes. The air was filled with the earthy aroma of aged tobacco, blending with the faint scent of whiskey and leather.

I scanned the room, spotting Manuel in an oversized, comfortable leather chair in the corner. My eyes narrowed as I recognized a few members of the Viper Crew scattered throughout the bar.

Taye hung back at the bar, ordering a drink while I approached Manuel. As I drew closer, he leaned back. "Mythic," he greeted with a sharp nod.

"Manuel." We shook hands before I sat in the seat across from him, clasping my hands in front of my face as my elbows rested on the arms of the chair.

Leaning forward, he told me, "Let's cut to the chase. I know you were the last to see Diego and his crew," Manuel said, his gaze piercing.

He didn't need me to deny it; he was certain, so I maintained my cool composure, refusing to show any hint of vulnerability. The way Manuel laid it out felt almost like a game, one I was more than willing to play.

"Now, they have gone missing, but..." Manuel shrugged a shoulder so nonchalantly that it was surprising. "Diego was a hothead, which was why he didn't have the sense to ask for permission before he approached you with his disputes. That's on him."

Though I was shocked, I remained cool, nodding smooth and confidently.

Manuel sat up. He took one of the copitas from the row that was sitting in front of him on the table and threw back a shot.

The liquor must have been smooth as hell because he didn't even wince or squint as it went down. Then he sat back, telling me, "You're good with us, Mythic. You've been a valuable distributor for the Viper Crew. I know you don't make stupid decisions."

"I appreciate that. I have no intention of getting involved in any unnecessary shit. I'm here to do business, not to deal with weak motherfuckers' egos."

Manuel's smirk was menacing as he leaned forward, tapping the rim of his empty glass. "Good. Because if it turns out you *did* have something to do with Diego's disappearance, then this little partnership of ours ends with blood."

He stood, adjusting his jacket, and gave me one last look. It was a look that made it clear the conversation wasn't over, just postponed.

I stayed seated as he walked away. His men fell in behind him like shadows.

Taye approached a second later. "That sound like a threat to you?"

"Manuel's just fishing. He doesn't know shit." My eyes stayed on the door Manuel had disappeared through. "He just *wants* to.

And by the time he figures out he never will, I'll be ten moves ahead. But if Manuel suspects the truth, this meeting wasn't about peace. It was a warning. And the next time we sit across from each other, one of us might not walk away."

## AVIANA SCOTT

**Mythic:** *How are you?*

As I stared at his text, my pulse quickened. The text had been just three simple words. It was a question he often asked, especially after everything that had happened with Mia. But after that night we shared, it felt as if those words had more meaning. They were loaded with unspoken thoughts and feelings. He *really* wanted to know how I felt about what had transpired between us. He was reaching out across the distance that had grown between us since then, trying to bridge that gap without saying too much.

I knew he was being respectful, not wanting to put everything in a text message, but it left me frazzled and unsure of how to respond. So, I didn't. Instead, I scrolled through my Facebook app.

I scrolled to Mythic's page. He hardly used the app, but the few pictures he had were striking, though I had seen them many times. Some, I had even taken myself. I clicked on one that showcased his tall, muscular frame, and the way his chocolate skin glistened under the light. He was so undeniably attractive, and I could feel a heat rising in my cheeks as I remembered the intimate moments we had shared just a few nights ago. I was salivating over the sight of him, the way he made me feel, and the connection that lingered even in his absence.

As I continued scrolling, I stumbled across a photo of me, Mia, and Mythic. It felt like a lifetime ago. We were all smiles, carefree, and naïve to the chaos that would soon follow. My heart ached for that bond that had once felt unbreakable. No matter what Mia had done, I missed her. I missed the laughter, the inside jokes, and the support we'd always given each other.

Tears pricked at the corners of my eyes as I reminisced about the good times. Everything had changed so drastically, and I wasn't sure if it could ever go back to what it was before.

I heard the click of the suite's door, which thankfully forced my mind off the hurt. I closed the app, rolled off of the bed, and padded out the bedroom to meet Damar in the living room. I had only been there for about an hour since arriving after work, so I still had on the maxi dress I'd worn to the office.

As I approached Damar, I noticed the tremor in his hands. His fingers fidgeted restlessly at his sides. Despite his nervousness, he smiled warmly, opening his arms to greet me. We hugged tightly, and I could feel the rapid thud of his heart against my chest.

I pulled back to look him in the eye. "What's wrong?"

"I'm fine," he replied, though the shaky smile didn't quite convince me.

I scanned him over, taking note of the beads of sweat glistening on his forehead. "You look a little shaky and sweaty."

He chuckled lightly, brushing it off. "I had it out with Jeremy again. I caught him outside with the 111 Boyz. I just can't get through to that kid. He's insistent on hanging with them niggas. I'm scared something is going to happen to him."

"I'll try to talk to him again."

"Thank you, baby, but he's got his mind made up apparently. This is a lesson he's going to have to learn on his own."

As I nodded, he shifted the focus back to me. "What's wrong with you?" His gaze was intense, studying me as if he could see right through to my thoughts.

I hesitated for a moment, feeling silly. "I was just looking at a picture of me, Mythic, and Mia," I admitted as sadness crept into my voice. "Is it silly that I miss Mia?"

"Not at all," he assured me softly. "No matter what Mia has done, she's been your best friend for years. You don't just forget that. You've shared so much together. Now you have to get accustomed to not having her around. You need to mourn her, in a way."

I nodded, but before I could dwell on it, he changed the subject. A smile broke across his face. "What do you want to do for your birthday?"

It dawned on me then that my birthday was next week. With everything that had been happening, I had barely noticed it was coming. "Honestly, after everything that's happened with Mia, I just want a quiet, intimate birthday with just you."

Damar's expression brightened. "I can do that. You want a new car for your birthday?"

My eyes widened excitedly. "*Really?* You'd do that?"

"Hell yeah."

Blushing, I replied, "But I don't know what I want."

"Let's go look at cars right now then."

As I grinned, the heaviness of the past few weeks lifted slightly. "Okay. Let's do it."

I turned to grab my shoes, but I felt Damar's hand gently wrap around mine. I looked back, curiously.

"Are you ovulating?" he asked with a playful glint in his eye and a sneaky grin spreading across his face.

I felt my cheeks flush hot at the question. "*Um,* yes."

"Then we need to wait to go to the car dealership," he said teasingly.

I pouted. "But I was looking forward to it."

He stepped closer as he pulled down his pants. "Oh, we're still going. I just need a few minutes."

A few hours later, we were at the second car dealership, and I was taken aback by the cars Damar was showing me. He led me from one luxury vehicle to another, pointing out the sleek lines of a high-end Range Rover and the sporty elegance of a Porsche. I couldn't afford the note on these cars, but he assured me that he was buying the car, so the note would be his responsibility.

Now we were at the Tesla dealership.

"Come on. Let's check out that Tesla X," Damar said with a boyish grin spreading across his face as he pulled me by the hand toward the sleek vehicle.

I smiled, watching him have way more fun with this than I was.

As we approached the vehicle, I was taken aback by its futuristic design. It had sleek curves and a glossy finish. The falcon-wing doors opened upward, giving it an otherworldly appearance.

"Wow. It's beautiful," I said, stepping inside.

"Just wait until you see the features," Damar told me as he settled into the driver's seat and adjusted the steering wheel. "It practically drives itself."

I settled into the passenger seat, feeling the plush material envelop me. "Seriously? That's wild."

He nodded enthusiastically. "Yeah. It's got all these safety features too. You can even summon it to you with your phone. Imagine no more walking through the parking lot looking for your ride because you forgot where you parked."

I laughed, picturing the car navigating its way to me. "Baby, I don't need this fancy-ass car."

Damar scoffed. "Girl, I ain't buying you this. I just wanted to look at it."

As we burst out laughing, his phone started to ring.

While he answered, I drifted off into my thoughts. His generosity was overwhelming. A blend of excitement and guilt hit me. I had cheated, and now, sitting next to my good husband who loved me and was doing his best to please me, I felt like a fraud.

Things between us might not have been perfect, but he was trying. He was putting in the effort to make me happy, to show me that he cared, and yet, my heart still ached for someone else. I beat myself up for allowing Mythic to consume me, for letting my desires cloud my judgment.

Suddenly, I was snatched out of my thoughts as Damar erupted, his voice loud and filled with anger. His loud bark drew the attention of everyone in the dealership, and I turned to see him with his phone pressed to his ear as he wore an expression of disbelief and heartache. "No. You're lying. This shit ain't true."

I cringed with embarrassment. Every eye in the dealership was on us. Suddenly, Damar started to shake with a look in his eyes that I had never seen before.

"Damar, what's wrong?" I asked, reaching out to touch his arm to ground him, but my words seemed to fall on deaf ears. He dropped the phone and slammed his fist into the steering wheel with such force that I feared he might break it.

The sound was deafening, and my heart raced as I bent down to pick up the phone. I glanced at the screen and saw it was Stephanie on the line.

"Stephanie?" I called out for her as I put the phone to my ear. "What's going on?"

But all I could hear was her sobbing on the other end, and my stomach dropped. "What's happening?" I repeated as panic crept into my voice.

"Aviana…" she gasped between cries. "Jeremy…my baby."

My eyes bulged. "What happened to Jeremy?"

"He's dead. Somebody killed my baby."

# CHAPTER 13

## MYTHIC GREY

AFTER DROPPING TAYE off, I was cruising through the city on my way to Enchant as I checked on Lelani.

"Hey, Mythic."

I cringed when I heard how weak she sounded. "Hey. How are you feeling?"

"My head is still killing me, and I've been nauseous all day."

"Is the edible that I got you helping any?"

"A little. I actually got hungry and ate something."

A smiled a bit. "Good. I know it's tough, but I also know that I don't completely understand since I'm not in your shoes."

I wanted to say more. It pissed me off that I wasn't there for her at that moment because her mother wanted to be. I had left my own house to ease the tension and make it easier on Lelani.

But, instead, I simply told her, "I hate that you have to go through this."

She blew a heavy breath, saying, "The doctor said that my symptoms will get worse until I have surgery."

"I just wish I could be there with you. It feels wrong to be away while you're going through this."

"It's okay, Mythic," she reassured me. "Trust me, you and my mother in the same room will only make matters worse." Then she chuckled a bit.

Despite her laugh, it didn't feel okay. I felt like less of a man for not being there to support her through the worst of it. No matter my lack of true unconditional love for her, I was obligated to be her rock, to hold her hand and take some of that burden off her shoulders.

"I know you're strong, but I'm here for you. If you need anything—*anything at all*—just call me, and I'll come home. Your mama don't scare me."

She giggled weakly. "I know. But I don't need the stress of you and her bickering over my head. I'm sick enough."

As I lightly chuckled, my other line rang. I glanced at the screen, and I felt so much relief when I saw Aviana's name flashing on my dash. We hadn't spoken since that night I finally felt her again, and the longing to hear her voice had been building inside me like a violent storm.

"I get it," I told Lelani, trying not to sound like I was rushing her off the phone. "Let me answer this other call though. I'll call you back in a minute."

"You don't have to. Hopefully, I'll fall asleep soon. I'll just see you when you get home."

"Okay. I won't stay at the club long. I'll be there in a few hours, so tell your moms she got a time limit."

She snickered and replied, "Okay. See you later."

As I clicked over, my chest started to hammer with need and anticipation. Suddenly, I felt like a hypocrite. I was worried about Lelani and her health, yet Aviana and how much I craved her presence superseded both.

"Aviana." I even grinned as I said her name. "What's up?"

Instead of the familiar warmth of her voice, I was met with uncontrollable sobbing.

My heart dropped. "Avi? What's wrong?"

"My–Mythic!" Her voice trembled and was filled with distress.

Hearing the pain and desperation, a knot formed in my stomach. "Avi, take a deep breath and tell me what happened."

She cried to calm down, but she couldn't control the tears. The sound of her anguish was gut-wrenching. I wanted nothing more than to reach through the phone and pull her into my arms. I had no idea what was going on, but I knew I needed to be there for her.

"I'm here, Avi. Just tell me what's going on."

Aviana fought to regain her composure. Each breath came in ragged, shaky gasps. She inhaled deeply, as she desperately fought to steady herself. "Jeremy…" She finally forced out. "He's–He's dead. He was murdered."

Shock flowed through me like ice water as I struggled to process her words.

Shaken, I pulled over to the side of the busy street. "*What? No, Aviana…*"

Her sobs resonated through the phone, and she could hardly speak. Her words tumbled out in fragments. "I'm outside…on the porch at Stephanie's house. I just…I needed to tell you…"

"Where is Damar?" I asked as my protective instincts kicked in. "I need to come see you."

"I'm with Damar," she replied, "but I had to step outside to call you. I didn't want you to find out on social media or something."

As her voice broke again, my heart ached for her.

"Aviana, listen to me. You're not alone. I'm here for you. I want to be there. Just tell me what you need."

As she took a shaky breath, I could hear the turmoil in her silence. "I don't know what to do, Mythic. I don't know how to comfort Damar and Stephanie. This is crazy."

"What happened to him?"

"No one knows yet, but we're sure he was with those damn 111 Boyz. Damar caught him outside with them earlier, but he made Jeremy get in the car. Damar said that he dropped him off at home, but Jeremy must have just left again. He was found in an alley around the corner. He was shot in the head...twice..." Whimpers took over as she tried to continue. "He was found in a fucking alley. They just left him in the alley like he was trash. That poor baby. This is unreal. This is un-fucking-real!"

As I sat there listening to her unravel, I felt like my hands were tied. Showing up at Damar's baby's mother's house to comfort his wife would complicate things even more. All I could do was offer my support through the phone.

"Aviana, listen to me. You have to be there for Damar and Stephanie right now. They're going to need your strength more than ever." Her sobs were gut-wrenching as I continued, "I've lost a lot of friends to the streets, and I know how devastating this can be. You have to hold on to the good memories. It's okay to grieve, but don't forget that you're not alone in this." I recalled the pain of losing both my parents at an early age, a feeling that had shaped who I was. "I've been through this too, Avi. It doesn't get easier, but you can find a way to navigate through it. You have to stay strong for Damar."

Slowly, I could hear her breathing begin to even out, and her sobs softened as I spoke. I was relieved to know that my words were reaching her. "I'm going to check on you later, okay? Just take a moment for yourself and breathe."

"Okay." Her voice was fragile but steadier than before.

I ended the call with Aviana and made a quick U-turn. I headed straight for the 111 Boyz' hood. The streets were a blur as I sped through the city.

I arrived in minutes. As I pulled up to the corner where the familiar convenience store stood, I spotted a group of the 111 Boyz loitering outside. They looked up as I jumped out of my ride, and I was met with respectful nods.

"Yo, Mythic," Murdock called out, stepping forward. "What's good?"

We shook up as I greeted the rest of them with a nod. Then I got straight to the point. "What happened to Jeremy?"

The group exchanged glances, confusion etched on their faces. "We don't know, man," Trell told me. "He was a good dude. He never got involved in our shit. He just wanted to hang out."

"He wasn't part of our crew or any beefs," Reggie added, crossing his arms. "We were shocked when we heard he was killed, especially for it to have happened in our hood and we not hear anything about it. Shit don't add up."

"There weren't any drive-bys today?"

"No," Reggie answered.

"Nobody was out here robbing people?" I pressed.

"Not that we know of," Murdock replied.

I studied their expressions, noting the sincerity in their eyes. They seemed genuinely hurt and stunned by the news. "You're sure he wasn't caught up in any street shit?"

"We're positive," Murdock insisted. "On my mama, on gang 'nem, he was just trying to live his life. We wouldn't have even let him get close to any real shit. None of us have heard anything about him being in the wrong place at the wrong time."

I groaned, frustrated. "This doesn't make sense."

"Facts," Murdock replied as a grimace crossed his face. "It ain't right that he went out like that. Jeremy didn't do nothing to nobody."

I took a deep breath, inhaling the confusion and grief. "If you hear anything, you let me know," I told them all. "We need to find out what really happened."

## AVIANA SCOTT

The last few days had passed in a haze of grief and disbelief. I felt like I was trapped in a hellish fog. Each hour blended into the next, filled with sorrow. Jeremy wasn't my biological son, but the bond we had developed since Damar and I got together felt as strong as any blood connection. He was a bright light in my life, full of potential and dreams, and now that light had been extinguished.

It hurt as if I had lost my own child. I could barely fathom the idea of bringing a child into this dangerous world, knowing that I could one day face the agony of burying that child. The thought twisted my insides, leaving me feeling hollow and terrified. My heart ached, and each breath felt like a struggle.

I had spent most of the past few days comforting and supporting Damar. He had been a mess, but each day he was becoming stronger and stronger. Today was the first I had been alone to drown in my thoughts and sorrow because Damar was busy with Stephanie making arrangements for Jeremy's funeral.

I had tried to distract myself, but nothing seemed to alleviate the crushing sadness. I spent most of my day in a daze, sitting on the couch with my phone in hand, staring at the screen without truly seeing anything. It wasn't until my parents called me on video call that I remembered what day it was.

"Hello?"

*"Happy birthday to you! Happy birthday to you!"* they sang. Their voices were filled with joy that felt so distant from my reality. The ritualistic tune echoed through the phone, but all I could feel was the burden of my sorrow.

"Thanks, guys," I replied weakly. My words felt so empty, lacking the excitement and celebration I should have felt on my birthday.

As I sat there, their faces began to blur as my eyes glassed over. I could barely muster a smile for them, knowing how much they wanted to celebrate me, but my heart was heavy. It felt wrong to be celebrating anything when the world felt so dark and unforgiving.

"How are you managing, sweetie?" my mom asked with a tone and expression full of concern.

"Barely."

"We're here for you," my dad added gently. "Always."

I swallowed hard, wishing that the comfort of their words could somehow ease the pain. But all I could think about was Jeremy and the void his absence left.

As I continued to talk to my parents about Jeremy, the pain of his loss spilling out with each word, a notification dropped down on my screen. All day, I had been ignoring calls and messages, people wishing me a happy birthday and offering empty clichés, but this one caught my attention because it was from Mythic.

I hesitated for a moment before opening it. His message simply read, *Happy birthday, Avi.* Still, my heart fluttered as if it was a message full of sweet sentiments, and I felt a small warmth cover me despite everything. I replied with a simple thank-you, adding a sad face emoji that mirrored how I felt inside.

As I resumed my conversation with my parents, my other line rang. It was Mythic with a video call. I quickly ended the call with my parents and answered his.

The moment his handsome, chocolate complexion filled the screen, a small smile broke through the heaviness I had been carrying. He looked concerned, his brows slightly furrowed, and that expression made my heart ache in the best way.

"What are you doing?" His deep rumble was so warm and inviting.

"Nothing," I replied, trying to keep my tone light, but I knew he could see through it. "Damar is with Stephanie. They're making arrangements for Jeremy's service and going shopping for his clothes to be buried in."

His face softened, and I could see the disappointment in his eyes. "You shouldn't be alone on your birthday, Avi."

I shrugged sadly. "I don't even care about celebrating. Nothing feels right. Mia is missing, and Jeremy is dead. There's really nothing to celebrate."

"Listen to me," Mythic said firmly but still gentle. "You need to get out of that house. Slip on something comfortable because I'm coming to get you."

At first, I hesitated, wanting to refuse. The thought of going out felt wrong and inconsiderate. But I knew being with him would be the perfect medicine. "I don't know, Mythic…"

"Just for a little while," he urged with a voice that would convince me to do anything. "You need some fresh air. Let me take your mind off everything for a little while. It'll be good for you."

As I looked into his eyes, the warmth and concern radiating from him was undeniable.

After a moment, I sighed, feeling the tension in my chest ease slightly. "Okay," I finally said. "I'll get ready."

"Good. I'll be there soon," he replied, a hint of relief washing over his face.

Mythic had taken me to Reggie's on the Beach. The restaurant sat right on the lakefront. The sound of the waves gently lapping against the shore was like a soothing balm for my troubled soul. As I took a deep breath, the smell of grilled seafood mixed with the fresh breeze. The salty air kissed my skin. Listening to the waves allowed a calm that I had been yearning for to wash over me. For the first time in days, I felt a bit of peace.

Sitting across from Mythic, I watched as he ordered our drinks with an admiring smirk. His confident demeanor made me feel at ease. The way he moved, the way he spoke brought a sense of comfort I always needed.

"Thanks for bringing me here," I said, smiling into his eyes.

A hint of a smile tugged at his cocky yet sexy smirk. "I had to make sure you had a happy birthday, even with everything that has happened. You deserve it, Avi."

I could feel the tension in my chest slowly dissipating. The sun was beginning to set, painting the sky in shades of orange and pink, and I wished that every day could be this easy, this beautiful. For a moment, the worries about Jeremy and Damar faded into the background, and I let myself enjoy the moment.

As we waited for our drinks, Mythic reached into his pocket and pulled out a small, neatly wrapped box.

"What's this?" I asked, eyeing it suspiciously as he handed it to me.

"Just a little something for your birthday."

My heart raced with curiosity as I opened the box carefully. A delicate diamond necklace lay inside. A small charm shaped like a wave hung from it.

I gasped, my fingers brushing over it. "My God, Mythic. This is beautiful."

"I figured you could use a reminder of how calming the waves can be," he said, his voice low, "especially with everything you've been through lately."

I felt a swell of emotion rise within me. "It's perfect. Thank you so much." I looked up at him, genuinely touched by his thoughtfulness. For a guy like him, so gritty and tough, it was impressive how well he understood me and what I needed. Staring at it, I told him, "This was so thoughtful. You didn't have to do this."

He shrugged, a hint of pride in his smile. "Yes, I did. I have to show my appreciation for the finer things."

As we sat across from each other, the silence between us felt smothering, like it was holding on to all the words neither of us dared to say. Mythic's eyes were filled with the same longing and love that always had me caught up. His gaze was deep, searching mine like he could see straight into my soul, and my heart was racing, pulling me toward him even though I knew I shouldn't. I couldn't ignore how he made me feel, like I was the only one in the room, like I was seen, loved, and completely his, even when I knew the reality of my life was pulling me in another direction.

Finally, I tore my eyes away, desperate to gather my composure and the ability to speak again. "You managed to make me smile today. Thank you."

He leaned back in his chair with a satisfied grin spreading across his face. "That was the plan."

# CHAPTER 14

## DAMAR SCOTT

**BEING IN THE** church was so damn suffocating. The pews were filled with Jeremy's friends and family. Their faces were engraved with sorrow. At the end of the row, Stephanie was wailing. Her high-pitched screams stabbed through the air like a knife. She was wrapped in the arms of her boyfriend and father. Both of them tried to hold her together while she fell apart.

Sitting there staring at Jeremy's casket, I still couldn't wrap my head around the fact that all of this had spiraled from messing around with Mia. I would've never thought one choice would end with me murdering not just Mia, but my own flesh and blood too. But it wasn't my fault. If Mia had just been cool, none of this would have happened. And all Jeremy had to do was mind his business and be obedient, and he'd still be alive.

For days, I'd waited to feel remorseful, but all I felt was irritation with Jeremy for forcing my hand. He'd left me no choice.

It hurt to lose my son, but he'd brought this on himself. If he'd stayed in his lane, he'd still be breathing. Instead, he'd made a decision that cost him his life. I didn't put him in that coffin—his own choices did.

Luckily, Jeremy's association with the 111 Boyz hid what I had done. His death had been immediately linked to the streets. Though his homies insisted that his murder couldn't have been related to their crew, Stephanie and our families assumed that Jeremy was killed because of his association with them—or the streets had gotten to our child.

Comforting everyone had been the greatest act I had ever pulled off. I offered my condolences, cried with them, and wrapped my arms around those who needed support. I could see the pain in their eyes, feel their despair, and yet I was the one who had caused this tragedy.

As I glanced around the church, my eyes landed on Mythic sitting nearby with Lelani. Every time I looked at him, I felt myself about to explode.

When Aviana told me she'd stepped out with Mythic for her birthday, I had been consumed with the going through her phone ever since. I could hardly focus on anything else. Each message I read only pissed me off more. Things still seemed friendly between them, but I could feel the tension in each message they sent each other. She repeatedly thanked him for the necklace he had given her, which she hadn't mentioned to me.

The first time she was hiding something from me related to Mythic. It felt like the start of what I had been fearing all along. And I refused to let Mythic win my woman. I had a right to Aviana, and I was determined to keep her. The way he was always around felt like an insult. He was a constant challenge that taunted me to prove myself worthy of *my* wife.

Every time I caught a glimpse of him, the territorial instinct in me flared up. I wanted to confront him, to lay down the law and remind him that Aviana was mine, but I couldn't do that without revealing my own secrets. Instead, I simmered in my frustration and forced myself to focus on the service while stewing in anger.

I was now more determined than ever to protect what was mine, no matter the cost.

# AVIANA SCOTT

As the repast carried on, I finally found a moment to myself. There had been a nonstop line of friends and loved ones giving their condolences, but finally, I found myself alone at the table sitting in front of a plate I hadn't touched.

Sighing, I stood and hoped that I could slip out of the hall without anyone noticing me. I was craving a breath of fresh air to clear the heaviness that clung to me like a veil. Being at Jeremy's funeral felt surreal. It had been an unmistakable reminder of how short life could be. Each moment I spent there pulled at my heart, making me reflect on my own life.

In addition, I had come on my menstrual cycle that morning, so my hormones were making me even more emotional.

As soon as I stepped into the vestibule, I bumped right into Lelani, who was just coming back from the bathroom. We almost collided, but I caught myself and managed a small smile. "Lelani, hey."

She smiled back, her eyes soft but tired.

"Hey, Aviana," she said gently. "I'm so sorry for your loss. My heart goes out to you and your family."

"Thank you," I replied, my heart aching a little. "I appreciate that. And, listen, I'm praying for you. You got this."

Although she had the man of my dreams, I truly felt sorry that she was fighting cancer, especially at such a young age. I knew that she was wracked with fear since she'd lost two family members to cancer as well.

Lelani's smile tightened, but she nodded. "Girl, I'm taking it day by day. Thank you, though. It means a lot."

We shared a smile before she turned and headed back inside.

I took a deep breath as I stepped outside. It was a brief moment of calm, just what I needed before going back in.

I leaned against the cool brick of the building, letting the warmth of the June sun soothe me. Watching Jeremy's casket lower into the ground made me feel like I was wasting my life. I had yet to pursue the career I truly wanted, and watching Mythic with Lelani all day made it painfully clear that I didn't have the man I truly desired either. The thought nagged at me.

Just then, the doors of the church swung open, and there was Mythic, stepping out in a fitted black polo and jeans. The diamonds decorating his body sparkled in the sunlight, catching my eye as he approached. Relief covered his features when he finally spotted me.

"There you are." His voice was soothing, wrapping around me like the warmest embrace. "Why are you out here alone?"

"I just needed some air and some time to think."

He raised an eyebrow. "About what?"

I looked up at the sky, taking a relaxing deep breath. "About how short life is. Jeremy's death has really made me realize that I want to live my life to the fullest. But I'm not. I don't have the career I want, and I don't have you."

My heart raced as I spoke those words. The confession hung in the air between us. My eyes left the clear blue sky and found Mythic. Surprise blanketed his face as my honesty settled in. "Avi," he began, clearly taken aback, "what do you mean you don't have me?"

"I've never stopped thinking about you," I confessed, my voice trembling. "I've always loved you, but I'm in a marriage that deserves my commitment. Damar hasn't done anything wrong. He's not perfect, but he's been a good husband. The only thing he's done wrong is not being you."

Mythic stepped closer and wrapped me in his arms. The grief faded as I drowned in his scent. For a moment, everything felt right, and I could have stayed there forever, feeling safe and cherished. But reality crashed down as I remembered where we were, and I reluctantly pulled away.

"We can't be seen like this," I murmured with a shaky breath.

"I know," he replied as his eyes searched mine.

His gaze made my feelings spill out like a dam bursting. "I've always loved you, Mythic. My feelings for you never changed, no matter how much time has passed. I crave you."

His intense, steadfast gaze burned into me. "I love you too, Aviana. I need you in a way that consumes me." The heat of his stare made my heart race. Exhilaration and nerves coursed through me. I felt exposed under his glare, yet strangely safe. "I love you enough to respect however you choose to handle your feelings for me." His tone softened as he searched my eyes for understanding.

"Thank you," I whispered.

He nodded, the corner of his mouth lifting in a gentle smile. "Let's go back inside."

I felt a twinge of reluctance at the thought of leaving this bubble we'd created, but I sighed and agreed. "Okay."

He gave me an encouraging smile. He squeezed my hand softly and quickly, causing me to swoon. But before I could completely unravel, he opened the large door of the event space.

As we walked back inside, I noticed Lelani craning her neck to watch the front door. Her eyes locked onto us as we entered.

Before we parted ways, Mythic looked at me with those intense eyes and said, "If you get a chance, call me this evening after you get settled."

"Okay."

He stared at me long enough for someone to notice. Then luckily, he finally walked away. I watched him for a moment, noticing how he turned to glance back. I felt a twinge of reluctance as I began to walk away. It felt like I was leaving a constant state of bliss.

As I turned my gaze back, I noticed Lelani staring at us with an unreadable expression.

I turned away as a knot formed in my stomach, knowing that I was stepping back into a reality filled with complications and unspoken truths. I took a deep breath, trying to steady myself, but the peace I had just felt with Mythic clung to me.

After Jeremy's repast, Damar insisted that we stop by our home to get more personal items. Renovations were due to start soon on our bedroom, but I was honestly enjoying the luxury of the hotel and wasn't pressed to return to basic living.

As Damar and I drove home, I sat in the passenger seat, consumed by the heaviness of the day. Now that all of the family and friends were gone, it was just the two of us, facing the somber reality of our lives without Jeremy. I could feel Damar's deep sorrow. I felt so alone, so I knew that Damar especially did. We were both lost in our own grief. I knew that I had to set aside my feelings for Mythic for now. I needed to be there for Damar, to support him through this dark time.

As we approached our neighborhood, a sharp pain shot through my stomach. I winced, cringing at the sudden cramp.

Damar glanced over, concerned. "What's wrong?"

"I have cramps," I admitted reluctantly.

His expression shifted, disappointment shadowing his features. I felt a pang of sympathy for him. He had so much to deal with already, and I was giving him yet another piece of bad news.

"It's okay," he insisted, but I could see it in his eyes—the hope that had been crushed yet again. I knew he was still holding on to the dream of us starting a family, and my body was just another reminder of how far we were from that.

"No, it's not." I sighed. "I know you really want this baby. Maybe we can try—"

As we pulled into our driveway, a large SUV parked in it caught my attention. My annoyance flared up; I really didn't feel like dealing with company right now. I assumed it was family or friends coming by to support Damar. But as we got closer, my eyes widened at the sight of a pristine white Range Rover parked out front, a big red bow perched on top like a gift.

"What the hell?" I muttered under my breath. My ballooned eyes bounced between Damar and the truck.

Damar watched me proudly as he smoothly said, "Happy birthday."

I turned completely toward him, bewildered. "Wh–What? That's for me?"

He lay a soothing, comforting hand on my thigh. "Of course."

Tears filled my eyes as I began to stutter. "H–How did you do this? W–Why did you do this, especially today of all days?"

"I needed something to make me smile, and so did you. You deserve it." As tears slid down my cheeks, he explained, "I paid the dealership to drop it off for me."

The initial shock began to fade, slowly giving way to excitement. Without thinking, I jumped out of Damar's car. "I can't believe this," I shrieked excitedly.

As he stepped out and joined me, his gaze softened. "You have no idea how much I love you, Aviana. I really appreciate everything you've done for me and Stephanie during this time."

A rush of guilt flowed through me. His words squeezed my heart like a vice, reminding me of how much he truly cared. Now, more than ever, I wanted to confess everything about Mythic, but I couldn't bring myself to shatter the fragile temporary peace we had.

I could hear sirens in the distance, a wailing sound that grew louder as we stood there. Damar continued to speak, pouring his heart out, but the noise drowned out his words.

"I adore you, Aviana," he said, his voice straining to break through the blaring noise.

Then the sirens reached a deafening pitch. Suddenly, multiple squad cars sped into the driveway, their lights flashing and sirens blaring.

Two detectives rushed out of a blacked-out SUV. Their serious expressions instantly raised the hairs on the back of my neck. Confusion covered me as I looked between the detectives and Damar, who stood frozen with a blank expression on his face.

The male detective stepped forward, reaching for Damar's arm. "Damar Scott, you're under arrest for the murder of Jeremy Scott."

I felt like the ground had been pulled out from beneath me. "What? No," I shouted. "You can't be serious."

As the detective took his cuffs from his waist, I erupted, "What the fuck is going on? Damar, tell them you didn't do this."

My mouth dropped watching Damar surrender without a word or fight. He turned, allowing the detective to put his arms behind his back and cuff him.

"Damar," I screamed, stepping toward him, but the female detective softly grabbed my arm, stopping me.

As the detective began to lead Damar away, he walked with them willingly, and my confusion turned to rage. "Why are you going with them?" I shouted, disbelief flooding my voice. "You didn't do this. You couldn't have done this."

Panic rose, causing my breath to come in sharp gasps. The female detective stepped in front of me and placed her hands firmly on my arms. "Calm down, ma'am. We need you to step back."

"Get your hands off me," I screamed, struggling against her grip. "You don't understand! That's Jeremy's father. He wouldn't kill his own son."

"Well, he did."

I guess the female detective felt sorry for me. She introduced herself as Detective Randall and offered to escort me into the house to explain everything. As she followed me, I could sense her genuine concern.

"Aviana, I need to ask you some questions," Detective Randall said gently, guiding me toward the living room. "We need to talk about Mia and Damar's connection."

"Wh–What connection?" I stuttered. "They were friends because she was my best friend since high school."

"Why would he have her phone?"

I shook my head, bewildered. "I don't know," I spat as I plopped down on the couch, holding my face with my hands. "I have no idea why he would have it. Mia has been missing for a while—"

"We know." Detective Randall sat carefully next to me. "When she came up in our investigation of Jeremy's murder, we did some digging."

My expression balled up with utter confusion. "How is any of this related to why Damar was arrested for Jeremy's murder?"

Detective Randall's expression hardened slightly, but her tone remained calm. "While investigating Jeremy's death, we went through his phone and found a recording made the day he was killed. In the recording, Jeremy questions his father about why he has Mia's phone, and then there's a scuffle followed by gunshots."

The world around me spun as her words sank in, each one cutting deeper than the last. My stomach churned violently, and I felt the blood drain from my face. A wave of nausea crashed over me as the realization hit—this wasn't just a simple misunderstanding. Damar was entangled in something far darker than I could have ever imagined.

"Oh my God…" I gasped, and my breath hitched in my throat. I sprang to my feet, causing Detective Randall's eyes to bulge. I then stumbled toward the guest bathroom as panic set in. The walls closed in around me, and suddenly, it felt like I was being smothered. I barely made it to the toilet before I bent over and retched, the contents of my stomach spilling out in violent waves.

The shock and dismay crashed over me like a tidal wave. Each heave brought with it a fresh wave of despair. I felt as if the ground had been ripped from beneath me, leaving me grasping for something—anything—to hold on to. As the sobs erupted from my chest, I couldn't shake the images of Jeremy, Damar, and Detective Randall's horrifying allegations. It was all too much, and I felt utterly lost in the chaos.

# CHAPTER 15

## DAMAR SCOTT

STARING INTO THE cold, judgmental eyes of Detective Harris, I sat back in the old metal chair in the interrogation room. The metal of the handcuffs bit into my wrists, reminding me how low my life had reached.

Detective Harris leaned against the table, his eyes narrowing as he studied me like I was a puzzle he was determined to solve.

"Where's Mia?" he asked.

My stomach knotted up at the mention of her name. I had spent so long trying to distance myself from the chaos of my double life, but I had now found myself caught in the web of my own making.

"I thought this was about Jeremy."

Detective Harris smiled with one side of his mouth. "I don't have many questions about Jeremy. Like I told you, your son was smart enough to record you all's altercation. I heard everything, how you choked him to death, then killed your own son—your own flesh and blood."

My nostrils flared as I stared at the wall behind him. Jeremy was still defiant beyond the grave. When the detective told me about the recording, I couldn't fucking believe it. I wanted to think that the detective was lying, but the way that he acted as if Jeremy's case was open and shut, I knew in my gut it was true. Jeremy had recorded his own murder.

"I do want to know how a man can kill his own child. What level of desperation caused a man to wrap his hands around his son's throat and squeeze until he couldn't breathe anymore? And it's obvious that that desperation has something to do with Mia. So…tell me, Damar. Where is Mia?"

My tone sounded innocent, even as my heart raced. "I don't know where she is."

Detective Harris leaned in closer with his scowl locked on me. "We've got her phone records, Damar. We know you were sleeping with her. Did she threaten to tell your wife?"

I swallowed hard, trying to maintain my composure, but I could feel the walls closing in. "I didn't do anything."

"Why did you have the phone of your missing sidepiece?" he pressed. "Did you kill her? Where is she?"

Panic crept in, but I forced myself to respond. "I want a lawyer."

As the detective's gaze hardened, I couldn't shake the guilt that gnawed at me—not just for Mia, but for Jeremy too. I thought about how I had failed him, how my choices had led to this moment. It was all spiraling out of control, and I was trying to act innocent while the truth clawed at me from the inside.

"Let's cut the games, Damar," Detective Harris said, his tone shifting. "You're in way over your head, and it's time to come clean. Confess, and maybe you can get a deal."

I couldn't. I wouldn't. I had to protect myself. As the reality of my situation settled in, I felt sick knowing that I was teetering on the edge of a cliff that could lead to my undoing. "I want a lawyer."

# MYTHIC GREY

I sat at the bar of Enchant, nursing a glass of Don Julio 1942. The smooth liquid slipped down my throat like silk. It was a Tuesday, and the place was quieter than usual. The low hum of R&B music barely cut through the silence. A handful of patrons dotted the lounge, but the vibrant energy I was used to on weekends had temporarily vanished.

As I took swigs of my drink, my mind drifted back to everything Aviana had shared at Jeremy's repast. The sincerity and genuineness of her words stalked me and softened places of my heart that had been rigid for a long time. I was ready to claim her, to make her mine, but the existence of Damar and Lelani loomed over us like a dark cloud. In the past, I might not have cared about leaving Lelani behind, but I wasn't heartless enough to add to her heartbreak, especially given everything she was already facing. I understood that while Aviana loved me, her principles meant even more to her. She wasn't the kind of woman who would hurt someone else for her own selfish desires. I knew it would be incredibly difficult for her to walk away from Damar, no matter how deep our connection ran.

Taking her from him—forcing her hand—would only add more stress to this already complicated situation, and I loved her too much to do that.

While I was lost in thought, I caught sight of a group of men entering the club through the mirror behind the bar. My instincts kicked in, and my posture stiffened as I recognized one of them. Fury, the leader of the Urban Enforcers, strolled in wearing a smirk that told me that he was on bullshit. His gang was notorious in Chicago, known for their savage but immature violence, and I didn't like the way they carried themselves. Their crew was reckless, unorganized, and unhinged.

As they moved deeper into the club, my bouncers trailed closely behind, keeping a watchful eye. The members of my security team discreetly positioned around the venue began to shift, their presence becoming more pronounced. The tension in the club began to thicken. The atmosphere shifted from casual to charged.

Fury approached with a serious yet respectful demeanor. "Mythic, got a minute?"

I regarded him coolly as I set my glass down on the bar with a soft clink. "Depends on what you want."

"Just wanted to talk business."

"You could have called first to arrange a meeting."

He leaned in slightly with a grin that didn't reach his eyes spreading across his face. "Thought it'd be better to discuss it face-to-face."

I knew better than to take him at face value, but curiosity piqued my interest. "All right. Let's hear it."

Fury motioned toward the barstool next to me. "Can I have a seat?"

I shrugged a shoulder, giving him permission to sit. "I need to purchase weapons from you," he told me.

I rose an eyebrow. This wasn't shocking. Like most of the new era's inner-city gangs, the Urban Enforcers lacked the sophistication and finances of past gangs and the cartel. Instead of making legitimate purchases from arms dealers, they usually resorted to stealing guns, street trades, or they would use people with clean records to buy firearms on their behalf. The thugs of today don't operate like the gangsters of the past—they had no code or honor and would get me caught because they would easily and quickly turn me in to spare themselves.

Keeping my brow dramatically arched, I sat back on the stool. "What makes you think I'd sell to you?"

Fury's eyes narrowed, and he gnawed on his bottom lip, clearly trying to choose his words carefully while maintaining his cool composure. "We're currently at war with the Crimson Order. We need a large quantity of weapons to level the playing field."

"I've heard. The Crimson Order is savage and ruthless, and it's no secret that they are winning. You're desperate, and desperation makes men dangerous." I smirked wickedly as Fury's nostrils flared. "You don't have the kind of money to purchase from me anyway. And even if you did, I'm not about to arm a bunch of wild, uncontrollable foot soldiers who think they can shoot their way out of anything."

Fury's expression hardened, but he pressed on. "We have the money—"

"But your crew lacks a moral code. You think I'd let weapons slip into the hands of a gang that has no regard for innocent lives? The collateral damage from your operations would come back to haunt me."

"Come on, Mythic! We're talking about survival here," Fury argued, frustration creeping into his voice. "You know how it is. This is the game we're in."

I leaned closer. "This isn't just a game for me. I won't be responsible for the bloodshed that your men would cause. The answer is no."

Tension sparked in the air between us, and I could see Fury's anger simmering just beneath the surface. He opened his mouth to protest, but I cut him off. "Get out of my club, Fury. If you don't, I'll end this war for the Crimson Order right here, right now."

His eyes narrowed, and for a moment, I could see the gears turning in his head, but I stood my ground, unyielding. "Leave before I decide to change my mind about what happens next."

With that, I watched as Fury's expression shifted from anger to reluctant acceptance. He took a step back, and I knew he understood that I wasn't fucking around. "I'll be back because you're my only option."

"No, you won't," I shot back, watching him turn and walk away.

As Fury and his crew walked out of Enchant, I saw Draven approaching with a questioning look. "What was that all about?"

I let out a cynical laugh, shaking my head. "Fury thinks he can play with the grownups."

As Draven chuckled, my phone buzzed on the bar. I glanced down to see Aviana's name and picture flashing on the screen.

I hurriedly answered. "Avi…"

The sound of her tears on the other end sent a chill down my spine. It felt like déjà vu.

"What's wrong?" I asked gently, knowing she needed me.

"Can you come over?" She sniffed, her voice trembling. "Damar's been arrested, and I don't want to be alone."

Surprised, my head reared back. "Arrested? For what?"

"Jeremy's murder," she said, and the shock of her words hit me hard.

"Where are you?"

"I'm back at the hotel."

"I'll be there right away."

As I held Aviana on the couch in the living room of the suite, I wrapped my arms around her tightly, letting her rest her head against my chest. She felt fragile in my embrace, and I could feel the turmoil consuming her. My fingers gently traced her back, trying to soothe the confusion and fear that radiated from her.

The warmth of her body against mine was comforting, but it only heightened the anger simmering beneath the surface of my skin.

I couldn't wrap my head around the fact that Jeremy had recorded his own death. It all sounded so unbelievable that I made Aviana recount what the detective had said at least three times, each time hoping I'd hear something different. But it got more real with every repetition, and the anger inside me began to flare to boiling hot.

I was a ruthless man with a lot of blood on my hands. But I couldn't imagine taking the life of my own child. The rage I felt knowing that Damar had taken Jeremy's life was dangerous and uncontrollable. Jeremy and I hadn't been very close, but he didn't deserve to die, especially at the hands of his own father. Damar was lucky that he was in a cell, otherwise he would have been six feet deep.

As Avi had explained everything to me, I texted Timmy. I told him to confirm the recording's validity and to get a copy of it.

"Why would Damar have Mia's phone?" Avi's voice trembled with uncertainty. "And why would he kill Jeremy just for knowing he had it? It doesn't make any sense."

I could see the wheels turning in her mind, her brow creased as she tried to piece it all together.

"He obviously has something to hide." As she continued, she looked up, searching my eyes for answers I didn't have. "He obviously didn't want anyone to find out that he had that phone."

"I'm sure they are investigating Mia and Damar's connection."

"They are, but she wouldn't tell me anything because it's an ongoing investigation. I'm sure they only told me about the recording because they wanted me to tell them anything I knew."

"I'll find out." I was furious at the thought of Damar being a snake, manipulating everyone around him while hiding behind a facade that had even tricked me. I knew that he was a bitch-ass nigga, but I hadn't seen this coming.

Aviana looked up at me with her eyes wide with worry. "Do you think he'll get out on bail?"

I shook my head. "With the irrefutable evidence against him? He'll probably be denied bail. If he's smart, he should take a plea deal when it's offered."

She sighed as relief and worry crossed her features. I couldn't blame her for feeling torn; I was just as conflicted.

I held her a little tighter, protecting her like a shield.

As I held her close, I felt Aviana's stomach growling softly.

"Have you eaten?" I asked, placing a soft kiss on her shoulder, savoring the warmth of her skin beneath my lips.

She shook her head. A hint of frustration crept into her voice. "I don't have an appetite."

"I didn't see you eat at the repast either," I said, pulling out my phone to order some food. "You're getting something to eat."

"But I can't—" she began to whine.

I cut her off with a firm yet gentle tone. "You will eat, Aviana. You need to take care of yourself."

"Mythic—"

"Don't play with me, Avi."

She finally submitted, a small nod indicating her acceptance. "Okay."

I ordered one of her favorite meals from a nearby restaurant through the food delivery app. Once I placed the order, I glanced at the clock and realized it was almost midnight. "You're still in those funeral clothes," I said, my voice softer now as I took her hand. "Let's get you cleaned up."

I stood and gently pulled her to her feet, guiding her toward the bedroom. Even amid the confusion and chaos of the night,

I admired the way her curves moved beneath her clothes. I led her into the master bathroom, then I turned on the shower and adjusted the temperature until it was just right.

As the water began to cascade down, I turned to her. I helped her undress. My fingers brushed against her skin as I peeled away the fabric. I was captivated by her. As each piece of her toffee-colored skin was revealed, I wanted to taste it—to devour it.

Once she was completely undressed, I took a moment to appreciate her beauty—the way the light danced on her skin and how every curve told a story.

"You're stunning," I murmured, unable to hold back the admiration.

Her weary eyes looked up at me. A small blush traced her cheeks, but I could still see the confusion and worry weighing down her shoulders.

"Get in," I softly ordered.

I watched her as she stepped through the glass doors.

As the water bathed her, she looked at me with pleading eyes. "Don't leave me."

Her need for me made my dick start to rise. When I began to undress, she at first looked surprised, then glad that I was not only staying, but joining her.

After stepping in with her, I wrapped my arms around her waist and pulled her close. I wanted her to know that even amid all this chaos, she was safe in my arms. I held her tightly as the water flowed down over us, providing a tranquil escape from the mayhem outside.

After a hot bath and some comforting food, Aviana finally managed to drift off to sleep. Even in her sleep, she clung to me with her head in my lap on the couch.

I stared out at the busy downtown below. The city lights sparkled like stars against the dark canvas of the night. My thoughts were chaotic as I tried to wrap my head around what Damar was hiding. The fact that Mia had been missing since shortly after her arrest gnawed at me, leading me to believe Damar might have murdered her. If he could murder his own son, he was capable of anything. But I wondered what would drive him to do any of this.

As I continued to try to mentally put this puzzle together, my phone lit up. It was on silent, but I could see Lelani's name flashing across the screen. She had called three times already. Sighing, I knew I had to go, but the last thing I wanted to do was leave Aviana.

As I carefully slid off the couch, trying not to disturb her, I felt her stir slightly.

"Are you leaving?" she mumbled sleepily.

I looked down at her, seeing the reluctance etched across her face. She had been the only woman to ever make my heart ache. I didn't want to be anywhere else at that moment but with her.

Our eyes locked, and in that instant, we both understood. Neither of us wanted me to go, but we knew I had to. I knelt beside her and brushed a strand of hair from her face. Then I leaned in, capturing her lips in a slow, sweet kiss as I savored the taste of her tongue.

"I promise I'll be back first thing in the morning," I whispered against her lips as I softly palmed the back of her head. "Okay?"

With our foreheads touching, she nodded. As I stood, the fervor lingered, making my dick hard, and I knew that no matter what happened, Avi was mine, and I would always fight to protect her.

As I left the suite, I felt so much regret and still longed for her. I could still feel Aviana's warmth on my skin, and as I closed the door behind me, it gnawed at me that I was leaving her. My phone continued to ring in my hand, and I sighed, knowing I needed to answer it.

"I'm on my way home. I just locked up at the club," I said quietly as I inched away from the suite.

But instead of the familiar voice I expected, I heard Rachel's bitter voice. "Mythic, I've been calling you for hours."

My heart dropped as I heard the urgency in her tone. "What's going on?"

"Lelani and I were in a car accident earlier this evening."

"Is she okay?" I shot back, already dashing down the hall toward the elevators.

"She'll be okay. She needed emergency surgery. We were on the way home, and another car ran a red light. We're at Rush Hospital."

# CHAPTER 16

## MYTHIC GREY

LELANI HAD SUFFERED significant injuries during the car accident—her side had taken the brunt of the impact when another vehicle t-boned them. The doctors had to perform emergency surgery to repair a lacerated spleen and some internal bleeding. It was a severe injury, and she would need to stay in the hospital for a few weeks to recover.

Her mother had only sustained a few cuts and bruises.

I stayed with her overnight. Her mother was too groggy on her own pain meds to battle with me over that.

Lelani was in and out consciousness all night as the anesthesia wore off, but by the next morning, she was fully awake and aware of what had taken place.

The monitors beeped steadily as the nurse checked her vitals.

"I can't believe this shit." Lelani pouted as she attempted to adjust her position in bed, but moving made her wince in pain.

*"Unt-uh,"* her nurse grunted. "You should be still. Let me help you if you need to move."

Lelani's pout deepened. "If I didn't have bad luck, I wouldn't have any."

"You're lucky," her nurse told her. "At least you were able to come out of that accident with your life."

Lelani rolled her eyes, though the nurse wasn't looking as she was diligently adjusting the IV drip.

I knew that Lelani was moreso upset that all of this had happened on top of what she was already dealing with. I wanted to comfort her, to hold her hand, but I felt a loyalty to Aviana that I couldn't shake. My protection was for her.

Luckily, the door of the hospital room opened, and a doctor in scrubs and a white coat entered, preventing me from having to be loving to a woman who didn't own my heart.

As the doctor strolled in, the nurse looked at him, and they both smiled a greeting as if they were familiar with each other.

"Good morning, Lelani. I'm Dr. Collins," he introduced himself as he tapped on the iPad in his hand. "I was your surgeon." He looked up from the tablet and glanced at her. Taking her in, he smiled a bit. "You're looking as well as can be. How are you feeling? Are you in any pain?"

"Not really."

"On a scale from one to ten, what's your pain level?'

She thought for a second. "A five."

His smile widened as he gave her a quick nod. "Well, that means the pain meds are working. But we'll increase the dosage to get that down to zero."

"Thank you," she said weakly.

"I want to go over a few things with you, then I'll be out of your hair so that you can continue to get some rest."

As he spoke, I leaned closer in order to hear every detail in case she didn't remember.

"You suffered a lacerated spleen during the accident," he explained. "The surgery went well. Expect some pain and fatigue as you recover. We'll monitor you closely, and I'll prescribe medication to help manage any discomfort."

Lelani nodded with heavy eyes. She was trying to process everything he was saying, but her expression shifted slightly as she listened.

"Will she still be able to get her biopsy?" I asked. "Her appointment is in like two weeks." I looked at Lelani for verification, but strangely she nervously avoided my eyes and the doctor's.

Dr. Collins looked confused as he glanced down at her chart on the iPad. "Biopsy?" he echoed, brows furrowing.

"Yes. On her brain tumor."

Dr. Collins' eyes bucked. "That's not mentioned anywhere here. There seems to be a mix-up."

I turned to Lelani, concerned when I noticed she had suddenly gone quiet and the color had drained from her face.

"Lelani?" I pushed. "When is your next chemo appointment? Shouldn't it be in the chart since you see your doctor here?"

My brows knitted together as Lelani shut her eyes, regret etching her face as if she wanted to hide under the covers.

Dr. Collins continued to review the chart, but I was focused on Lelani who looked increasingly distressed.

"Cancer?" the doctor asked, looking up at her with concern. "None of your blood work indicates cancer, and there's no info in your chart."

She opened her eyes, and they were filled with tears as she shook her head, barely able to whisper, "No."

"The fuck? What you mean no?" I snapped.

As Lelani began to sob, Dr. Collins interjected. "I'll step out to give you some privacy."

The sudden tension in the room had caused Dr. Collins and the nurse to turn crimson red as they rushed out.

I took a deep breath, trying not to explode in this hospital. "Lelani, what the fuck is going on?"

"You love her," she cried so low that I could barely hear her.

Frowning, I asked, "What are you talking about?"

"Aviana," she snapped, slamming her hands down on the bed. "You love her. You want to be with her. I always knew it. I could tell by the way you looked at her. You are fucking obsessed with that girl, and I caught you all in the stairway at the club that day. Y'all were about to kiss. I was scared that you were going to leave me for her, so I made something up to keep you."

I shot up out of my seat, making her eyes bulge. "Are you fucking serious? That's some sick shit to lie about."

I was roaring so loud it made her cringe. "Would you be quiet?"

I laughed psychotically. "Why? You don't want these people to know how diabolical you are?"

"Being with someone who loves someone else will make you do some diabolical shit. You never loved me. You never looked at me the way you look at her. I was just a clone—something you used to try to replace something that never could be replaced."

I couldn't believe that she was telling this much truth. But I figured that her pain meds weren't letting her think straight, so I kept asking her questions.

"So, there were never any doctor's appointments? The headaches and throwing up was fake?"

She whimpered. "I faked all of it, okay? I was just leaving the house so that you thought I was going to the doctor. But that's how much I love you, Mythic. I didn't want to lose you, baby."

I scoffed, shaking my head in disbelief I had never felt before. "Well…at least you weren't lying about everything. You really are a sick bitch."

She began to sob. I met the eyes of concerned staff and nurses who were standing around the door. I pulled my rage-filled eyes away from them all and charged down the hall.

Filled with rage, I felt the heat of betrayal surging through my veins as I looked at Lelani. My mind raced with anger and disbelief. I felt used, like a fool and like I had been set up. I prided myself on being a smart man, but this felt like a sucker punch. I had let a snake into my own backyard.

Every instinct in me screamed to kill her, to make her hurt for the way she had deceived me. I could see the fear in her eyes, the tears that streamed down her cheeks, and it only fueled my frustration.

I took a step back, forcing myself to breathe through the anger boiling inside me. I could hear the dark thoughts whispering in the back of my mind, urging me to take drastic measures, to end this snake's existence once and for all. But I fought against it. I needed to get away before I did something I would regret—before I crossed a line I swore I never would.

With a final glance at Lelani, I turned and walked out of the room, clenching my fists to keep my emotions in check.

I could still hear her sobbing, calling out for me. "Mythic, please don't leave me. *Pleeeease.*"

Every step as I stormed down the hall of the ICU was fueled by a simmering rage. Lelani's cries grew fainter as I reached the exit of the unit. As I stalked through the hospital, I could feel the concerned looks from the staff, patients, and visitors. My towering figure—a large, pissed-off Black man—drew attention, and I could see their judgment and worry. I was a storm about to break, and they could see it.

I reached the elevator and pressed the button, pacing impatiently as I waited for the doors to slide open. Just as I was about to lose it, my phone buzzed in my pocket. I pulled it out and saw Timmy's name flashing on the screen.

"What, Timmy?" I answered.

"Whoa. You good, boss?"

"Just tell me what you need."

"Check your email," he replied cautiously. "I got the evidence from Mia's investigation and a copy of Jeremy's recording."

I grumbled a simple, "All right," before ending the call.

## AVIANA SCOTT

Emotionally and physically, I was all over the place. When I woke up that morning, I called off work and planned to for the next few days. I had used Jeremy's death as an excuse to take some vacation time, when in actuality I needed time to process that my husband had killed him. It all felt unreal, like I was in a hellish nightmare that I would soon wake up from. I couldn't do anything. I could taste the funk on my breath. I hadn't even had the energy to brush my teeth that morning. My hair was a tangled mess. I had spent all morning just lying in bed, drowning in my own confusion and disappointment.

Then Mythic returned to the suite some time ago and changed my world forever. He told me that Timmy had used his connections at the police department to get the evidence in Mia's investigation that was linked to Damar. My heart sunk when he mentioned that Timmy also got a copy of the recording of Jeremy's death. Hearing Jeremy struggle to breathe, followed by the gunshots that stole his life, made my stomach turn. It was unbearable. And knowing it was his own father who had done it was even more crippling.

But what crushed me the most were the text messages I had read between Damar and Mia. Each word cut deeper than the last, revealing that they had been having an affair and that Damar had been the one to teach her how to steal from Dream Realty. My best friend and my husband had betrayed me in the worst way possible. I felt like I was drowning in a sea of betrayal and heartache.

And she was pregnant by him. While trying to purposely get me pregnant, he knew that my best friend was carrying his child.

Lying in bed, wrapped up in Mythic's arms, I felt like a complete mess. My face was buried in Mythic's chest as I let the tears flow freely. Every breath I took pulled his scent into my nostrils. It was a comforting reminder that he was here, that I wasn't alone. I clung to him like a lifeline, my body shaking as I cried. I didn't want to face the reality outside these walls. I just wanted to hold on to him and forget about the pain, if only for a little while.

"I'm sorry," I whispered into Mythic's shirt.

"Why?"

"I feel bad that you're lying here comforting me while I cry over another man."

"You feel bad because you know the feelings that I have for you. But despite how much I love you, I'm still and will always be your best friend, so you don't have to feel bad about shit."

The warmth of Mythic's love and attention wrapped around me like a comforting blanket. He was so loving and attentive. His gentle touch and comforting words were a soothing balm, making me feel cared for in a way I hadn't felt in a long time. It hit me how much he truly cared for me, despite the chaos surrounding us. I could feel his strong heartbeat beneath my head, reminding me that I wasn't alone. Even in my darkest hour, he was there, ready to hold me together when everything felt like it was falling apart.

He was giving me space to grieve for another man while holding me. He was giving me space to let my guard down.

"I can't believe I was so blind. How could I not see Damar and Mia deceiving me right in front of my face?"

Mythic shifted slightly. I soon felt his fingers running through my hair. I closed my eyes, enjoying the touch of his fingertips on my scalp.

"You shouldn't feel stupid, Avi. Some people are just master manipulators."

I sniffled, wiping my tears with the back of my hand. "But how did I not notice? I thought I knew them both. I thought I could trust them."

"You trusted them because you're a good person. That's not a weakness," he said, rubbing my back gently. The way he touched me made me feel safe, like I could let my guard down.

"Thank you for being here for me," I said weakly. "I don't know what I would do without you. I would be so alone if it weren't for you because I can't even bring myself to explain any of this to my parents. I have no strength for that. They'll want to know what's going on, and I can't even wrap my head around it myself."

He sighed softly. "I get it. You don't have to explain any of this to your parents right now."

I leaned into him, finding comfort in his presence. "I just feel so lost," I admitted, letting my emotions spill out. "It's like everything I thought I knew has been turned upside down."

"You can feel lost, but know that you're never alone because I'm right here," Mythic reassured me as his fingers still raked gently through my hair. "I got you, baby, I promise."

Standing on Stephanie's porch felt surreal. Even breathing took effort. The weight of this death and betrayal was on my chest like bricks. I squeezed my eyes shut briefly, trying not to crumble where I stood. If I felt this suffocated, I couldn't imagine what Stephanie was going through. Jeremy was only my stepson, and still, the grief felt unbearable.

I reached out and pressed the doorbell. As I waited, I wondered if Stephanie would even answer. I knew the detectives had already delivered the same horrific news to her.

My palms turned cold as footsteps finally approached on the other side of the door. When Stephanie opened the door, her appearance took my breath away. Her eyes were swollen. The whites of them were bloodshot from endless tears. She looked fragile and broken, as if a gentle breeze might even cause her to collapse.

"I'm so sorry, Stephanie," I choked out as tears pooled quickly in my eyes.

Before I could finish, Stephanie broke down completely, burying her face in her hands. Instinctively, I stepped forward and wrapped my arms around her, pulling her against me. Her body shook as she sobbed.

We stood there for a moment, crying in each other's arms.

"Come inside, Avi," she finally whispered between shaky breaths, pulling away slightly.

She closed the door softly behind me and led me toward the living room. My eyes immediately fell on the couch. It was scattered with used tissues and crumpled blankets. There was a noticeable indentation where Stephanie had obviously spent days curled up on it. The sight made my heart ache even more.

"Have you been alone all day?" I asked quietly. "Someone should be here with you."

Stephanie sounded exhausted as she exhaled slowly. "I sent everyone away. I wanted to be alone."

I nodded in understanding. "Then I won't stay long. I just had to come check on you."

She sank down heavily onto the couch. Fresh tears slipped silently down her cheeks. "The detectives told me everything. They played the recording for me." Anguish carved deep lines into her face. "The gunshots...God, those gunshots just keep playing in my head over and over again. I can't even imagine how Jeremy must have felt." She cringed and shuddered. "The fear, the betrayal... It was his own father."

Her words came out so broken. My chest tightened painfully. Nausea swirled in my stomach. I sat down beside her, gripping her trembling hand.

"I feel like I don't even know who Damar is anymore," I admitted shakily. "I'm sick to my stomach thinking I've been married to someone capable of this. Jeremy was only my stepson, but the pain—I can't even imagine yours."

Stephanie's shoulders shook violently as her sobs deepened. "I don't know how I'll get through this. Only God can help me now." Pain and fury battled openly across her face.

"I don't know what to do with all this rage inside me. It's eating me alive. I can't sleep. I can't breathe without thinking about what Damar did to my baby. And I know exactly what he was thinking—he thought nobody would care. Because of our neighborhood and Jeremy getting caught up with those boys, Damar thought the police would just sweep my son's murder under the rug." She paused, taking a shaky breath. "But Jeremy was smart. He knew to record that conversation, even though..." As her voice cracked, my heart broke even further. "Even though he didn't know he was recording his own murder."

"Honestly, I can't believe Damar didn't take Jeremy's phone."

Stephanie scoffed bitterly. "He probably never even considered Jeremy would be smart enough to record him. But my baby proved him wrong." Fresh tears spilled down her face, but I could still see the pride in her eyes. "I'm so proud of Jeremy. Even now, even after everything, my son is the reason the truth came out."

I nodded softly as tears ran unchecked down my face. We sat there in shared grief, helpless in these dark shadows of everything we'd lost.

# DAMAR SCOTT

Standing in line for the shower at Cook County Jail, I felt like I was losing my shit. It was only a few days since they'd denied my bail, and already, I could feel the walls closing in. I wasn't built for this, and deep down, I knew I wouldn't survive long in here.

My lawyer had come by earlier. The state's attorney had offered me a plea deal of twenty years—the minimum for first-degree murder. I couldn't wrap my head around it. Twenty years was still a lifetime, but it was better than the alternative. If I turned it down, I'd be looking at sixty years, and I knew I couldn't handle that. I couldn't imagine spending one more day in this hellhole, let alone decades.

The thought of being locked up for twenty years felt suffocating. I'd be missing out on everything I had killed to maintain. I wasn't willing to do twenty years—or sixty.

As I shuffled forward, my eyes met those of a few 111 Boyz. They'd been whispering and glaring at me since I got here. I assumed that they'd heard that I had been charged with Jeremy's murder. They shared the same loyalty and bond of the 111 Boyz that Jeremy hung with.

"This bitch-ass nigga." One of them sneered. He had that dangerous glint in his eye, the kind that told you he was itching for a fight.

I tried to ignore them, focusing on the ground and shuffling my feet. I knew better than to give them any reason to come after me, but they were intent on fucking with me.

"You think you can just walk around like you didn't kill one of our homies?" another voice cut in, louder this time. The group started closing in as their taunts grew more hostile by the second.

Before I could react, one of them pushed me hard in the back. I stumbled forward, trying to catch my balance, but it was too late. They were on me. Fists and boots flew, each hit landing with bone-jarring force. I barely had time to raise my arms to protect myself before the first punch connected with my ribs, sending a jolt of pain through my body.

"This for Jeremy, nigga," one of them spat as another kick landed on my side. I could feel the sharp sting of every blow. My vision blurred from the pain. I was gasping for air, trying to curl up into a ball to protect myself, but the hits kept coming.

It felt like the world was collapsing around me with each punch and kick. I wanted to scream, to fight back, but the relentless and merciless hits just kept coming. The sounds of their taunts mixed with the pounding of my heart, and I couldn't keep track of how many times they struck me.

The pain was so intense that I hoped and prayed that I would pass out. It felt like they were trying to beat the life out of me, and I was powerless to stop them.

All I could think was that this was how it was going to end for me. The realization hit me hard, leaving me gasping for breath as the assault continued.

# AVIANA SCOTT

I slowly stirred awake. The soft rhythm of Mythic's breathing brought me back to consciousness. His arms were wrapped around me, and it felt like the safest place in the world. I had been dozing on and off all day. It was as if now that I finally had some answers, my body relaxed, letting me sleep. Mythic had been out cold for hours. He'd told me he hadn't slept at all the night before, so he needed the rest.

When he'd gotten to the suite earlier that day, I could sense something was off with him. It wasn't just the drama with Damar and Mia; there was a shadow hanging over him that he was trying to hide in order to be there for me.

Now, it was around the time that he usually opened Enchant. I rolled over. We had been spooning, so now I was nose to nose with him.

I gently nudged him, whispering, "Mythic…Mythic, get up."

He slowly began to wake up, groaning as his eyes fluttered open. Even with a groggy frown on his face, this man was beautiful.

As his eyes adjusted and focused on me, his full lips curved upward into a small smile. "What's up?" he croaked.

"You've been sleeping for hours. It's getting late. Don't you need to open the club or check in with Lelani?"

He shook his head as a slight scowl crossed his expression. "Nah. I don't have to do either."

Confusion creased my brow, and I wanted to push for more answers, but before I could, he leaned in and pressed his lips against mine. It was a gentle, lingering kiss that washed away all my worries. I moaned softly into the kiss, and for a brief moment, everything else faded away, leaving just the two of us in our little bubble of peace and serenity.

When we finally pulled away, his eyes locked onto mine, and I could feel the flirtatious tension sparking between us. I broke the gaze as my cheeks flushed with heat.

"I–I need to shower," I stammered, suddenly feeling shy under his intense gaze.

He softly pinched my side as I sat up. "You hungry?"

I looked down on him, allowing my hunger to show in my gaze. But I wasn't hungry for just food. Having him here—near me, touching me, holding me—without the feeling of shame or guilt was so electrifying that it was only increasing my desire and longing for him.

"Actually, I am."

Mythic raised an eyebrow in response to the longing twinkling in my eyes. His lips curved into a smirk. "I'll order something then." His deep rumble was low and teasing, and his eyes glinted with perverted mischief.

I was unable to hide the way my heart raced at the way he looked at me. I exhaled slowly in relief of the peace this man gave me. I bit my lip as I glanced away, feeling the heat creep up my cheeks. "Okay."

His gaze locked onto mine like he was searching for something deeper. "What are you in the mood for?"

I shrugged, trying to maintain my composure. "Surprise me."

Mythic chuckled softly as he watched me with eyes filled with admiration and something much more intense. "I know what you like. I got you."

I felt a flutter in my stomach. The tension was suffocating as we exchanged flirtatious glances, each moment stretching longer than the last.

I playfully shook my head and tore my eyes away from his. As I slipped into the bathroom, I realized that everything was shifting between us, and I wasn't sure what it all meant. But for now, I just wanted to savor this moment and ride the wave.

# CHAPTER 17
## AVIANA SCOTT

WE HAD SPENT the night like two best friends, laughing, drinking, and reminiscing about old times. Every now and then, I would slip back into reality and vocalize my wonder in how Damar and Mia could have betrayed me for so long, how Damar could have killed his own child. But every time I did, I felt like Damar and Mia didn't deserve to be able to taint my and Mythic's peaceful bliss, so I would change the subject.

Having learned the truth about Damar and Mia, I was overwhelmed. My heart ached. But above it all, I knew that Mythic's touch and penetration made me forget it all for just a little while.

All night, there was intense sexual tension between us, but it felt as if he were trying to be respectful of my turmoil or my state of mind.

But as I woke up the next morning, I couldn't take lying next to that perfection any longer without feeling it on top of me, inside of me.

Even as he slept, his massive tool danced under the sheets, rock hard with a morning wood. I began to stroke it softly, purposefully waking Mythic up.

He squinted as his eyes tried to adjust to the morning sun, then he looked at me with an arched brow and a smirk that invited me to continue.

I pulled his dick out of his boxer briefs, which fit his ass so right, then I crawled between his legs. Kneeling between them, I took all of his swollen manhood into my mouth. It was a stretch to fit all of him in—the corners of my mouth stung with pain as they stretched beyond capacity. He hissed as my wet mouth sucked him into my throat. His fingers found my scalp as I repeatedly brought his tip to kiss my tonsils and then sucked every inch of him to the tip where I kissed his head slowly.

"*Gaaawd* damn." It was an ego boost to have such a dominant, hard man like Mythic succumb to me, to writhe under my touch because I was sucking the ego out of him.

My hand slid around his size as my mouth glided effortlessly up and down on his shaft. He had an intoxicating, addicting taste. He was far better than any drug but just as exhilarating as heroin running through my veins. He was my new high, which I never wanted to escape from, and I desperately hoped I would never have to.

My tongue slowly ran down his thick base, tasting him and the oozing drip of his stickily sweet pre-cum. The way he gnawed his bottom lip made delighted goosebumps prickle my skin. I wanted more of that, more of his reactions. I indulged in his taste, bobbing my head up and down, accepting him at the back of my throat.

His addicting dick constricted my breath. Saliva dripped down onto my fingers, which stroked him. I wanted to feel every vein, every single detail of him that I could barely wrap my fingers around. My tongue delicately teased his tip, slowly running over his slit and tasting that delicious ooze.

*"Unt uh."* He grunted, tapping my shoulder. "I want to feel you."

His penetrating eyes told me things he wanted to do that made me shudder.

I released him from my oral embrace and climbed on top of him. As I slid down his length, he took one of my breasts into his mouth, then the other.

"Oh my god," I whimpered as I rode him slowly, feeling his dick kiss my cervix.

His large hands gently followed the curves of my body. I bent down, resting my forehead on his and slowly rocked my hips.

"You feel so good, Mythic."

We kissed again as we gently fucked, moaning into each other's mouths with every slow stroke.

Mythic held my ass in his hands and helped me ride. I got faster and faster as more and more pleasure filled my body. I could feel a release about to come. He felt it too because he lifted me and started thrusting hard from below.

Before I could cum, he drove deep inside me and rolled over, flipping me onto my back. I shrieked in shock at the way he easily handled all of my weight and then moaned as he started fucking me hard. I screamed out as he held me down and thrust harder and harder, pumping his dick inside my warm, wet center.

I wanted to feel bad for sleeping with and enjoying another woman's man, but no one had given a fuck about deceiving me, and I was over putting others above my own happiness. I just knew that eventually Mythic and I would have to have a talk about him having to end his relationship with Lelani if he wanted to continue things with me. But for now, I was going to enjoy the one thing that brought me peace and happiness, especially when everything else around me was crumbling.

I sat on the edge of the bed pouting as I watched Mythic get dressed. He was pulling on a fitted black shirt that hugged his muscles just right. Disappointment tugged at my heart with the thought of him leaving. When he left, I would have to face the chaos and heartache again.

"What's with the pout?" He chuckled, glancing over his shoulder at me with that trademark grin of his.

"I don't want you to leave. These last two days have felt like I've been living in a bubble with you. Despite everything that's happened, I've actually been content."

He turned to face me fully, and I could see the warmth in his eyes, but there was also a flicker of something else. "I get it," he said, nodding. "I feel the same way. I don't want to leave this peace either…" Just then another glimmer of something deeper flashed in his eyes.

I watched him pull on his jeans, still feeling that nagging sense that something wasn't quite right with him.

"Are you okay?" I asked, wrinkling my brows.

I could see the tension in his shoulders, even as he tried to keep it cool.

"I'm okay," he replied, but there was an edge to his voice that made me doubt it. "Just worried about you. I hate to leave you, but I've been laid up with you for damn near two days. I got business to take care of."

I nodded, but I knew that he was hiding something else. But, despite the reality that the other two closest people had completely deceived me without me knowing, I knew that whatever Mythic was hiding would never hurt me. So, instead of probing, I watched as he reached into his pocket and pulled out a set of keys.

"Here," he said, handing them to me.

"What are these for?" I asked, raising an eyebrow as I took them from him.

"It's the condo you showed me on 21st and Indiana. You don't have to be in a hotel. You can stay there instead," he explained, his gaze steady on mine. "If you want to stay at the hotel, I'll pay for it, but I'd prefer you at one of my spots."

I felt a flutter in my chest at his offer. "I want to be wherever you want me to be," I said, meeting his eyes with sincerity.

His smile widened, and for a moment, his tension seemed to ease. And even as uncertainty loomed over us, I felt a flicker of hope that maybe, just maybe, we could find our way through this mess together.

## MYTHIC GREY

That morning, as I sat across from Aviana eating breakfast, I sent Taye a quick text instructing him to get some movers over to my place ASAP and pack up all of Lelani's things.

After leaving the hotel, I drove over to Rachel's house, where the movers were waiting for me. I stepped out of my truck, the June sun shining down on what felt like a new beginning for me and Aviana. Though this opportunity had come with tragedy and betrayal, it felt like the universe had finally put us together at a time where we didn't have to be ashamed or feel any guilt. The last two days with her had been further confirmation that she was mine. That woman was not only mine, she was also my peace and my home. I was upset that Lelani had lied to me, and I was upset with myself for not having my guard up. But her accident was my blessing because I didn't have to feel bad for kicking her to the curb so that I could finally be with the woman that owned me.

As I walked up to the moving truck, the movers were unloading boxes. I had told them to only pack up any feminine clothes and products, so there was only about twenty boxes.

"Yo, leave those boxes on the lawn," I instructed.

One of the movers looked up, confusion written all over his face. "*Uh*, shouldn't we take them inside? It'd make it easier for you."

I shot him a glare that could cut glass. "Nah. I said leave them out here. Just do what I said."

The second mover chimed in, trying to diffuse the situation. "Look, man, it's just a suggestion. We can help you—"

"Do I look like I need your suggestions, motherfucka?" I snapped back, feeling my temper rise. "Just put the boxes on the fucking lawn and keep it moving."

They exchanged glances, probably debating whether they wanted to push back or just get the job done. I glared at them as they finally reluctantly complied and started to drop boxes on the grass. As they did so, the front door swung open, and Rachel stormed out fuming, with her usual disgust for me painted all over her face.

"What the hell is going on here? What are you doing, Mythic?" Her sharp, piercing tone was so high that it cut through the afternoon quiet.

I leaned against my truck coolly. "I'm giving your daughter's things back. She should be lucky I'm even doing that."

"Why are you doing this?" she asked as she stormed toward me.

"Because your daughter lied to me about having cancer just to keep me from breaking up with her. Had me all worried about her and shit, faking like she was sick, throwing up and shit, when ain't shit wrong with her except that she's fucking diabolical."

The movers paused for a second as their eyes widened in shock while they listened.

Rachel's jaw dropped, disbelief flooding her features. Stunned, she paused her approach, stopping in the middle of the lawn among the boxes that now scattered it. "You're lying!"

"I don't have to lie to you about shit." Then I shrugged. "I don't give a fuck what you believe."

"I knew you weren't a good man for her," she growled. "You're just a ghetto thug who was never good enough for my daughter."

I didn't flinch at her insults. I'd heard worse on the streets. Her anger only seemed to fuel my persistence. "You can think what you want, but it doesn't change the truth. I might be a thug, but your daughter is a lying ass bitch who needs therapy."

Rachel crossed her arms as her frustrations boiled over. "Can you at least have the movers put the boxes inside?"

I leaned back slightly, smirking. "Hell no. They'll leave them right where they are."

She turned to the movers, asking, "Can you please place the boxes in the house?"

I locked eyes with the guys. My gaze dared them to listen to her. They glanced at me, then back at Rachel.

"Sorry, ma'am," one of them told her. "We have to listen to the man who's paying us."

"This is insane," she quipped.

I chuckled tauntingly. "No. *Your daughter* is insane."

Rachel's mouth opened. She was probably about to unleash some long-winded speech defending Lelani, but I was already done listening. I pushed off the truck and took a few slow steps toward her. "She faked an illness to manipulate me. She played with emotions I don't even let most people see. And now?" I gestured to the boxes littering her lawn. "She can sit in this mess and figure out how to rebuild her life without me in it."

## AVIANA SCOTT

As I stepped into Mythic's condo, my breath caught in my throat. The moment the door swung open, I was met with overwhelming luxury. I had toured so many places since I'd shown him this one, so I showed myself around to refresh my memory.

The first thing that caught my eye was the open layout of the living space. The floor-to-ceiling windows flooded the room with natural light, offering a breathtaking view of the city skyline. I took a moment to just soak it all in, feeling a flutter of excitement in my chest.

I set my bags down at the front door and took off my shoes, respectful of the polished floors. Then I wandered over to the kitchen. My fingers glided over the cool marble of the island. It was polished to perfection, gleaming under the sunlight, and I couldn't help but admire the high-end appliances that lined the countertops. Everything was immaculate, like a scene straight out of a magazine.

The hardwood floors were smooth beneath my feet. The living room was cozy yet sophisticated with a plush sectional that looked perfect for lounging and a large flat-screen TV mounted on the wall. A few pieces of art hung around, each one telling a story of its own.

As I made my way to the two bedrooms, I was struck by how calm and inviting each space felt. The master bedroom was a sanctuary, complete with a king-sized bed dressed in soft, luxurious linens. The second bedroom was just as nice, perfect for guests or even a home office if Mythic ever needed one.

I stepped out onto the large balcony, taking in the fresh air and the view. I could see the rooftop pool and terrace of the building. It looked like a tempting oasis that made me wish I could dive in right then. I leaned against the railing, feeling as if I was in a movie. This place was a reflection of who he was—ambitious, stylish, and unapologetically bold.

I turned away from the balcony, basking in the sense of peace that washed over me as I walked back inside. I headed toward the front door to grab the bags I had left behind. As I approached the foyer, something on the table caught my eye. A note lay there, neatly folded, and curiosity pulled me closer.

As I picked it up, I noticed a credit card sitting beside it. My heart skipped a beat as I read the note: *Use the card to fill the fridge and get whatever else you need. Treat this like it's your house.*

My smile was so wide that my cheeks stung from the strain. For Mythic, this was such a simple gesture, but it meant so much to me. God was showing out for me, even amid all the hurt and disappointment I was carrying. Mythic was so loving, so attentive, that I had to remind myself that I was living a nightmare.

I took a deep breath, clutching the note and card tightly, knowing that I needed to focus on the good as long as it lasted.

## MYTHIC GREY

I could feel the tension of the day easing away as I got off the elevator at my condo on Indiana Avenue. I had left my manager at Enchant to close up for me, and honestly, I didn't even care about the club or the streets right now. All I wanted was to be with Avi. Spending these last two days with her had shown me the difference in being with a woman you want to be around. Nothing else really mattered, and it was hard to focus on anything or anyone else.

The moment I walked in, a savory, appetizing aroma invaded my nostrils, and I smiled. I followed the scent into the kitchen, and there she was—Aviana, my beautiful distraction—standing at the stove. Her hair was pulled back into a lazy, messy bun, and she was wearing one of my shirts, which barely covered her.

The sight of her was everything.

I leaned against the doorframe, allowing the moment to sink in.

She turned around, surprise flashing across her face. "What are you doing here?"

"This is my crib," I jokingly reminded her. "I can't come to my own crib?"

Aviana glanced at the clock above the refrigerator, then she looked at me, tilting her head dramatically. "It's late. Don't you need to be at home?"

I shrugged a shoulder. "I am home."

Her brows creased as she stirred whatever was cooking. It smelled like pasta.

"How have you been able to spend so much time with me?" I knew that question had been on the tip of her tongue for the last two days, but she didn't want to burst our bubble by bringing up Lelani.

I hesitated for a second, then decided to finally tell her. "Lelani faked having cancer," I said, watching her reaction. Her face dropped. "What? Why would she do something like that?"

"Because I love you, and she knew it."

Aviana stopped stirring and then slowly faced me. Her expression was a blur of admiration and surprise.

"She didn't want me to leave her. She felt like it was going to happen at any moment, so she lied to keep me. Guess she figured I would never leave her at a time like that, and she was right. I was about to leave her. You hadn't even mentioned leaving Damar, and I knew you probably wouldn't have, but I knew that I wasn't giving her my all because I was in love with you."

Aviana's shoulders sank as a pout of admiration formed on her lips.

"She must have felt that shit," I went on, "so she made up having cancer."

"But her head was always hurting. You said that she was sick and throwing up and shit."

I chuckled wryly. "I guess she was just pretending. She must have taken something to make her throw up."

"That's crazy. How did you find out?"

"She got in an accident the other night."

Aviana's eyes bulged.

"I was in the hospital with her all night. That's why I hadn't gotten any sleep. When her surgeon came in explaining that she would be in there for a while, I asked if she could still get her biopsy. That's how it all came out. They had no record of her having cancer."

"Oh my God. That's insane."

"I got her stuff moved out of my crib today and took it to her mother's house."

I stepped away from the doorway and made my way into the kitchen. As I approached Aviana at the stove, she held me in a tight embrace.

"I'm sorry," she murmured.

I chuckled, pulling back slightly to look down in her eyes. "For what?"

"I feel responsible for what Lelani did to you," she said as her gaze dropped to the floor.

I shook my head as I smiled. "Nah. Don't do that. I'm actually happy it happened. It feels like God made a way for us to be together. We both loved each other but respected our significant others. Now we can be together without feeling guilty."

She hesitated, biting her lip with her brows furrowed in thought. "I don't know if I'm in the right headspace to be in another relationship. Damar and Mia have left some scars, and I'm scared that I will bleed on you."

"I know," I gently told her.

"But I need you," she admitted, her eyes searching mine for understanding.

Relieved, I told her, "I know that too. That's why I'm going to take it slow with you."

Her expression softened, and I could see the glimmer of hope, longing, and love in her eyes. I reached out, brushing a strand of hair behind her ear, causing my thumb to graze her cheek.

As I pulled Aviana closer, the moment was suddenly interrupted by the shrill ring of her phone. She glanced at the island where it sat, and I caught a glimpse of Carol's name flashing on the screen.

"Answer it," I told her, but I felt a spasm of disappointment as she stepped away from me. The warmth of her body was gone, and I couldn't help but laugh at myself for feeling so possessive.

As she lifted the phone to her ear, I turned my attention to the stove. I grabbed the stirring spoon and dipped it into the bubbling pot of alfredo sauce. The spicy kick hit me, and I realized she was making rasta pasta.

Suddenly, I heard Aviana inhaling sharply, and my heart dropped. I turned just in time to see her collapse onto a stool with her hands gripping her head.

I rushed over, asking, "Avi, what's wrong?"

She held the phone to her ear as her expression shifted from surprise to devastation. "They found Mia." Her voice trembled as she struggled to process the news.

My pulse quickened. "Where is she?"

Her gaze lowered when she saw the hope in my eyes. Her eyes were wide with shock as she covered the speaker of her phone. "She's dead. She was found stuffed in a suitcase in the lake."

# A MONTH LATER

# CHAPTER 18

## AVIANA SCOTT

**SINCE LEARNING OF** Damar and Mia's deception and Mia's death, I reverted to my roots and started to lean on God more than ever. I couldn't wrap my mind around how two of the people that I loved the most in the world could betray me so savagely. I had been attending church with my parents every Sunday and praying more than I ever had before.

This Sunday had been no different. After church, I followed my parents back to their house for dinner, which my mother had prepared that morning.

I sat at my parents' dining table with the appetizing aroma of pot roast wafting through the air.

"So, when are you going to move out of Mythic's place?"

I sighed heavily as my mother waited for an answer. During the silence, I could see my parents stealing concerned, worried glances at each other. They hadn't wanted to let me out of their sight since the truth came out about Damar's involvement in Jeremy and Mia's murders. Their trust in my judgment was shattered, and I could sense their disapproval, especially when Mythic's name came up.

I sighed, knowing where this was heading. "I don't know. After everything that happened, I feel safest there, and he's been really supportive. I don't see a reason to leave."

Mom furrowed her brow as her fork paused mid-air. "Avi, you know how we feel about him. He's a gangster, and we remember what he was like in high school. You really should be careful spending so much time with him."

I bit back my irritation. "He'll never let anything happen to me. He's been there for me through all of this. I'm not going to push him away because of his past."

"Baby, it's not just about his past," my dad interjected. "It's about your safety. We want you to make good choices, especially now, after everything that's happened."

Their words struck a nerve. I understood their concern, but they didn't see the side of Mythic that I did. He had been my rock during this storm, and it hurt that they couldn't see that. I swallowed hard, trying to focus on the food in front of me instead of the growing tension in the room. I wanted to yell that I was a grown woman capable of making my own decisions, but I respectfully held my tongue about that too because I had clearly not been the best judge of character when it came to Damar and Mia.

As I pushed the mashed potatoes around my plate, my dad's voice broke through the tension. "So, what's going on with the divorce? How does that process work with Damar being in jail?"

Looking into his eyes, I saw the usual flash of anger that appeared every time Damar's name came up.

When my parents found out about the affair between Mia and Damar, I had never seen them so furious. I wanted to keep the news from them—to protect them from the chaos—but it was impossible; the story had exploded all over the news and the Internet, and the gossip was relentless.

Our friends and loved ones, even neighbors, were whispering and speculating. Everyone looked at me with eyes filled with pity. It felt like I was living in a reality show I never signed up for. Everyone seemed to think they knew the truth, and the speculation was always the same: Damar had murdered Mia, but he had yet to make a confession, and the investigation was still ongoing.

"Well, since he's locked up, it's a bit complicated. I've filed the divorce petition through the court, and it's different when the spouse is incarcerated. I've been working with a lawyer who specializes in these kinds of cases. He said I'll need to serve Damar with the divorce papers, even if he's in jail."

Mom frowned, clearly worried. "But how will you do that? Is he even going to respond?"

I shrugged. "He has a right to respond, but it might not matter. I can still move forward with the divorce if he doesn't. The lawyer said that as long as I can prove he's been served, I can request a default judgment since he can't show up in court."

"Do you have any idea how long it will take?" Mom asked.

"It could take a few months, depending on how things go. I just have to stay strong and keep pushing through the process. It's just one more thing I have to handle on top of everything else."

Their silent support was comforting, but I could still feel their concern. I hated that I was making them worry. I wished I could retreat into my own world, far away from the prying eyes and the constant chatter. I felt suffocated by my parents' worry and the public scrutiny.

I took a deep breath, both reluctantly and willingly changing the subject. "I'm going out of town with Mythic." The moment the words left my mouth, I could sense the immediate shift in my parents' demeanor. Their eyes widened, and I braced myself for their reaction. "He's taking me on a vacation because I need to relax and clear my mind after everything that has happened."

I had been wrestling with the urge to lie about who I was going with. I could have said I was going alone, but I knew that wouldn't fly. My parents would never let me rest if they thought I was going off by myself, and I had no other friends to lie and say that I was going with.

"*Unt-uh.* I don't think that's a good idea," my father fussed.

"I really need this vacation right now. I promise I'll be careful."

My mom exchanged a worried glance with my dad, and I could see the doubt written all over their faces.

"Avi," my mother said with the high-pitched tone that always sent chills down my spine, "haven't you had enough of being connected to the wrong people?"

"Well, we all thought Mia and Damar were good people, and we were clearly wrong about that. So, obviously, none of us are in the position to judge," I shot back with a hint of frustration creeping into my voice.

My dad raised an eyebrow as a stern expression covered his face. "Watch it."

"We're only looking out for you," my mother quipped. "We don't want to see you hurt again."

"I'm sorry," I quickly told them. "I didn't mean to get smart. It's just… It's been a lot lately, and I really think this trip will help me."

The tension hung in the air for a moment before my parents nodded. Their expressions were still worried but slightly more understanding.

"We just want what's best for you, honey." My mom's voice was gentler now.

"I know," I replied, feeling a little calmer. "And I appreciate it. I really do. I just need some space to figure things out." I bit my tongue, fighting the urge to tell my parents that I was in love with Mythic, that he was not only being supportive, but he was also putting his dick in me every chance he got. But I wouldn't dare give my parents heart attacks. I couldn't bear to lose them too after everything else I had already lost.

## DAMAR SCOTT

I slouched in a chair in the dayroom, half-heartedly watching some old sitcom on the flickering TV. It was just background noise.

Just months ago, I was a promoter, living the high life, surrounded by the glitz and glamour of the club scene. Bottles popped like fireworks every night. I mingled with the city's elite. I was living like a king in a world where money and status meant everything.

Now, I was stuck in Cook County Jail, and reality hit me like a punch to the gut every morning when I opened my eyes. This place was far from the vibrant nightlife I once thrived in.

I glanced around at the other inmates. All of them were hardened by their circumstances. Their faces were etched with lines of suffering and regret. They wore their misery like a second skin, and I couldn't help but feel a sense of superiority, even if I was locked up with them. Sure, I had made my share of mistakes, but I did what I had to do for survival. I didn't just throw my life away; I made calculated moves, and the only reason I had gotten caught is because it turns out that my son was smarter than I thought.

Every day here felt like a prison within a prison. The food was bland and tasteless, served on trays that reminded me more of a school cafeteria than a place meant to rehabilitate. The stench of every room was a mix of sweat and despair that clung to my clothes.

As I stared aimlessly at the TV, the same crew of 111 Boyz who had jumped me the first day I got locked up strolled in. Their crew had grown since then as more and more of them got arrested every day. Their taunting laughter echoed off the walls as they came in. They were always on the lookout for a chance to make my life hell. They'd been terrorizing me day in and day out. It was no longer just about avenging Jeremy's death; they treated it like a game, and I was their favorite target.

Each time they spotted me, I could see the twisted thrill in their eyes of making me feel small and weak. They'd throw insults my way, trying to get a rise out of me, laughing at my every flinch. They'd corner me in the yard or during meals, pushing me around like I was nothing. Just a few days ago, they'd jumped me again, and I still hadn't fully healed from the bruises they'd left behind. Every painful movement I made reminded me of their fists connecting with my skin as their laughter rang in my ears.

I felt the tension building inside me as they closed in. Fear crept up my spine. Every time we had an altercation, I wondered what if this time was worse. I wondered what if they decided that particular time to kill me. The thought made my heart race so intensely that a sharp pain shot through my chest. I was living in a nightmare that I couldn't wake up from.

"Look at this bitch-ass nigga."

"Weak bitch."

As the 111 Boyz closed in around me, their taunts bounced off the cold concrete walls. I could feel their eyes boring into me. Their laughter was like a pack of wolves circling their prey. Just when I thought they were about to make a move, a correctional officer stepped into the room.

"Scott!" the officer barked my last name as he looked around the room.

Just as I discreetly exhaled with relief, his eyes finally found me. "Your lawyer is here to see you."

"O–Okay." I wasted no time getting out of there.

"You lucky, bitch. But we'll see you around," one of the 111 Boyz gritted as I carefully made my way through their huddle.

I followed the correctional officer through the maze of the jail. The fluorescent lights buzzed overhead, casting a harsh glare on the grimy tiles below. The hallways were lined with heavy steel doors. The air smelled stale and hopeless. I could hear the faint sounds of shouting and the clanging of metal.

We finally reached the visitation room, a small, dimly lit space with a few plastic chairs and a thick glass partition separating us from the other side. I could see a couple of other inmates sitting with their visitors having conversations that were muffled through the glass.

When I stepped into the visitation room, my lawyer, Bradley, was already seated at the small table wearing a serious expression. I could tell he wasn't here to share good news. I took a seat across from him and braced myself for what he was about to say.

As I sat down at the table, a sharp pain shot through my ribs, making me flinch. Bradley noticed. His brow wrinkled with concern as he glanced over my bruises. "Are you okay?"

"Could be better," I muttered, forcing a sarcastic grin that didn't quite reach my eyes. "Had another encounter with the 111 Boyz."

Bradley leaned in closer. "What happened?"

I shook my head, groaning. "They just don't let up, man. It's like they're bored or something. I swear, every time I turn around, they're in my face, taunting me, pushing me around. It's a fucking game to them at this point."

Bradley frowned as concern deepened in his eyes. "You need to be careful. I can't have you getting into more trouble while we're trying to sort this out. You already have enough on your plate."

I leaned back in my chair, wincing again as the movement jostled my ribs. "Yeah, well, it's hard to stay out of trouble when they're actively looking for a reason to fuck with me."

Bradley nodded. "I get that, but we need to focus on getting you out of here. Just try to keep your head down. I'll do what I can on my end."

I appreciated what he was saying, but keeping my head down was becoming increasingly difficult.

Sighing, Bradley sat back. "Damar, we need to talk. In light of Mia's body being found, you are the DA's prime suspect. They are forming a case against you. Given that, the DA has taken the previously offered deal off the table for Jeremy's murder."

Panic struck me. "I can't be stuck in this hellhole while we go to trial. The 111 Boyz are on my back. They're making my life miserable in here."

Bradley nodded, understanding my panic. "I get it, but right now, you have a couple of options. You can enter a straight guilty plea, which could help you get a lighter sentence, but—"

"But what?" I pressed. "I don't want to sit here for a lengthy trial. I don't have time for this."

He leaned forward, lowering his voice. "Look, I can't promise you anything. The DA is working hard to gather the evidence they need to charge you with Mia's murder. If that happens, you'll still be stuck in the county while you wait for trial."

The room felt like it was closing in on me. I couldn't stand the thought of staying in this jail for what felt like an eternity, especially with the constant threat of the 111 Boyz looming over me. "What if I just confess to Mia's murder?" I blurted desperately. "I'll do whatever it takes to get out of here."

Bradley looked taken aback. His brows wrinkled in concern. "Damar, that's a serious decision. You need to think this through.

Confessing to two murders will guarantee a very lengthy sentence. You'll most likely never get out of prison."

All I could think about was the hell I was living in every single day. "I don't care! I can't take this anymore. I just want out of here."

## MYTHIC GREY

I was geeked as I pulled up to Enchant. I was ready to get this night over with so I could pack for my vacation with Aviana. It felt wild, thinking about it—me, a street nigga, heading out of the country. I'd always been stuck in the grind, taking business trips here and there in the states, but this was going to be different. This was about making memories, about breaking free from the chaos of our lives for a minute.

Before climbing out of the car, my phone lit up again with Lelani's name flashing across the screen. For the past month, she'd been blowing me up nonstop, calling back-to-back until I had no choice but to block her number. That hadn't stopped her, though. Soon after, she started calling me through Instagram. Sitting there, I thought about blocking her there too, but with me and Avi about to go on vacation, I figured I'd better settle this once and for all. I didn't need Lelani interrupting our peace on our trip.

With a heavy sigh, I picked up the call. "What, Lelani?"

She breathed as if she were relieved I finally answered. "I'm sorry," she whispered. "I shouldn't have lied to you."

I scoffed with a chuckle. "You didn't just lie. You made up a whole damn disease."

"I know," she said softly as if she were ashamed, "but admit it, Mythic, you've been in love with Aviana the whole time, haven't you?"

Now that I finally had Aviana, I was never going to deny my feelings for her again. "Yeah, I have, but Avi and I didn't cross any lines until recently. I only just told her how I felt about her right before your fake diagnosis."

"I knew it," she gritted. "I was right all along."

"The day you said you had cancer, I was planning to leave you because I felt like a good woman like you deserved a man who actually loved you." Then I laughed at my own naïveté.

She scoffed bitterly. "I *am* a good woman, Mythic. You don't get to judge me for doing what I had to do to hold on to the man I love. I was desperate."

"Look, what's this call even for?"

She sighed again. "Closure, I guess."

"Well, you got it now, so don't ever call me again. If you do, I swear to God I'll break every finger you use to dial my number."

I hung up before she could say another word and climbed out of my SUV.

Since the whole situation with Lelani blew up, I hadn't even gone back to the place we used to share. Instead, I'd been focusing on Aviana, while taking things slow. She had been through so much heartbreak, and I didn't want to rush her into anything. But spending every day with her felt like we were practically living together already. She lit up my world, and I wanted to show her how much she meant to me with this vacation.

As I stepped out of the truck, a car pulled in behind me. I turned to see Fury, the leader of the Urban Enforcers, sliding out of a Honda Civic. He was clearly trying to keep it low-key, probably because his crew was still losing that war with the Crimson Order. Most of their lieutenants had been gunned down. Many of them had lost family members and friends to the violence, and Fury had a bounty on his head.

My security team was on point, emerging from their spots like shadows.

As Fury closed the distance between us, I cut him off right away. "If you're here to convince me to distribute to the Urban Enforcers, you might as well turn the fuck around and walk away."

His face contorted with rage. "I can't just walk away. My crew, my family, my friends are dying out here. We need those weapons."

I stood my ground, unfazed. "*No* is a complete sentence, motherfucka. You shouldn't have started a war you couldn't win. Your stupidity and desperation are why I won't work with you."

As Fury stepped closer, his voice dropped to a menacing growl. "Then you're just as much to blame for their deaths as the Crimson Order. You're playing a dangerous game, Mythic."

I could see the fire in his eyes, the wild desperation of a man backed into a corner. "You're threatening me?" I challenged with an icy tone. "You know I could take your life right here, right now."

My security team began to close in, surrounding me with a wall of muscle.

Out of the corner of my eye, I spotted a police car cruising down the street. The officers stared at the scene as they slowed their speed.

Fury glanced over his shoulder, noticing the police presence too. "This isn't over, Mythic," he warned as he turned to walk away. "You'll see me again."

I watched him go, knowing that this wouldn't be the last I heard from him.

# CHAPTER 19

## AVIANA SCOTT

A FEW DAYS later, Mythic and I were being absorbed by the Caribbean Sea. The sun hung low in the sky, painting the horizon in hues of orange and pink as the ocean waves lapped at our bodies. I floated beside Mythic in the warm water, feeling completely at ease, as if we were the only two souls in the world. The private island he'd rented for us was a literal paradise. It was the kind of place you only dream about.

I still didn't know exactly how he got his money. I just knew that no matter what, I was safe. But I did always know Mythic was financially comfortable, but these last few weeks had opened my eyes to a whole new level of wealth I never imagined. The luxury surrounding him and the expense of his life were overwhelming. I found myself wondering if I truly belonged in his world of lavishness, if I deserved it, if I fit in.

But every time I caught Mythic's eye, I felt that uncertainty melt away. He was grounded and real and completely down-to-earth despite the riches surrounding us. He looked at me like I was everything he wanted, and I could feel the sincerity in his voice when he assured me that I fit perfectly into his world.

"You deserve this, Aviana," he would often tell me. "You deserve all of it."

I appreciated the way he listened to me, how he took his time to understand my fears and worries. His patience made me feel safe, like I could open up without judgment.

As Mythic and I floated in the crystal-clear water, the gentle current cradled us while we shared laughter and playful splashes. His laughter was like music, pulling me further into this moment that felt so perfect, it was almost surreal.

My heart raced as he swam closer, the muscles in his arms and shoulders flexing effortlessly with each stroke. It was almost poetic to see a man with such a rough exterior immersed in the beauty of the ocean, transforming him into something dreamlike. The way the sunlight glinted off the water as he moved, paired with the gentle waves crashing around him, created a surreal image that was a complete difference from his tough demeanor. The muscles in his arms and shoulders caught the light, making him look like a sculpture carved from marble, while the serene setting acted as a background, softening the edges of his hard personality. In that moment, he was both a fierce warrior and a gentle soul, a perfect harmony of strength and tranquility that left me captivated. I remembered the young and reckless boy he used to be. Now, he had grown into a confident, successful man. The man I saw before me was not just a former crush; he was someone who had learned from his past and was ready to love deeply and with intent.

"Hey you." His voice was so inviting, breaking through my thoughts. He swam closer until the tips of our noses nearly touched. The warmth in his dark eyes sparkled like the ocean around us. "Remember when we used to sneak into the pool at the park district after hours, just you and me?"

I chuckled, nodding. "Yeah, and you nearly got us caught every time."

His smile was so genuine. "I was just trying to impress you. You always made me feel like I had to level up."

His words sent a thrill through me. "And look at you now. You've definitely leveled up since those days."

He moved closer, wrapping his arms around my waist and pulling me against him. The warmth of his body seeped into mine, and I felt a flutter of excitement as his lips brushed against my forehead. "I've always wanted to impress you, Avi," he murmured with his breath against my skin. "But this time, I want to do more than just show off. I want you to know how much you mean to me."

As he spoke, it was just us, floating in this beautiful ocean, the sun kissing our melanin, the rhythm of the waves providing a soothing soundtrack to our reunion. I felt so connected to him in that moment, as if the years had only deepened our bond.

"I can't believe we're here again," I whispered as my heart swelled with emotion. "It feels like a dream."

"It's not a dream," he said, looking deep into my eyes with a sincerity. "This is real, and I'm not going anywhere this time. I want to build something with you—something that lasts forever."

I felt a rush of warmth, my cheeks flushing as I searched his gaze for any hint of doubt. But all I saw was determination and love. "You mean it?"

"Absolutely." He dipped his head, his lips just inches from mine. "I've waited long enough, Avi. I'm ready to make up for lost time."

Our lips met, and a spark ignited between us. It was soft and cautious at first, but soon it grew into a passionate kiss that left me breathless. The taste of saltwater mixed with the sweetness of his lips sent a wave of desire through me. I wrapped my arms around his neck, pulling him closer as the ocean flowed around us.

As we finally broke apart, I looked into his eyes and saw the promise of a future filled with love, laughter, and the kind of connection we had always wanted. In the heart of the ocean, with the sun setting above us, I knew that this was just the beginning of our story.

"Fuck. I love this pussy," Mythic lowly growled with his mouth to my ear and his hand gripping the back of my neck as I rode him.

"It's yours, baby," I swore.

"Is it?"

"Yes," I whimpered as the tip of his dick flipped the switch of yet another orgasm.

With his grip on my neck, he pulled me back, demanding my eyes on his. "Promise?"

Locked in his intense gaze, I nodded feverishly. "I promise. I promise."

He smiled wickedly. "Good girl."

Permanently locking his eyes on mine, he bit down on his bottom lip and smacked my ass...hard.

*"Mmmm!"* I exclaimed as the impact sent chills all over my tan skin.

When we finally left the ocean, we made our way over to the beach showers by the villa. The cool water washed over us and rinsed away the day. As I watched Mythic under the shower, I couldn't take my eyes off him. His brown melanin seemed to glow in the fading light as the water dripped down his skin.

The way the water cascaded over him, mixed with the sun's glow, made him look powerful and untouchable, but somehow all mine. I couldn't stop staring at how effortlessly he owned the moment. Watching him like that, with the sun setting behind him, I felt an overwhelming need to be near him, to feel his strength, his warmth. It was like the sun itself was admiring him, and I was right there with it, completely mesmerized.

Being with Mythic like that, spending all day on the beach, drinking, talking…it felt more intense. Like something had shifted between us—something real and final—and I couldn't get enough of him. All I could think about was feeling him inside of me. I was pulled to him, couldn't keep my hands off him if I tried. I grabbed his hand and led him over to one of the beach chairs, sitting him down before I climbed onto his lap.

I didn't even think twice about it. The moment felt too right. His skin was still damp from the shower and warm under my touch. Everything about him just made me want more. My lips found him, and that was it. We were lost in each other as we became tangled up in the passion, heat, and connection that felt like it had been building all day.

His eyes remained locked onto mine, and I couldn't look away, even if I wanted to. It was like he had me under a spell, completely frozen in that moment. Every inch of me felt drawn to him, like nothing else existed but the space between us.

Then, he said, "I'm so in love with you, Avi." Though I heard him say it before, those words hit me deeper in this moment. I had never heard them spoken to me with so much meaning, so much weight behind them. It wasn't just something he said—it was like he was pouring his whole soul into those three words, and I felt it in every part of me.

I melted all over him. My center flooded his rod as I bounced slowly on it. "I love you too, Mythic."

## MYTHIC GREY

It had only been two days on this private island, but I was already addicted to the peace it offered. There was no looking over my shoulder or worrying about the streets. It was just me and Aviana living in the moment.

Over the last two days, I made it my mission to show Aviana a side of life that felt miles away from the mayhem we both had been going through. We started our mornings with breakfast on the balcony while the sun rose. We'd sit there, laughing and teasing each other with the sounds of the ocean creating a calming soundtrack to our morning. One afternoon, I took her for a private boat ride. We anchored the boat in a secluded cove and swam while exploring it. I watched her face light up as she dove into the water, carefree and glowing, and it filled me with pride to see her truly enjoying herself after weeks of sadness.

In the evenings, I set up a romantic dinner under the stars, complete with candles and the sound of waves lapping against the shore. I wanted to create an atmosphere where she could forget everything, even if just for a moment. We shared our dreams and fears over Belizean food. The connection between us grew deeper with every passing hour. After dinner, we strolled along the beach, and I pulled her close as we gazed up at the stars. Each moment with her was a reminder of what I had been missing, and I made it my goal to make her feel cherished and loved in every way possible.

This morning, I let her sleep in since I had been keeping her busy fucking her all over the island. I stood at the edge of the pool outside our private villa with the morning sun warming my dark skin. The sound of the water lapping gently against the side of the pool was a soothing background to my conversation with Taye.

"Shit is getting real with the Urban Enforcers. Fury's girlfriend got caught in a shootout last night. She didn't make it."

"Damn. That's rough," I replied, pushing off the edge of the pool and beginning to pace.

"I'm worried he might try to rob us. He's desperate, and you know how these guys get when they lose someone close to them. They lash out." Taye paused and took a deep, anxious breath. "I don't want him coming for you."

I smirked a little. "I appreciate your concern, but I've got our security team on high alert. You know they're like hawks, man. Plus, the warehouse is well hidden. If Fury thinks he can pull something, he's in for a rude awakening."

"Just watch your back, ah ight? You know how these streets are. Desperation makes people do crazy shit."

"I feel you. But we're good. That motherfucka isn't clever enough to get past our team."

As Taye wrapped up the call, I walked toward the villa. The moment I entered, I was met by the sheer luxury of the place. It was massive, with high ceilings and floor-to-ceiling windows that let in the sunlight. The living room flowed into the dining area. It was decorated with dope, luxurious furnishings and decor. It was extravagant as hell, almost too much for just the two of us.

As I made my way through the villa, the aroma of breakfast wafted through the air, leading me to the kitchen. The private chef was hard at work, cooking up a storm. He glanced up at me and gave me a nod with a friendly smile before turning back to the sizzling pans. Just then, Aviana emerged from the hallway. She looked like a vision even in her sleepy state. Her hair was a tousled mess, falling perfectly around her face, and she wore a silky, short robe that barely covered the beautiful curves I couldn't get enough of. I felt my breath catch for a moment, admiring how effortlessly stunning she looked. She rubbed her eyes, still waking up, and in that instant, I knew that this was exactly where I wanted to be—right beside her, in this slice of paradise.

I walked over to where she was leaning against the kitchen counter.

"*Buenos días,*" she greeted the cook.

He turned toward her, smiling. "*Buenos días.*"

I gently took her hand and led her toward the patio door.

"Where are we going?" she sleepily mumbled.

"Just follow me."

I led her out to the balcony where we had been spending most of our mornings. Without saying a word, I pulled a small speaker from my pocket and connected it to my phone. I found a song that always took her back to simpler times, back when we were young and the world wasn't as complicated. As the first few notes played, I watched her eyes light up as a small smile curved her lips.

"May I have this dance?" I asked, taking her hand in mine.

She laughed softly, nodding as I pulled her closer. We started to sway gently to the rhythm. My arms wrapped around her, holding her like I never wanted to let go. I whispered the lyrics in her ear, just loud enough for her to hear, and I felt her relax completely in my arms. It was just us, moving slowly under the morning sun with the sound of waves crashing in the background.

I held her tighter, resting my forehead against hers. "I'm gonna make sure you feel like this every day, Avi—safe, loved, and appreciated…like the queen you are."

She looked up at me, her eyes shining, and I knew right then that this was real, and I was going to do whatever it took to keep her feeling like this, like she was my everything. Because she was.

I LOVE YOU TOO MUCH


## DAMAR SCOTT

A week later, I was sitting across from Detectives Harris and Randall in that cold visitation room. Bradley sat beside me. The room was bare—just a metal table and a couple of chairs bolted to the floor. I was sweating. My mind was racing, wondering if I was really about to do this. But then I thought about being stuck in this hellhole, surrounded by the 111 Boyz for a year or more while a trial dragged on. The thought made my stomach churn. I couldn't go through that. I wasn't built for that life. So, I knew what I had to do.

Detective Harris leaned forward, his eyes never leaving mine. He looked like he'd seen a lot in his years and I wasn't about to surprise him with anything I had to say. Randall, on the other hand, was almost too calm. She reached into her pocket and pulled out a small recorder. She turned it on, and the red light blinked to life.

"All right, Damar," Harris said, flipping open his notepad. His pen was ready to take notes. "Let's hear it."

I slowly turned my head, looking at Bradley. He nodded, giving me a nonverbal signal to proceed.

I took a deep breath as my hands clenched and unclenched under the table. "Okay. I'm gonna tell y'all everything."

Harris nodded, his eyes steady on me, while Randall sat back, letting the recorder do the work. "We're listening," Harris said.

"I was having an affair with Mia." I could hear my voice shaking and could feel the room getting smaller with every word. "I taught her how to embezzle from Dream Realty. She didn't know shit about that kind of thing until I showed her how to do it. It was supposed to be just a little hustle on the side, something to put a few extra dollars in our pockets. But then she started getting greedy. She wanted more money and more of my time. When she found out she was pregnant, she saw it as her ticket to lock me down. She wanted me to leave Aviana. After she was arrested, she told me that she was going to tell Aviana everything because she was convinced that Aviana had snitched. But it was me. I made the anonymous tip to the twins at Dream Realty because I was trying to get rid of her."

Randall shifted in her seat, leaning forward a bit. "What happened next, Damar?"

I swallowed hard, feeling the pressure of their stares. "When she picked up her phone to call Aviana, I knew she would really do it. I knew I had to do something to stop her. I couldn't let her ruin everything I had, so I killed her in an apartment we would sneak off to. This was the night that she got fired from Dream Realty."

"How did you get her out of the building?" Harris asked.

"In the suitcase she was found in." I waited for them to respond with disdain or surprise at my actions, but their expressions remained stoic, as if they had heard this all before. "Somehow, the anchor I had tied to it must have come loose, and it floated to the surface."

"Go on," Randall pressed.

"After I killed her, I pretended to be her to make it seem like she was still alive." The words came out in a rush, almost like I was trying to push them away from me. "I started texting Aviana, making it look like it was Mia sending those threatening messages."

Randall raised an eyebrow, finally speaking. "So, you were the one behind the car and the fire?"

I nodded. "I paid some chick to do it. I just wanted to make it seem like Mia was still alive."

Randall clicked off the recorder. They stayed silent for so long, as if they couldn't believe the lengths to which I had gone.

"You're looking at a long time, Damar," she said, almost like she was reminding me of the fate I'd just sealed with my own words.

"I don't care," I replied, staring down at the table. "I just can't be in here for a year, maybe more, fighting for my life every day. At least this way, I got a chance."

The detectives exchanged a glance, and I knew they had what they needed. My confession was out there now, and there was no taking it back. But at least, maybe, just maybe, I could find a way to survive prison without fearing for my life every day, even if it meant doing time for the rest of it. Anything was better than rotting in this place with a target on my back.

# CHAPTER 20

## AVIANA SCOTT

As SOON AS we landed back in Chicago, Mythic headed straight to the grocery store. Having that private chef in Belize had been amazing, no doubt. The food was delicious, but after a week of it, we were both ready to get back to some real food—Black American food. I was craving it like crazy, and apparently, so was he.

We were walking through the produce section, picking up stuff for the meal we had in mind—fried chicken, collard greens, and sweet potatoes.

As I reached for some bell peppers, I smirked at him flirtatiously. "You know," I started, "I never imagined you'd be this soft."

He looked at me with one eyebrow cocked and that grin of his showing just how cocky he could be. "Ain't nothing soft about me," he shot back, his deep voice dripping with that usual swag.

I giggled, tilting my head to the side. Then my eyes slowly grazed his tall frame from the top of his head to where I knew his impressive manhood hung. "You're right about that shit, baby."

Biting on his bottom lip with a devilish smirk, he pinched my stomach. "Don't start no shit in this store. I'll have you bent over the lettuce."

I giggled and put space between us as I pushed the cart farther down the aisle. "I didn't mean soft like that. I meant, I never imagined a street dude like you would be so…attentive. You know, loving, affectionate. You've been spoiling me all week, and now you're out here grocery shopping with me. It's cute, but I'm shocked."

He stepped closer, sliding his arm around my waist with his lips just brushing my ear. "I can be a gangsta and still be the man you need. I ain't gotta choose between loving you and the streets."

I smiled up into his eyes with a gaze filled with appreciation for his presence in my life. He wasn't just saying these words. He meant them. He could be tough when the world demanded it, but here, with me, he was something else—something I hadn't expected but couldn't resist.

Given everything I had just been through, I should have been more guarded, more skeptical about putting so much faith in him. My parents would've called me a fool. They would've warned me that trusting too easily only leads to more hurt. But deep down, I knew there wasn't any reason to build walls with Mythic. With him, it felt different. My heart told me he was the one place I didn't need to keep my guard up, and despite everything I'd learned the hard way, I believed it. Completely.

I smiled, leaning into him. "Yeah. Let's stop before you have me bent over the lettuce."

"Yeah. 'Cause you got my dick harder than life right now," he teased with that cocky grin still playing on his lips. Before I could even respond, his hand slid from my waist, gently cradling the back of my head. He pulled me in, and when his lips met mine, soft yet commanding, a moan escaped my throat. I got lost in the way his lips moved against mine, like he knew exactly how to make me melt. All I could do was savor the way he kissed me, as if he owned me.

My lips were still pressed against Mythic's when I heard my father's disapproving tone cut through the air like a whip.

"Aviana." The way he said my name sent an ice-cold chill down my spine, just like when I was a little girl caught doing something I had no business doing, knowing I was about to get in trouble.

I froze. My whole body stiffened against Mythic's. His hand was still on the back of my head, but I was snatched out of the moment. I reluctantly turned as my stomach knotted up. My father stood a few feet behind us with a cart with disappointment written all over his face like he'd just seen something he couldn't unsee.

My voice was small and nervous as I greeted him. "Daddy." I couldn't even look him in the eye. My eyes kept bouncing between his and the floor.

"Come here," he said with a flat tone.

I stepped away from Mythic, the heat of his kiss still lingering on my lips, and moved toward my father.

Mythic didn't back down. He nodded at my dad, saying, "How you doin', Mr. Bennett?"

But my father didn't even look at Mythic, didn't acknowledge him—nothing. He just ignored him, eyes locked on me like Mythic wasn't even standing there. My cheeks flushed with embarrassment.

"What the hell are you doing, Aviana?" he gritted, full of judgment. "So, you're dating him?"

Despite the utter disappointment in my father's eyes, Mythic had been too good to me for me to ever deny him. "Yes."

My father scoffed, frowning. "Are you serious? After all you've been through, you make a decision like this? He's who you want to be with? Do you remember how he treated you? How he broke your heart?"

"Daddy, that was a long time ago. We were kids back then. Things are different now."

He shook his head, his face hard, like he wasn't hearing a word I was saying. "A man like him doesn't change. He hurt you before, and he'll hurt you again. I don't care how much time's passed."

I swallowed hard. "Daddy, I'm grown now. I know what I'm doing. I wouldn't be with him if I didn't trust him."

He sighed, looking at me like he wanted to say more but was biting his tongue. "You can think you know all you want. But I'm telling you, a man like that, he doesn't care about you the way you deserve."

I felt the sting of his words, but I stood my ground. "I hear you, Daddy, I do, but you don't know him like I do now."

My father's eyes looked toward Mythic for the briefest second, then back to me. "You're right, Aviana; you're grown. All I can do is pray for you."

With that, he turned and pushed his cart past us, leaving me standing there, feeling like I was ten years old again, caught between the man who raised me and the one who had my heart held hostage.

As my father walked away, I felt Mythic's presence come closer. His eyes were filled with sympathy and concern. He didn't say anything, but I knew he wanted to. I wasn't sure how much of my father's conversation he had heard.

Just as he reached for my hand, my phone rang. I glanced down at it, and my heart sank when I saw the name *Detective Randall* flash on the screen.

I stood there frozen for a second, not wanting to deal with more stress after that confrontation with my dad. I knew Detective

Randall could only be calling about Damar's case. The thought of it twisted my insides. That case had been like a constant storm over my life I couldn't escape.

Without saying a word, I answered and fixed the volume so Mythic could hear too.

I sighed heavily, answering, "Hello, Detective Randall."

"Hi, Aviana. I hope that I'm not disturbing you. I only need a moment of your time."

Mythic stepped closer and leaned down so that he could still hear.

"I'm doing some grocery shopping, but you can go ahead."

"I just wanted to inform you that Damar confessed to Mia's murder."

My fingers gripped the edge of the cart. Mythic's brow furrowed, his eyes flicking between me and the phone. It was obvious that he'd killed her, but hearing her say the words made it real.

"He told us everything," Detective Randall continued. "He confessed to killing Mia. He killed her the night that she bonded out. He admitted to posing as her when you received those threatening messages to make it look like she was still alive. He was behind the explosion of your car and the fire at your home."

I waited for my world to tilt, but I felt nothing. No shock. No anger. No sadness. I was numb. After everything Mia and Damar had done, it was like nothing could hurt me anymore. My heart didn't even flinch.

"He has a court appearance this afternoon where he will be pleading guilty to both murders. He should be sentenced right away."

Mythic's eyes searched my face, waiting for some kind of reaction, but I had none to give. "Thank you for letting me know,"

I finally managed, my voice flat. I ended the call and slipped the phone back into my purse.

Mythic stepped closer. He rested his hand on the small of my back.

"You good?" he asked gently.

I nodded, staring down at the cart like it held all the answers. But deep down, I knew there was nothing left to feel. Damar and Mia had taken enough from me already. I wasn't going to give them anything more.

After that mess at the grocery store with my dad and the call from Detective Randall, Mythic wasn't about to let me out of his sight. He could feel something was off, and honestly, I wasn't about to fight him on it because I didn't want to be alone. So, after I cooked us dinner, I went with him to Enchant.

Everyone around me was vibing, dancing, laughing, living it up like they didn't have a care in the world, but I just couldn't get there.

I sat at the bar, nursing yet another glass of Rosé. My mind was spinning, stuck on everything Detective Randall said. Damar's confession didn't shock me, but hearing how deep his lies ran was mind boggling. His level of deceit was disgusting, and no matter how much I tried to shake it off, it clung to me.

I swirled the wine in my glass, watching the bubbles rise. My father's voice echoed in my head. His words stabbed at my sense of judgment. How did I miss all the signs? How did I let myself get played like that? It made me doubt my judgment, my common sense, my ability to see people for who they really were.

Was I just too gullible? Too trusting?

I sat there, questioning myself, wondering if I'd let my heart blind me from the truth for too long. Maybe my dad was right. Maybe I *was* a fool.

I couldn't even muster up the energy to pretend like I was having a good time. I took another sip of my Rosé, feeling the buzz but knowing it wasn't enough to drown out the noise in my head. I didn't want to be alone, but being in this loud, crowded club wasn't doing me any favors either. The music was too loud and the laughter too carefree. I wanted to be home with Mythic.

I slid off the stool and started moving through the crowd. My irritation grew with every step. Folks were dancing like they had no sense and bumping into me left and right, spilling drinks without a care. Somebody's elbow hit me in the side, and I shot them a look, but of course, they were too busy wilding out to even notice.

I kept moving, dodging and pushing through the bodies. I figured that Mythic was in his office, handling business, or speaking to some staff. That was his usual routine.

Finally, I spotted him upstairs in VIP, and for a second, I was relieved. But then I squinted, staring hard. There was a woman right up in his face, smiling and laughing like she didn't have a care in the world.

And just like that, the memories of him being a player, cheating, all the lies I had let slide in the past hit me. I felt my blood start to boil, and before I knew it, I was charging upstairs. I didn't even think; I just drunkenly reacted.

As soon as he saw me coming, he came toward me. His expression was painted with concern as I lashed out at him.

"Who the fuck is she?" I spit as I tried to walk around him. My eyes were staring a hole into the woman. I was so drunk that I wanted to hear it from her that she was fucking my man.

But Mythic stopped me with a stern arm stretched out, blocking my path. "Whoa, baby. What you doin'?"

"Who is she?" I hissed, glaring up at him.

His eyes narrowed with concern. "I don't know—"

I scoffed. "*Mumph.* You don't know?"

"No, baby. She's just some chick who wanted to get bottle service. I just happened to be walking by." Then he laughed at my rage.

"Ain't shit funny," I snapped.

He shook his head slowly. "You're drunk."

"No! I'm done being a goofy bitch. You played me before, and let's not forget that you were fucking me while you had a woman."

Now, his humor was gone. Had I not been so drunk, I would have noticed the offense in his eyes. But as he took my hand, I snatched away from him, "Let me go!"

But I didn't get far before he had a firm grip on my elbow. I winced at how hard he held me as he drug me out of the VIP section and then down the flight of stairs.

"Let me go, Mythic!" I tried to scream over the bass.

"You got me fucked up," he barked.

He pressed me up against the wall in the hallway. He'd brought me to his office. He continued to hold my arm as he unlocked his office with his other hand. He pushed the door open and then forced me inside to the point that I tripped a bit over my own feet.

"Fuck is wrong with you?" he snapped as he slammed the door.

"You—"

He was so furious, he didn't even let me finish, just cut me off. "Nah. You said enough. So, you think I'll go through all I did to have you again just to play you? You think I'm stupid enough to fumble you again? You think I wanna lose you?" My heart skipped a beat, and my eyes widened as I watched him march toward me with rage flickering in his eyes like fire. Each step he took sent a jolt of fear through me, and for a second, I couldn't breathe. The intensity in his stare had me frozen in place and unable to speak.

He grabbed my face with one of his large hands. He forced my head up and my eyes on him. "Who do I love?" he demanded, but still, I was too scared to speak. "Who do I love, Avi?"

"M–Me," I whimpered. I cowered. I clung to him, but he pushed my hands away.

"Nah."

"Mythic…I'm sorry," I whined.

"You got me," he confessed, seemingly against his will. His shoulders lowered as if he were losing a battle. "You fucking own me—"

I leaped toward him. I stood on my tiptoes and wrapped my arms around his neck. He tried to push me away, but I locked my arms around him and brought his lips to mine. "I'm sorry," I professed against his lips, drinking in his air as we kissed.

We crashed into a heated, fiery kiss, the kind that made my heart race and my whole body come alive. His lips were demanding, pulling every bit of breath from me.

As we kissed, Mythic guided me backward. Each step brought us closer to his desk. His hands gripped me tighter, and I could feel the electricity between us building with every touch.

He spun me around and pushed me down with his hand in the small of my back. I creamed and moaned as I could feel his nails running down my thighs as he pulled my denim shorts down. I wasn't able to brace myself for his impact before he was diving inside of my center, delivering brutal, deep strokes that made me wail.

"Who do I love, Avi?" he panted.

Tears filled my eyes as I exclaimed proudly, "*Me*."

I lay on Mythic's couch in his office, staring at the ceiling. My pussy was throbbing and my head still spinning, not from the alcohol, but from all the regret and doubts clouding my mind. Mythic had left me alone to sober up, but honestly, I didn't need more time to sober up—I needed time to think. My mind was on fire, and no matter how hard I tried, I couldn't shake it. Damar and Mia had been a poison in my life, and even though most of my days had been good because of Mythic, today wasn't one of them.

Today, everything about their betrayal was eating at me. What Damar did, the lies he told, how far he went, those details from Detective Randall just wouldn't stop playing on a loop in my head. I hated feeling this way, but Damar's deceit had me questioning everything, and I was embarrassed by it. Embarrassed that I was letting those old wounds mess with my head like this.

I didn't want to be here anymore. I needed to be alone—away from Mythic's staff, away from the noise, away from all of it—so, I slipped out of his office, making sure no one saw me because I knew Mythic would stop me. I knew the layout of the club like the back of my hand. I knew where all the bouncers and security posted up outside, so I moved through the shadows, staying out of sight as I slipped out of the club and down the block. As soon as I was clear, I pulled out my phone and called an Uber.

I started walking down the block, still keeping my distance from where Mythic's security could see me. The Uber app was loading, and just as I confirmed my ride, a car screeched up out of nowhere. The headlights were so bright they blinded me, and before I could even react, three men jumped out.

My heart slammed in my chest. I assumed I was about to get robbed. My mind started spinning, thinking maybe I could toss them my purse and run.

But instead of asking for money or my purse, one of them rushed me. He grabbed me before I could scream. His hand clamped down over my mouth. His grip was so tight I could taste the dirt on his skin. I kicked and struggled, but he was too strong, and the other two were closing in. My screams were muffled against his hand as he carried me toward the car. My feet kicked uselessly in the air.

"Damn. This big bitch is heavy." He grunted as he struggled to carry me.

"You sure this her?"

"Yeah. I watched them in club more than once. *It's her.*"

The trunk popped open. When I saw the dark, empty space waiting for me, I really started to panic. I fought harder, twisting and thrashing, but it was no use. There was no way I could win against three men. They threw me into the trunk like I was nothing, slamming me down before I could catch my breath. I tried to scream again, but another one of them started wrapping duct tape around my mouth, sealing off my only way to cry for help.

"Hold her still," one of them barked, and I felt them grab my hands, then my feet, taping them up too. My arms ached from trying to fight, but I couldn't break free.

As they finished taping me up, one of them leaned in. As he spoke, his voice so cold. "All he had to do was work with me. Now, I have to take from him the way he took from me."

Then the trunk slammed shut, and everything went dark.

# CHAPTER 21

## MYTHIC GREY

**I STOOD NEAR** the entrance, looking around as the night started to wind down.

I signaled to Tyiesha, and she made her way over.

"Yo, I need you to close up tonight," I told her. "I gotta get Aviana home."

Tyiesha nodded. She was about to say something, but JD came rushing up out of nowhere, breathless, his face serious. "Mythic, we got a problem. Aviana was just abducted."

Everything inside me froze for a second, but then the anger hit me like a freight train. "What the hell do you mean abducted?" I snapped with my voice low but treacherous.

JD looked rattled but kept talking. "She got past security somehow. By the time we spotted her, they were already putting her in the trunk."

"How the fuck did she get past security?" I growled as my blood began to boil.

JD shook his head, scrambling for an answer. "I don't know, man. We didn't see her slip out until it was too late. We didn't wanna shoot—didn't want her caught in any crossfire."

I clenched my fists, but I knew JD was right. The last thing I wanted was Aviana gettin' hit because someone was too quick on the trigger. "All right. Good call," I muttered, even though I was still heated.

"Draven's on them, though," JD added quickly. "He's following the car, keeping his distance so they don't know. He'll let us know where they're headed."

That eased some of the rage, but not enough. I needed to see her—to know she was safe.

Without another word, I turned and started toward the door. JD was right on my heels.

As JD and I pushed through the club, I could feel eyes on us. Staff and partygoers gave us curious, concerned looks. I didn't slow down as I pushed my way past everyone. The second we hit the exit, I was already moving, rushing toward my truck like my life depended on it. And in a way, it did.

I grabbed my phone from my pocket and dialed Taye.

The second he picked up, I blurted, "Taye, follow my location. Aviana's been abducted."

There was silence on the other end for half a second, then Taye's voice came through, urgent and serious. "I'm on it."

I hung up, my heart pounding in my chest like it was trying to break out. I couldn't think straight. The fear hit me hard—harder than I wanted to admit. The idea of losing her was suffocating. I couldn't breathe, couldn't even focus. All I could see was her face, and the thought of her being taken by some niggas who had no damn business with her… The thought was like a weight crushing my chest.

I hopped into my truck, not caring about the looks I was getting as I peeled out of the lot. As I sped down the street, I knew the cars in my rearview were my security team following me just like I'd trained them to. But it didn't calm me. Nothing would calm me until I had Aviana back in my arms—safe.

I followed Draven's location, speeding through the Southside streets until we pulled up to what looked like a trap house, deep in Urban Enforcers' territory.

I already knew Fury was behind this. He and his crew had been a thorn in my side for too long, and now he'd gone too far. Taking Aviana was a line he was gonna live to regret crossing, but he wasn't going to live for long.

We didn't park right in front of the spot. Instead, we pulled up two blocks away in a deserted parking lot.

We climbed out of our rides, and they all stood around me, waiting for orders. But I wasn't thinking about strategy. I wasn't even thinking straight. They had my heart, the love of my fucking life. All I wanted was to storm in there and take those motherfuckers out, one by one.

"We go in blazing with all of the artillery we got," I told them. "We're gonna burn that place down and take every one of them out."

"You need to relax, Mythic. I get you want to make these motherfuckers pay—hell, I want to too. But this ain't the way. You don't want Aviana to get hurt in the process. You're not thinking rationally right now."

"I'm not thinking rationally? Damn right I'm not," I snapped. "I don't think rationally when it comes to her. *They took her,* Taye. And you're expecting me to be calm?"

Taye stood on business. "Yeah, I am. 'Cause if we go in there wild, with no plan, she's the one who's gonna pay for it. You want her getting caught in the crossfire? You think you'll be able to forgive yourself if she gets hurt because you couldn't keep your head on straight?"

I clenched my fists as my chest started to heave. He was right, but it didn't stop the rage burning in me.

Draven stepped up. His voice was more level than mine. "We can't rush in blind. Let's be smart about this. We got the drone with us. Let's use it to look through the windows, see where they're at inside the house, then we can make a move without putting her at risk. If we locate Aviana before going in, we have a better shot at getting her out alive—and tearing Fury apart after."

"All right," I said through clenched teeth. "Let's send the drone in and see what we're dealing with. But the second we spot them, it's game on."

## AVIANA SCOTT

I was tied to a damn chair in some old, cold basement that looked like it hadn't seen daylight in years. The air was damp, and I could feel the chill in my bones. My hands and feet were bound tight. The duct tape cut into my skin, and my mouth was still covered. I was breathing heavily through my nose, trying to catch my breath.

I could hear the idiots who took me. They were upstairs arguing. They didn't have a clue what they were doing. As I listened closely, every word made my stomach turn. One of them was pissed. He kept talking about how Mythic wouldn't distribute weapons to him, and because of that, his woman got killed. Now, he wanted revenge—an eye for an eye. He wanted to kill me.

The other wanted to use me as ransom, thinking they could trade me for the artillery they were after. I could hear the frustration in his voice, though, like he knew it wouldn't work. "Even if we get the weapons from Mythic, we'll still be at war with him," he said, sounding like he finally realized just how deep they were in. "This was a bad idea. I told y'all this was stupid! He's got too much firepower for us to survive this."

"Then we gotta kill him," the first one shot back, and my heart dropped.

"Y'all chill," another voice said. "We made sure that nobody saw us snatch her, so we got time to figure this shit out."

I realized then that I wasn't making it out of this alive. They were reckless, thinking with emotions instead of sense. One wanted revenge, the other wanted artillery, and neither of them had the brains to see this whole thing was a suicide mission. And I was stuck in the middle.

I closed my eyes for a moment, trying to steady my breathing. I had come to terms with it. I was going to die down here. My body trembled as I tried to block out the panic creeping in. I started praying, begging God to spare me.

*Lord, please…don't let this be how it ends. Please spare my and Mythic's lives.*

The truth about Mythic—about who he really was—hit me. The conversation I overheard let me finally know what he did in the streets. He was an illegal arms dealer. But as I sat there, helpless, I prayed anyway.

*God, I know what he is doing is wrong, but You had to put him in my life for a reason. Forgive me for loving a man like him, but please… don't take him from me. I trust You wouldn't have brought him into my life unless he was a good man.*

As I prayed, a loud blast shook the house. Gunshots rang out like explosions above me. My heart stopped, then started pounding again—pounding so hard I could hear it in my ears. I began breathing faster, panting with fear. It sounded like a war zone, like a straight-up battlefield both outside and inside the house. Windows shattered repeatedly. The shots kept coming one after the other, some sounding closer, some farther away.

I heard grunts, yells, and the sickening thud of bodies hitting the floor. My body jerked in the chair, buckling and pulling at the restraints, trying to get free, but I couldn't. The duct tape was too tight, cutting into my wrists. No matter how hard I struggled, I wasn't moving.

Tears welled up in my eyes as the chaos raged on around me. I kept praying, kept asking for mercy, even though I couldn't see how I was getting out of this alive. The sounds of the fight upstairs were getting closer, and all I could do was sit there helpless, trapped, and terrified.

The noises upstairs grew louder, almost deafening, like someone had kicked open the basement door. I froze. My breath caught in my throat. Then I heard footsteps, loud and fast, pounding down the old wooden stairs. My heart dropped.

One of the abductors burst into the room, wild-eyed, frantic, and his face drenched in sweat. His shoulder was bleeding. There was a dark stain spreading across his shirt where he'd been shot. He looked like a man on the edge and desperate.

Without a word, he stormed over to me, his breathing ragged. He ripped the duct tape from my mouth so fast I winced, and the sting made my eyes water.

I barely had time to react before I felt the cold steel of a gun pressed against my head. "I want him to hear you. I want Mythic to hear you scream and beg for your life while I kill you."

I could feel his breath on my face, smell the mix of sweat and blood coming off him, but I wasn't about to cower. I wasn't giving him that. My heart was pounding, but my anger was louder. Without thinking, I spat right in his face. My eyes locked on his with all the fury I had in me.

His expression shifted with pure rage. Before I could brace myself, his hand came down across my face, the force of the slap knocking my head to the side. Pain shot through me, and I tasted blood in my mouth.

The room spun for a second, and my cheek throbbed. I bit down, trying to swallow the fear. Even as blood filled my mouth, I stared him down, refusing to let him see an ounce of fear.

Just as his finger tightened on the trigger, a gunshot exploded nearby. The sound was blaring. I braced myself for the pain. I squeezed my eyes shut, ready for the worst. But when nothing happened—no pain, no burn from the bullet—I opened my eyes.

He stood there, frozen. His eyes were wide with shock. A gaping hole was in the center of his chest, blood pouring out, staining his shirt even more. He dropped to his knees, collapsing forward into my lap. I screamed and wiggled my legs frantically, trying to get him off me. I could feel his blood on my face and seeping through my clothes.

His body hit the floor with a thud, and I gasped for air, relief and fear battling inside me.

I looked up, heart pounding, and saw the basement window shattered. There was a jagged hole right where the shot must've come from. Everything upstairs had gone quiet. The gunshots and chaos had all stopped. All I could hear now were heavy, deliberate footsteps coming down the basement stairs again.

I held my breath, unsure of what was about to happen. But then, I saw Mythic. His tall, strong figure rushed toward me, and the moment I saw his face, I knew I was safe.

He was at my side in an instant. He ripped the duct tape from my wrists and ankles with a speed and focus I'd never seen before.

"I'm so sorry, baby," he whispered emotionally. His eyes were glistening, and I could see the regret he was holding back.

Seeing the tears in his eyes tore at me. "I'm okay. I'm okay."

Mythic's gaze dropped to the blood on my lips. With the gentlest touch, he caressed my cheek. His thumb brushed over my skin where I had been hit.

As a tear slid down his face, his torn voice croaked, "I should've never let this happen."

Before I could say anything, he scooped me up effortlessly, holding me tight against him as he carried me up the stairs. I pressed my face into his neck, feeling the strength in him, the protectiveness. And for the first time since this nightmare started, I felt like I could finally breathe again.

# DAMAR SCOTT

I had arrived at the supermax prison in southern Illinois. The gates were tall and intimidating. Razor wire glistened under the dull sunlight. It was like a fortress, built to keep people like me locked up for good. The types of people in this place weren't getting out. This wasn't county jail where people were waiting to see the judge. This was where they put you when they were done with you—murderers, gang leaders, and hustlers who'd been in the game so long they didn't know anything else but this life. And now, I was one of them.

I got thirty years for Mia, and another thirty for Jeremy. Luckily, I had gotten away with Marlene's murder, but I was still facing sixty years. *Sixty years.* I would most likely die in this place. There was no way around it.

The correctional officer walking me through the joint was barely paying me any mind. He just did his job, leading me down the cold halls with his keys jangling with every step. We passed a few cells, and I caught glimpses of the guys inside. All of them had hard faces and dead eyes. Some of them didn't even look up. They were already ghosts, just waiting for their bodies to catch up.

As we got closer to my cell, the officer slowed down and gave a slight nod to the dude inside. Dude was massive—built like a linebacker. He was sitting on his bunk, arms crossed, looking like he didn't want to be bothered.

As he unlocked the cell, the correctional officer casually greeted him like they were homies. "What's good, Bear?"

Bear just grunted, barely acknowledging him, but I noticed the way the officer wasn't even trippin', as if he had been dealing with him for years and probably even liked him.

Bear didn't even stand up. He just glanced at me real quick, sizing me up. I was half his size. He could snap me like a twig if he wanted to. The man had a hard, unforgiving look in his eyes—the kind of look that told me he wasn't about to make room for anybody.

"Inside," the officer barked, giving me a little push. The door clanged shut behind me. That metal-on-metal sound hit my ears like a death sentence.

After a few moments of silence, Bear finally turned to look at me. His eyes were cold and calculating. He stayed seated on his bunk, arms still crossed over his massive chest, like he owned the place—and I already knew he did. I was just a visitor.

"Listen up." His voice was deep and rough like gravel. "You're new here, so let me break it down for you."

I nodded slightly, trying not to look too eager, but I was terrified. Bear didn't miss it. He could probably smell fear like a damn shark smelling blood.

"First off, don't touch nothin' that ain't yours," he barked as he gestured around the small cell. "That bunk up there? That's yours. You don't sit on mine, you don't lay on mine, and don't even think about putting your shit near mine."

I glanced up at the top bunk, giving a quick nod. "Got it."

"And don't be in my space, either. Stay on your side of the cell. You step into my area for any reason, we're gonna have problems."

I could tell he was eagerly anticipating me fucking up, to break one of these ridiculous rules so that he could have some fun.

"Ah ight," I replied quietly. "I got you."

Bear leaned forward slightly, his eyes locking on mine for the first time since I got in here. "Good. 'Cause I ain't the type to warn twice. You talk when I say it's cool to talk. You sleep when I say it's time to sleep. You get that?"

I swallowed hard, nodding again. "Yeah. I get it."

"And another thing," he added, pointing to the small toilet in the corner. "You don't take a dump while I'm in here. You hold it until I'm out. Understood?"

I blinked, trying to process the insanity of what he'd just said. "You serious?"

Bear's face darkened, and he leaned in. His massive frame filled up even more space. "I'm real fucking serious. If you don't like it, go tell the CO and get yourself moved. But you'll learn real quick that they don't give a fuck about you in here, and the next cell might be worse."

I nodded, swallowing down the frustration. "I got it."

He stared at me for a few long seconds, then leaned back, seemingly satisfied. "Good. Don't test me. Understand?"

I nodded again, keeping my voice low. "I understand."

Bear stood up slowly, towering over me like a giant. "Just do what the fuck I say. The minute you forget that, we got a problem."

I clenched my fists at my sides, but I knew better than to say anything. This wasn't the place to start fights—not with this dude. So, I kept quiet, nodded, and took a deep breath, fearing that for the next sixty years, this was my reality.

As he sat back down, my eyes landed on Bear's massive forearm. He had biceps the size of my head. But what stood out was his tattoo—*111 Boyz* inked on his arm clear as day.

My blood ran cold.

If he was rocking that tattoo, he was deep in it. It would only be a matter of time before he got word of who I was. I'd be locked in a cell for twenty-three hours a day with a man who could decide to make me suffer for sport.

# CHAPTER 22

## MYTHIC GREY

**I LAY THERE** holding Aviana close. Her head was resting on my chest. Her breath was soft and steady. She was sleeping hard, but I hadn't been able to shut my eyes all night. Every time I closed them, I saw her fear, the pain, and the blood. And it was my fault.

My arms were wrapped around her, like if I let go for even a second, she'd slip away. I held her tight, protecting her, keeping her safe, but the guilt was eating me up inside. I had let my guard down, and because of that, my favorite person in the world, the only woman I'd ever really cared about, was almost taken from me. I couldn't get that out of my head.

I stared at the ceiling with my mind racing. I should've seen it coming. I should've known someone like Fury would try something this wild. I was too focused on handling business, too confident that nobody would be dumb enough to come for Aviana. But they did, and I wasn't there to stop it.

As she shifted a little in her sleep, I pulled her in closer. I couldn't believe I almost lost her. The thought of her being hurt—or worse—because of me was too much.

I glanced down at her, watching her breathe. Her face was calm and peaceful, like nothing had happened. But she had been through hell, and I wasn't there when she needed me the most. That shit burned deep. I let my guard down, and she paid for it.

I couldn't forgive myself for that.

Aviana stirred slowly, and I felt her shift against my chest. I looked down and saw that she was awake. She stayed quiet for a moment, just lying there, staring out the window.

Then, out of nowhere, she spoke softly. "So, you sell guns illegally?"

I cringed as my stomach lurched. I had never been ashamed of my profession, but hearing her say it hit different. For the first time, I was ashamed, and I couldn't look at her. I let out a deep breath, feeling that guilt sink deeper.

"Yeah," I said lowly, "but I don't sell to just anybody. I only deal with cartels, organized syndicates—businessmen who don't kill for no reason. That's why Fury came for you. I refused to sell to his crew, and they've been losing a war because they don't have enough artillery. His girl got killed, and he blamed me for it."

I waited, feeling the tension rise in the room. I expected her to be mad, to ask how I could do something like that.

But she didn't. Instead. She smiled a little, almost like she found it funny. "Mia and I always wondered what you did, but I would've never guessed this."

I was shocked at her nonchalant response. I lay there, blinking slowly, not sure how to take it. She wasn't yelling, wasn't looking at me like I was a monster. She was just...accepting it.

"You don't care?"

She waved a hand dismissively. "I spent years with the wrong man because I thought he was the safe choice, and he turned out to be the devil in disguise. Despite what happened last night, I trust you to protect me, just like you did. I can't imagine my life without you, Mythic. I don't want to spend my days longing for you. I want to spend them enjoying and loving you, so no, I don't care."

I looked at her—really looked at her—and all I could think was how I didn't deserve her. She was too pure, too good for someone like me, someone who lived in the shadows. She almost lost her life because of me, and on top of that, she'd already lost her father's respect. I couldn't put her through any more of this.

I sat up a little, pushing her off my chest gently but firmly. "You should go, Avi."

"Huh?" Confused, she watched me, blinking rapidly as she braced herself on her elbow.

"I ain't good for you. You almost died because of me. You need to get out before I drag you down with me."

Her eyes searched mine, as if she were shocked, but she didn't move. "Mythic, stop. I'm not going anywhere."

"Yes, you are. You're getting the fuck up outta here," I ordered, my voice hard, almost mean. I needed her to understand, even if it hurt her. "I'm no good for you. You'll end up hurt—or worse—because of this life I'm in. I can't protect you from everything, and I won't lose you because of my shit."

She shook her head, but her eyes never left mine. "You're not pushing me away, Mythic. I don't care about all that. I care about you."

I felt the anger rise, but it wasn't at her—it was at myself. "I ain't worth your life, Aviana. Can't you see that?"

But she didn't budge, didn't back down. "I'm not goin' anywhere," she repeated, bringing her face closer to mine. "You can try to push me away all you want, but I'm staying. I'm not losing you too."

For a second, I wanted to fight it, wanted to yell at her, make her leave, but the way she looked at me, like she saw right through the bullshit, I couldn't. I couldn't lose her either, no matter how hard I tried to push her away. So, I just sat there, staring at the only person who proved there was some good left in me.

I hated the hold she had on me. It was smart to make her leave, to give her to a nigga who was better for her, but I couldn't.

I couldn't understand how she could still want me after everything. Without thinking, I grabbed her face, pulling her close, and kissed her hard. It wasn't gentle. It was messy and full of anger and confusion. Her lips trembled under mine, and I could feel the desperation in the way I kissed her, trying to push her away with the same force I was pulling her in.

She winced when my hand brushed against the bruise on her cheek.

I froze, my breath ragged. I pulled back just enough to look at her, still gripping her face. "You want me to stop?"

Her eyes locked on mine, and without missing a beat, she whispered, "No. Please don't."

That was all I needed. I kissed her again, this time slower, but the heat, the hunger between us, didn't fade.

"Please don't ever leave me."

Her need made me yearn for her. I flipped her over and hovered on top of her. As I positioned my dick at her center, she held my face. As she cupped my beard, her fingers laced into the curly dark hairs.

"Don't ever leave me," she pleaded as I slowly pushed into her walls.

She gasped a bit, eyes widening from the stretch my entrance caused. "I promise I won't ever leave my home."

Aviana was my home. She was the only place I felt at peace, like I could finally breathe. Everything about her grounded me and made me feel like I belonged somewhere. She completed me in ways I didn't even know I needed. She was it for me. I had fantasized about her for years, watching her from a distance, aching to make her mine again. And yet, I let another man mishandle her, but I planned to fix everything he broke. Every crack, every piece of her that had been shattered, I was going to put her back together, piece by perfect piece.

# DAMAR SCOTT

The clanging of the cell doors echoed down the block as the correctional officer slid them open for the hour of free time. I watched Bear step out, barely glancing my way. He grunted at the CO and disappeared into the dayroom. I should've been moving too, but I didn't.

Once Bear was out of sight, I got up and quietly pushed the cell door back until it clicked shut. My hands were shaking, but I was intent.

I grabbed the sheet off my bunk. It was thin and worn. I started twisting it, wrapping it up as tight as I could, turning it into a rope. Every knot I made, I felt this strange sense of calm creeping in, like this was the only answer left for me.

I tied one end of the sheet around the top of the metal bunk frame. I made sure that it was secure, pulling it hard so it would hold. My fingers were numb, but I kept going, tying the other end into a noose. I stared at it for a second, feeling my throat close, but it wasn't from fear. It was like I was ready, like this was the only way to stop the unbearable fear and dread.

I climbed onto the bunk, slipped the loop over my head, and tightened it around my neck. My chest thudded with each beat, but I felt numb all over. Everything around me blurred as I stood there, on the edge of ending it all.

I couldn't take it anymore. It wasn't just the thought of spending the rest of my life in this cell that was eating me alive. Living under Bear's control, knowing every day was gonna be hell with him, was torture I couldn't face. I already knew what was coming. Bear didn't know who I was yet, but he would. Word would get around soon enough. He was 111 Boyz through and through, and once he heard my name and learned what I had done, it was game over. He wouldn't just beat me down; he'd make it a daily thing. I'd be his punching bag until I couldn't take another hit.

The thought of waking up every day in this cell, living under the shadow of this man was nerve ending. I was already living with the guilt of everything I had done to Aviana, to Mia, to my son. Now, on top of that, I had to live under Bear's boot. I'd rather end it here, on my own terms, before he turned my life into a living nightmare.

I felt the pressure around my neck, tighter with each passing second, my breath coming in short gasps. My heart was pounding like it was trying to fight its way out of my chest. This was it. I was supposed to let go and just let it happen.

But as the seconds ticked by, panic started to creep in. I felt the world closing in, the air getting thinner, and suddenly, I couldn't do it. My body wouldn't let me. I yanked at the sheet, my hands shaking, fingers scrambling to untie the knot. Tears started streaming down my face before I even realized I was crying.

I pulled the noose off and collapsed onto the bunk, gasping for air, my whole body trembling. I couldn't even end it. And now I had to face the reality of what was left. Sixty years in this place. Sixty years with Bear controlling every damn minute of my life. Sixty years of hell.

It all came crashing down, and I couldn't stop the audible sobs that racked my body. There was no escape for me. No way out. I was stuck in this nightmare, and the worst part was I knew I deserved every second of it.

I'd destroyed lives, betrayed the people I cared about, and now I was paying for it. But the payment wasn't death. It wasn't the easy way out I'd tried to take. My punishment was living through it, every single miserable day, trapped in this cell, under Bear's thumb, until the day I finally truly couldn't take it anymore.

And by then, nobody would care. No one would remember me, or what I did, or why I ended up here. I'd just be another forgotten soul.

## AVIANA SCOTT

I stayed lying in bed all day. The soft light of the afternoon streamed in through the blinds. I couldn't fathom what I had gone through last night, but I was still here, breathing, and I thanked God for that. I could've been gone, but I made it through. My heart went out to Mythic, though. He hadn't slept much since it happened because he was still weighed down by the guilt of it all. I felt so sorry for his regret and worry.

I should've been scared. Most women in my position probably would be, but I wasn't. That's when I knew that I was exactly where I was supposed to be—with him. I'd ignored all of the doubts I had about Damar, and I paid for it. I should've listened to myself back then. But with Mythic, I didn't have those doubts. I didn't feel unsure. He was the man I was meant to be with.

As the day went by, I realized that I hadn't talked to my parents, and that was strange. One of them usually called every day, but it had been silence since yesterday. I knew my father was pissed, and he'd probably told my mother. I could feel their disappointment without even talking to them.

But I still respected my parents and wanted them to know that this wasn't a decision that I would regret. Reluctantly, I picked up my phone, knowing I'd have a better shot at getting through to my mother. Since we're both women, I hoped she'd hear me out before shutting me down. Mythic was in his office handling payroll for the club, so I took a breath and hit the video call button.

When my mom's face popped up on the screen, I knew it wasn't going to be easy. Her mouth barely opened when she greeted me. "Hi." Her expression was already tight with disapproval. The look of disdain was written all over her face.

"Hi, Mama." I sighed.

She skipped past any further pleasantries. "I know that your mind is probably all over the place after what Mia and Damar did, but do you have to be this desperate? You can't find somebody else to screw?"

My eyes bulged at my mother's sudden vulgarity.

"What are you thinking, Aviana?" she said through gritted teeth.

"I'm thinking that for the first time, I'm sure about who I'm with. Mythic isn't perfect in you and Daddy's eyes, but he's good for me."

She didn't say anything right away, just stared at me like she couldn't believe the words coming out of my mouth.

"I let you and Daddy's judgment push me toward Damar, and look what happened with him."

Her head reared back as her eyes bulged.

"I let y'all's opinions keep me from the man I should've been with, but I'm not making that mistake again. I'm with Mythic now because I want to be—because I know what's real."

"Look at you." She sneered, shaking her head. "That thug got you disrespecting us already. Is it that good?"

I scoffed, in complete shock at my mother's hatred. My parents were so holy—until it came to getting what they wanted.

I smiled slowly, answering her. "It is. It's worth every inch."

My mother gasped a warning, "Aviana!"

"I have to go, Mama. I love you." I ended the call before she could say anything else, then I silenced my ringer. I was done making decisions based on my parents' approval. And if they couldn't respect who I wanted to love, then they wouldn't be around to witness it.

I finally rolled out of bed, feeling the cool air from the vent hit my bare skin as I stretched. I'd been naked all day, lounging and trying to get my mind together after what had happened. Facing death, staring it in the face like that, wasn't something I'd ever imagined for myself.

I spotted one of Mythic's shirts on the lounge chair near the bed and slipped it on. It smelled like him, so it was comforting. But it barely covered me since he was all about that slim-fit style. It hugged my upper body and barely lay over my massive, curvaceous hips.

As I padded through the condo, my feet bare against the cool floors, I was still amazed. I still wasn't used to this life—the luxury, the space, and the quiet. I'd come a long way from what I was used to, but every day, it felt like I was walking through someone else's world. It was his world, and thankfully, he welcomed me into it with open arms and an open heart.

Opening Mythic's office door, I found him behind his desk, focused while typing away. Even though I loved the swag that his dangerous persona gave him, it made me wet to see him behind a computer, crunching numbers like a nerd and sending emails.

When he saw me, his face softened. "Come here, baby," he said, leaning back in his chair. His eyes swept over me in that shirt like he was admiring his work.

I crossed the room and made my way behind his desk. Once I was in arm's reach, he grabbed me and sat me down on his lap.

"I'm hiring a private driver for you—at least for a while, until I'm sure you're not in any danger."

I shook my head instantly. "That's too much, Mythic. I can handle myself."

His head dramatically leaned to the side. "Can you?"

I chuckled a bit. "That was my fault. I shouldn't have snuck out of the club."

"Exactly. Don't ever do that again," he said firmly as he lightly smacked my ass.

"I won't. I promise."

"I'm not comfortable with you moving around without someone watching your back right now."

I sighed, but I knew there was no winning this argument.

"And I don't want you working anymore." He leaned forward as his eyes locked on mine.

I stared at him, overwhelmed. "Mythic, I appreciate you wanting to take care of me, but I like working. I want to be independent."

He leaned back, his gaze softening just a little. "I'm not saying you can't be independent. What I'm saying is, I want you to have the time to go after your real dream—nursing school. I'm gonna pay for it. You focus on that, and let me take care of the rest."

My heart bloomed with pure bliss. "I love you," I professed, grinning. "You already have me. You don't have to buy me."

He smiled, pulling me close as his hands rested on my waist. "I know you do. But this ain't about buying you, baby. I know you're already mine. But now that I've got you, I'm gonna spoil the hell out of you, so get used to it."

I wrapped my arms around Mythic's neck, letting myself sink into him.

"I got you," he whispered against my ear, like a promise he would never break.

And I believed him. I held him tighter, letting go of all the fears and doubts that used to cloud my mind. With Mythic, I didn't have to wonder if I was making the right choice, nor did I have to question where we stood. *I knew.*

As we sat there, wrapped up in each other, I realized that I was living in the fantasy I'd had for years. This was the kind of ease and passion I'd yearned for. This was the kind of love that didn't leave me guessing, that didn't tear me apart.

He was different from anything I'd ever felt before. With him, it wasn't complicated, it wasn't filled with doubt or second-guessing. It was right. Loving Mythic felt like breathing, like something I was always meant to do.

# EPILOGUE

## DAMAR SCOTT

As soon as I opened my eyes, I felt the dread. The cold metal bunk pressed against my spine, sending sharp pains through my bruised bones. Staring up at the cracked concrete ceiling, my heart began to pound with terror because I'd woken up another morning in this living hell.

"You awake yet, princess?" Bear's taunting chilled me to the bone.

I struggled upright, ribs aching from yesterday's beating. Bear leaned against the wall with his large arms crossed. His eyes were dark with sadistic amusement.

"Yeah," I croaked. "Can I get up now, sir?"

Bear smirked. "Look at you, askin' permission like a well-trained dog. Yeah. You can get up. We got work to do today."

I lowered my head, swallowing the lump in my throat. "What do you want me to do?"

Bear stepped closer. He was so tall that, though I was on the top bunk, we were damn near eye to eye. He reached for a tiny, filthy rag on the shelf, tore a corner of it off, and tossed it to me. "Get on your hands and knees. I want that floor spotless."

I stared at the pathetic scrap of cloth, then around at the grimy cell. The concrete was filthy, stained with my blood, old and new; urine; and God knows what else.

When I hesitated, Bear's eyes narrowed dangerously. He grabbed me by my throat, squeezing so hard I gasped and clawed weakly at his iron grip.

"Did I stutter, motherfucker?" he growled into my ear. "You want another lesson? Maybe I should break a few more ribs, huh?"

"Nah—" I choked out desperately. "I'll do it!"

He pulled me out of the bunk and threw me to the floor, slamming my head painfully against the concrete wall. Dizzy, I rested on my knees, grabbed the rag, and started scrubbing. My knuckles scraped against gritty concrete. Because the rag was so flimsy, my nails broke and my skin tore. Blood slowly seeped into the cloth as I scrubbed harder.

Bear watched with sick satisfaction.

It only took a few weeks for Bear to find out what I was in jail for. Ever since, he had been torturing me both physically and mentally. If it wasn't the endless beatings, it was waking up to his piss dripping on my face or being forced to eat from the floor like a dog while he kicked me in the ribs. Bear turned the cell into a cage, making me his personal punching bag whenever he got bored. Sometimes he starved me, letting me watch while he ate my meals slowly in front of me. Sometimes, at night, he'd keep me awake, whispering threats of what he'd do to me the next day, describing in sickening detail how he planned to break every bone in my body.

He'd made me his slave, forcing me to wash his filthy underwear by hand, scrubbing until my fingers bled. If I missed even one stain, he'd shove my face into the sink until I nearly drowned. Bear had stripped me of every ounce of dignity I had left. The worst nights were when he forced me to stand naked in the corner for hours, shivering and humiliated, while he laughed at my bruised body. Every second I lived was another second closer to wishing I was dead.

I couldn't tell anyone. No one would listen because Bear had most of the correctional officers on his payroll. I had tried to kill myself a few times, but I just couldn't go through with it.

"Matter of fact…" Bear stopped abruptly, grabbing my chin and forcing my head up. "Maybe you'd do better lickin' it clean."

I froze. "Bear, please—"

He smirked darkly. "Get to lickin', pretty boy. Floor better shine when you're done."

With trembling hands, I lowered myself onto the cold, filthy concrete. My tongue touched the surface, and I instantly recoiled from the vile taste. I gagged, nearly vomiting.

"Don't you dare throw up," Bear warned viciously. "'Cause you gon' lick that shit up too."

My throat burned as I fought to keep down the bile. Slowly, miserably, I dragged my tongue across the grimy floor, tasting blood, dirt, and filth as Bear laughed.

This was my life now. I had been reduced from a man who thought he had everything to a helpless animal forced to lick floors clean, praying for death to finally come and take mercy on me.

## AVIANA GREY

I stood there giggling as Mythic's hands covered my eyes. "Come on, Mythic. Hurry up!"

"Can you see?" he asked playfully.

"No. I can't see a thing, just hurry up. My feet are killing me!" I shifted my weight from one foot to the other, trying to ignore how huge and swollen I felt. I was now seven months pregnant, and I was starting to feel like a balloon. My feet ached from being on them all day. My ankles were swollen and uncomfortable.

Mythic's hands slowly pulled away from my eyes. "All right. you can look now."

When I opened my eyes, I was immediately struck by the beauty of the room. The nursery he'd set up for our son, Sire, was breathtaking. My breath caught in my throat as I took in every detail.

Mythic had made me promise to stay out of this room all week because he wanted me to be surprised by what the interior decorator had done.

The walls were painted in soft, warm tones of yellow and green, with a gorgeous giraffe theme that was perfect for our little boy. The furniture was all wood with a cozy crib in the center, adorned with soft linens in a giraffe print. There were matching shelves with stuffed animals, books, and little giraffe figurines. A changing table stood nearby.

But what took my breath away the most were the 3D letters on the wall. Sire's name was written in a playful yet elegant font. The giraffe theme continued on the wall behind the crib, where a mural of giraffes was painted. Their long necks reached up to the ceiling. It was soft, whimsical, and perfect for our little one.

Tears welled in my eyes, but I blinked them away. "Mythic... this is beautiful."

He stepped behind me, wrapping his arms around my swollen belly, pulling me close. "Not as beautiful as you."

I turned my head slightly to look up at him, and I could see the love and pride in his eyes. Even in my state—swollen with a dark neck and spreading nose—he made me feel like I was still sexy. His affection for me had never wavered, and in that moment, surrounded by the beauty he had created for our son, I knew I was loved.

"I love it," I said, turning in his arms. "It's perfect."

He kissed my forehead softly. "I'm glad. Now, take a seat, mama. You've been on your feet too long."

I smiled, feeling my heart swell again as I looked around the room that Mythic had so carefully put together. It was real now. This was happening. Our family, our baby boy, was coming, and nothing in this world could make me feel more blessed.

I settled down on the loveseat in the nursery. The soft fabric molded to my body as I let out a sigh of relief. Mythic sat next to me and immediately lifted my swollen leg onto his lap. His hands were warm and gentle as he began to rub my feet. I closed my eyes for a moment, letting myself relax into his touch. Then I opened them, looking around the room to take it all in again.

As I rubbed my belly, I noticed the glint of my wedding ring on my finger. It had been almost a year since we'd rushed to the courthouse to get married. Neither of us wanted to wait any longer, especially with everything that had happened between us. We planned to have a big wedding ceremony soon after, but with the pregnancy, we decided to put it off. We planned to have the ceremony once I had the baby, after my body snatched back, as I liked to say.

Mythic looked at me as he continued to massage my feet. "So, how is giving birth gonna affect school?"

"Hopefully, it won't since I'm giving birth in the summer. I just won't take any summer classes so that I can bond with Sire before school starts again in the fall."

"That sounds like a plan."

I was a year into my bachelor of science in nursing, and after I graduated, I had to work for a couple of years before applying to a certified registered nurse anesthetist program. Then I'd have to complete a master's program, and after that, pass a national certification exam. It was a seven-to-ten-year process, but I was so happy that I was finally following my dreams.

"I'm proud of you, baby."

I reached out, taking his hand in mine. "I appreciate you supporting me. I need your support to make this happen. You're not just helping me financially; you're helping me believe in myself, and that means more than anything."

"I wouldn't have it any other way, baby."

As Mythic gently rubbed my feet, the tension of the day melted away under his touch. The heat from his hands was soothing, and I was starting to relax. But then, my phone rang, pulling me out of the moment.

I groaned, struggling to fish the phone out of my pocket, cursing under my breath as it seemed to slip deeper inside. Finally, I managed to grab it and saw that it was my mom with a video call.

I tapped the screen to answer. "Hey, Mom."

When the screen came to life, both my parents were there, beaming at me. "We finally get to see the room!" my mom said excitedly.

I blinked, a little confused. "How did you know the room was done?"

"Mythic told me," my father replied. "He said he was going to show it to you as soon as you got home from class. We couldn't wait to see it."

I smiled at their excitement.

My parents and I had been estranged for a few months when I found out I was pregnant. I'd called them, and despite our differences, they were thrilled to hear the news. We reconciled quickly after that, and now, they were as excited as ever about becoming grandparents. They put aside everything and welcomed Mythic with open arms. My parents were hurt that they weren't able to witness my marriage, but they felt much better when they learned that there would be an official ceremony that they could be a part of.

"C'mon. Let us see the room," my mother urged.

Chuckling, Mythic took the phone from me and stood.

"Hey there, Mythic," my father greeted him.

"How you doin', Pops. Hey, Ma."

"Hi, baby." My mother beamed.

Once we reconciled, my parents took the time to get to know Mythic. They took him in, not only as my husband, but as their son-in-love. They still had some reservations about his line of work and often preached to him, but I was happy that they had accepted him.

As Mythic showed my parents the room, I just stared at him, grateful for this man. Despite everything that had happened, despite the heartache and turmoil, this was my life now. And with Mythic, with the support of my family, I knew I was exactly where I was supposed to be.

All the heartbreak, betrayal, and tears I'd endured had led me back into the arms of this man who loved me with a depth and purity I never knew was possible. Life had taken me through storms that seemed never-ending, through nights that felt darker than any night should. But now I knew every moment of pain had been worth it.

This was the love I'd always dreamed of, the kind of love that healed wounds instead of creating them. And even though the path had been rough, the end of this rainbow was brighter than anything I could've imagined.

# THE END

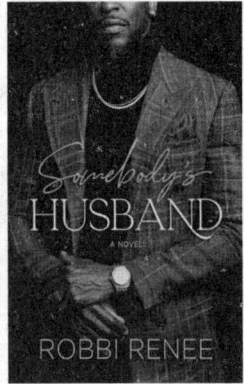